PENNED
The Fourth Kate Turner, DVM, Mystery

"Veterinarian Brady imbues this page-turner with authentic details about a vet and the critters she treats."

—Kirkus Reviews

CHAINED
The Third Kate Turner, DVM, Mystery

"The discovery of the remains of Flynn Keegan, who everyone in Oak Falls, N.Y., assumed left for Hollywood after graduating from high school a decade earlier, propels Brady's well-crafted third Kate Turner mystery...As Kate's digging turns up more secrets and long-buried lies, she has too many suspects and too little evidence. But when a high school classmate of Flynn's is murdered, Kate knows she's both perilously close to the truth and in grave danger. Brady keeps the suspense high through the surprising ending."

—*Publishers Weekly*

"A client's chance encounter with a bone involves veterinarian Kate Turner in yet another murder case in the beautiful but apparently not so peaceful Hudson Valley town of Oak Falls...Brady's years of experience as a veterinarian supply plenty of amusing stories and helpful hints for animal owners while her complicated heroine investigates a tricky case."

—*Kirkus Reviews*

UNLEASHED
The Second Kate Turner, DVM, Mystery

"Brady's sophomore effort is an appealing mix of murder and medicine. Kate is an amiable heroine with lots of spunk. Not willing to leave well enough alone, she joins the list of cozy amateur sleuths such as Laura Childs's Theodosia Browning and Jane Cleland's Josie Prescott."

—*Library Journal*

"In Brady's amusing, well-plotted second Kate Turner mystery, the Oak Falls, N.Y., veterinarian investigates the death of Claire Birnham, whose Cairn terrier was treated at the local veterinary hospital. Claire appears to have committed suicide, but it begins to look like a case of foul play after various pet owners reveal details about the woman's life...Turner treats a pot-bellied pig and a smelly cocker spaniel, besides getting chased by a flock of geese. Readers will eagerly look forward to Kate's further adventures."

—*Publishers Weekly*

"Now that curiosity has killed the cat, will it kill the veterinarian?... Kate's second is a treat for animal lovers. The plethora of suspects keeps you guessing."

—*Kirkus Reviews*

MUZZLED
The First Kate Turner, DVM, Mystery

"Here is a novel written with exacting authority, along with a frolicking sense of humor about life, animals, and the lengths to which someone will go to right a wrong, all while still maintaining a solid sense of tension and suspense. I look forward to future mysteries featuring the charismatic Dr. Kate Turner...and I'm sure you will, too!"

—James Rollins, *New York Times* bestselling author

"A delightful and lively mystery that introduces Kate Turner, a veterinarian with heart, humor and a new penchant for solving murders. A promising first novel that will leave readers begging for more."

—Earline Fowler, Agatha award-winning author
of the Benni Harper Series

"*Muzzled* is an enjoyable read for both the light mystery fan and the dog lover, and if they are one and the same, it's a double delight."

—*New York Journal of Books*

"Kate's debut has plenty to offer pet lovers and mystery mavens alike."

—*Kirkus Reviews*

Penned

Books by Eileen Brady

The Kate Turner, DVM, Mysteries
Muzzled
Unleashed
Chained
Penned

Penned

A Kate Turner, DVM, Mystery

Eileen Brady

Poisoned Pen Press

First Edition 2018

10 9 8 7 6 5 4 3 2 1

Library of Congress Control Number: 2018940608

ISBN: 9781464211096   Hardcover
ISBN: 9781464210815   Trade Paperback
ISBN: 9781464210822   Ebook

Poisoned Pen Press
4014 N. Goldwater Blvd., #201
Scottsdale, AZ 85251
www.poisonedpenpress.com
info@poisonedpenpress.com

Printed in the United States of America

To the Animal Medical Center in New York City,
who hired a young girl and changed her life.

Acknowledgments

I'd like to thank the wonderful people at Poisoned Pen Press for once again transforming my manuscript into a book. Kudos to the Poisoned Pen Bookstore, in Scottsdale, Arizona, that hosts book-signings, author events, and so much more. Communities are lucky to have bookstores like this one.

As always, it's been a pleasure to work with Annette Rodgers, my inspired editor, whose suggestions never fail to improve each book. Many thanks also to Barbara Peters for giving me the opportunity to tell Kate's story.

Readers often ask me where I write my books. Well, parts of this book were written on planes, a tour bus in Iceland (in the winter to see the Northern Lights), and in various hotel rooms on the East and West Coasts. Deadlines don't care if you are on vacation, sick, or feeling particularly uninspired—they have a life unto themselves. Thankfully, my worn and battered laptop held on until I sprinted past the finish line.

Penned had a rocky start. My critique group of fellow writers—Betty Webb, Sharon Magee, Art Kerns, Sonja Stone, and Charles Pyeatte—all hated the original beginning chapters of this book, encouraging me to scrap it and start over. They were right. Thanks again to the Sheridan Street Irregulars, one of the longest-running and most productive critique groups I know.

None of this would be possible without unwavering support

from my husband, Jon, encouragement from daughters, Amanda and Britt, and good wishes from the rest of the family.

I always think of my readers as I write, hoping to amuse, educate, and entertain you with animal antics and an intriguing plotline. Let me know if I succeeded, at: www.eileenbradymysteries.com. And remember, like Kate Turner, I believe any day looks brighter when served with a slice of really good pie.

Finally, we all, as humans, can learn something from the animal community, both wild and domesticated, that surrounds us and sustains us. Life is complex, yet ultimately simple. Take a moment to enjoy and cherish our beautiful world and the creatures that share the land, oceans, and sky with us.

The pen is mightier than the sword.

—Edward Bulwer-Lytton

Don't approach a goat from the front, a horse from the back, or a fool from any side.

—Folk proverb

Prologue

The killer envisioned the old woman lying in bed sleeping, a slight smile on her face. That smile would disappear when their eyes met.

It's not that he disliked her. On the contrary, she hadn't annoyed him that much, not like the other idiots who fluttered in and out of his life. So many weak people living useless lives, constantly getting in his way. Their overwhelming stupidity forced him to take control—sometimes in a subtle, manipulative way, sometimes not.

Fate's odd sense of humor had brought the old lady, one of the few people alive who might recognize him, to this tiny town in the Hudson Valley. One of them had to go.

He'd decided to stage the murder as a burglary gone wrong with dresser drawers opened, possessions scattered on the floor. Elderly women always hid their good stuff in the same places. All her jewelry and other valuables would disappear, including the gold wedding ring on her finger.

Strangling her would be fun for one of them.

It should take twenty minutes, flat. Too bad killing wasn't an Olympic event. No need to worry about cameras in the small older complex she lived in. Management had never gotten around to updating their security. Why should they? Oak Falls was as safe as safe could be.

It would be a perfect murder on a perfect winter's night performed by a perfect killer.

Chapter One

Blood dripped from the zombie's brown cracked lips. He staggered toward me. I dodged right only to spy a pair of vampires closing in on my left, their yellowed fangs bared and ready.

"Oops. Sorry," said the tiny Cinderella in a blond wig who collided with my leg.

It was Halloween night in the Hudson Valley, and the residents of Oak Falls had come out to play. With Main Street closed to traffic, kids of all ages could safely trick-or-treat. Even the shops got into the act with employees dressed as ghosts or elves or whatever, handing out samples and gift certificates to the crowd.

"Kate, isn't this great?" asked Mari, my friend and veterinary assistant. Dressed as Harpo Marx to take full advantage of her natural halo of curly hair, she'd dragged me out to experience this annual spooky celebration, which the town was famous for.

"Fantastic!" I yelled my reply over the lyrics of the "Monster Mash" blasted from speakers set up in the town square. A pair of tinfoil-wrapped robots broke into an impromptu dance. Passersby clapped and joined in. Everyday troubles faded for one night as young and old cavorted in the street.

She eyed my Halloween outfit. "I still think you should have gone with the Meryl Streep look. You'd look great with a pile of awards in your arms."

Mari was referring to the superficial resemblance I had to the famous actress. My straight blond hair, longish nose, and blue eyes were to blame, I supposed. Despite her suggestion I went to the costume school of throw-some-stuff-on-and-pretend-it-works.

My last-minute outfit consisted of an old pair of surgical scrubs smeared with clotted catsup blood. A greasy black wig provided by Mari paired with a stained surgical mask across my face made me unrecognizable as the local veterinarian from Oak Falls Animal Hospital. I'd insulated myself from the October cold with two pairs of long johns and tall green rubber boots, lightly sprinkled with more catsup. With my absentee boyfriend Jeremy's big tweed jacket pulled over everything, I'd morphed into an androgynous mad scientist.

This was my first Halloween in the village since being hired to run the Oak Falls Animal Hospital, while the owner, Doc Anderson, took an around-the-world cruise. Known as an artistic community, the town vigorously cultivated an eccentric and care-free vibe, making it particularly attractive to residents of nearby New York City. Only a two-hour drive away, but light years from the city's noise and pollution, Oak Falls attracted visitors, many of them ending up as weekend residents.

I'd been unprepared for the hectic workload of house calls and hospital appointments at an animal hospital. Although rewarding, being the only veterinarian on staff had proved quite stressful. My coping strategy of reckless pie-consumption and amateur sleuthing didn't help solve that problem, resulting only in tighter-fitting pants and alienating the chief of police. I hoped the coming winter might bring a sense of calm into my life.

I was wrong.

Very, very, wrong.

• • ● • •

Ten minutes later the lively crowd around us appeared to have doubled. Live music blared from the loudspeakers as a local group calling themselves the Ghouls performed classic hits.

Parents hoisted kids on their shoulders and the costumed audience rocked to the music. Mari called out something inaudible and disappeared. I walked onto a side street to check my phone only to discover its battery was low.

A harried Marilyn Monroe stepped out of the throng, a confused-looking elderly woman in tow. "Now wait here, Aunt Gloria," she said, gently guiding the woman toward the brick wall of a storefront a few feet from me, stroking her white hair to soothe any fear. "I've got to track down the kids."

"Is this a party?" Gloria asked. "Where's my drink? I'd like a martini, please."

"No drinks, Aunt Gloria. Please. Please just stay here for a few minutes." While the younger woman talked, her eyes anxiously searched the crowd.

"Excuse me." I lowered my bloody surgical mask. "If you like, I can wait here with your aunt until you get back. My name is Kate Turner. I'm a veterinarian at Oak Falls Animal Hospital."

Suspicion turned to relief at the magic word, "veterinarian."

"Oh, Dr. Turner. Yes, I recognize you now. I'm Irene Zeidman. We brought our cat Picasso in to see you a few months ago."

Her face looked familiar, but like most vets, I remembered the cat better.

"If you could help keep my Aunt Gloria company that would be great. My teenagers are running around here somewhere and deliberately not answering my texts. They're in big trouble, let me tell you." A frustrated scowl clashed with her iconic Marilyn Monroe get-up.

"Don't worry, I've gotten separated from my friend too." I'd expected Mari to pop up by now. "After you get back, could I text her from your phone?"

"Sure." Without a backward glance she secured her wig and disappeared into the crowd.

I took a closer look at my charge. Gloria appeared to be in her early eighties, her sweet face surrounded by a thin cloud of white hair. The top of her head barely came up to my shoulder.

"You look familiar, dear. Don't I know you?" Watery blue eyes stared into mine.

"I'm Picasso's doctor," I explained.

She patted my hand and shook her head. "You're much too young for that."

"For what?"

"For Pablo Picasso. He was before my time and I'm much older than you."

Feeling we were talking at cross-purposes I leaned in closer so she could hear me above the noise. "I mean Picasso, the cat."

A slow dawning of understanding spread across her face. "Oh, that makes much more sense. Pablo was a great artist, you know, but he's dead." A tut-tut sort of sound escaped her lips.

Frankenstein walked past and nodded in our direction, his dark eyes wide and weird.

"He looks very familiar. Don't I know him?" Gloria stared at the departing back.

"You might. Do you live here in town?"

"I live near my grandniece. She got me an apartment close to her family so they can keep an eye on me." Gloria's moving hand, dotted with age spots, beckoned me closer. In a conspiratorial whisper she added, "I'm getting older, you know."

"We all are." I gave her a hug. She smelled vaguely of dried lilacs.

Twenty minutes later the crowd started to thin out and the band wrapped it up for the night. The air felt colder. I hoped Irene wouldn't be too much longer. While I kept a watch out for Mari, Gloria rambled on.

"I've always loved the Hudson Valley, but I haven't lived here in many years. My husband and I sold our home to move to New Jersey to be closer to our daughter." Tears glistened for a moment in her faded blue eyes. "You plan and plan but then things happen...why, who knows?...they're all gone now...my husband, my daughter. Our grandsons are left, but one's in Indiana and the other is living in New Mexico. Irene is my sister's girl."

I wasn't sure how to respond.

A tall man in a New York Yankees baseball uniform complete with cap walked quickly past, in work boots instead of sneakers, almost knocking into my elderly charge.

"Excuse me." He reached out to steady her, his back toward me. "Are you alright?"

"Don't I know you?" I heard her ask him.

"I don't think so. Happy Halloween, ladies."

I tried to thank him but he crossed the street, narrowly avoiding colliding with a police officer, before continuing on his way.

"Why, I swear that's…what's his name? I haven't seen him in years."

I followed her pointing finger. Walking along the sidewalk I saw someone dressed as a creepy clown, the kind that gives kids nightmares, talking to a teen-aged girl wearing devil horns and carrying a plastic pitchfork. Another, more friendly Frankenstein, lurched behind them. The baseball player disappeared into the crowd.

Gloria grabbed my sleeve. "Of course I can't be positive… my eyes aren't what they used to be. I wonder what he's doing at my party? And when is Irene coming back with my martini?"

Obviously Gloria appeared able to focus on some things, but became confused about others. I started to explain that we were at the town Halloween party when she tilted her head and asked a familiar question, "You look familiar. Don't I know you?"

Her smile revealed suspiciously perfect white teeth.

"Yes, you do know me," I reassured her. "I'm Kate."

"I'm Gloria. Gloria LaGuardia."

"That's a famous name. Did you know…?"

"Mayor LaGuardia? No. But my husband swore he was his cousin, twice-removed." Her laughter reminded me of Glinda, the good witch of the North, tinkling like the top keys of a piano.

A couple dressed in full-length bunny costumes strolled by. "Let's stop for a second, honey," a muffled voice said. "It's stuffy in this thing." They leaned against the storefront across from us and removed their elaborate costume heads. The man, still wearing his pink rabbit nose, reached into a hidden pocket, pulled out cigarettes, and lit up.

"Yuck. You promised you were going to quit." The female bunny began fanning the smoke away with an exaggerated sweep of her hand, barely missing her companion's eye.

"This is only my second cigarette today." After sliding the rabbit ears off, his handsome face leaned into hers. With strong black eyebrows and curly dark hair streaked with silver, the male bunny cut a dashing figure. I guessed he was in his late forties or early fifties. His well-maintained girlfriend appeared slightly older.

Gloria stared at them in disbelief. "I'm confused. Are you really rabbits?"

They both laughed. "Don't I wish," the woman replied. "Life would be much more simple."

"All I'd need to keep you happy would be some carrots, and I don't mean diamonds," her boyfriend chimed in. He picked up her paw and kissed it.

"You look familiar. Don't I know you?" Gloria's attention now focused on the man with the cigarette.

I was beginning to realize that Gloria thought everyone looked familiar.

Before the rabbits could answer, Irene appeared with a teenage boy and preteen girl in tow, neither looking happy. I wasn't sure if the ripped jeans and dreadlocks the boy wore were a costume or his everyday look. On the other hand, the girl was definitely a witch.

"Wait. Is that you, Peter?" Gloria stared at her grandniece's children. Her demeanor became more and more agitated.

The boy scowled while the girl checked messages on her phone.

Irene gave her daughter the evil eye. "Put the phone away, Jillian."

"Mom," the girl whined. "Stop treating us like children."

"Don't press your luck," her mom snapped back.

Just in time, it was my turn to see a familiar face walking toward us. Mari/Harpo Marx and I waved to each other through the thinning crowd.

"Thanks so much for taking care of Aunt Gloria. Sorry it took so long." Behind Irene's back Jillian stuck her tongue out. Her brother slapped approval with a high-five.

Gloria started to mutter to herself.

I didn't envy Irene, this poor woman, who had her hands full with two scowling siblings and a senior citizen expecting a martini.

Irene waved them along and said in her happy voice, "Come on, everyone. Time to go home."

Gloria latched onto my arm. She stood on her tippy toes trying to whisper in my ear, eager to tell me something.

I leaned down.

"Kate," the elderly woman said, "I'm afraid."

Her eyes looked clear and focused even though her hands clenched and unclenched my arm. I felt her body tremble. "What's wrong?"

"It all came back to me just now. Someone evil is here. I saw him." She gestured to the costumed crowd streaming past.

I stared into the ghosts and goblins, witches and robots heading home. No one acted crazy or out-of-line. If evil walked in front of us, I didn't see it. Perhaps my elderly friend had had enough Halloween partying for one night.

"Who are you talking about?"

Instead of answering she moved away from me and told her waiting niece in a plaintive voice to take her home.

Irene gathered her little group together then shepherded them toward the town parking area, holding her aunt's arm while shooing the complaining kids along.

Bewildered by Gloria's sudden fear, I didn't know what to think. In the midst of the confusion Mari called out my name.

When I turned back toward the street the rabbits had disappeared.

Chapter Two

My patient wanted to kill me. I didn't take it personally. Phil, the sulfur-crested cockatoo, wanted to kill anyone who dared enter his home and disrupt the interspecies bliss he enjoyed with his human mommy/girlfriend.

He definitely did not want to get his toenails trimmed.

Our eyes met, his a glittering black, versus my determined blue. He ruffled his snowy feathers, head bobbing up and down. I smoothed my pale blond hair and flexed all ten fingers. He laid his expressive crest flat down in anger. I wiggled my eyebrows.

"Are we ready?" Veronica Goell, Phil's pretty mommy/girlfriend, asked. At the sound of her voice Phil turned on his perch, gently leaned over and nibbled on her hair. His neck curved in adoration.

I glanced down at my tools, spread out on the table. Two pair of nail clippers—one small, one usually used for cats—styptic pencils, styptic powder, and a metal nail file.

"Ready?"

Mari, my assistant, nodded back in confirmation.

Both of us watched as Veronica turned to Phil, explained it was time to trim his long nails, then expertly wrapped him up in a towel like a bird burrito. She was the perfect large bird owner, confident and completely bonded with her cockatoo. After many trial runs Phil had now become accustomed to the drill, which made it easy on everyone.

"Make sure you don't put pressure on his chest," I told his owner as we positioned the bird on the table. Mari held one leg with its impressive claws, and kept an eye out for the other. We didn't want the second leg escaping and scratching the heck out of us.

Veronica laughed. "How could I forget? You always remind me, Dr. Kate."

That was true, but due to their anatomy, birds can suffocate from too much pressure on their chests, especially small canaries and budgies.

"She's got you pegged," Mari agreed. "But better to be safe than sorry."

As I stared down at Phil's impressively curled talons I had to agree. Usually the pink quick in the nail where the blood supply ended was visible. Not so with our sulfur-crested cockatoo. His nails gleamed as black as his eyes. Slow and steady was the only way to safely trim the surprisingly thick nails. If I cut any too short, the styptic pencils and powder would stop the bleeding.

It took us only twenty minutes to finish our task, thanks to Veronica's expert handling skills. As we cleaned up she made nice with Phil and in a few minutes he became calm again, chuckling bird love songs to her.

"Where is Rita?" I asked as I packed up my gear. Rita was a fluffy mixed-breed rescue dog and Phil's other loving companion.

"She's at the groomer. Next time you've got to see their new trick, playing fetch. Phil pushes the ball with his head or throws it with his foot and she runs after it. I've got the whole thing running on YouTube."

Another silly pet video to add to my expanding list of silly pet videos.

"Did I tell you Phil is going for his therapy animal designation? I thought when he's ready I would take him out so he could cheer up some of the seniors I look after."

I knew Veronica worked as a nurse but didn't know much else.

She explained on our way down the hallway, Phil perched on her arm. "I do my regular four-day shift at Kingston Hospital, then on Fridays I work at the Oak Falls Community Center at their adult daycare. It's for independent geriatric patients who need daytime supervision and stimulation."

"That's a great idea. The socialization is also good for your bird." Phil danced back and forth in agreement. I idly wondered if a program like that might be helpful for someone like Gloria.

Mari cautiously opened the door and slipped out ahead of me. Even though the possibility of Phil flying out into the winter weather was small, it was one we didn't want to take.

"Say good-bye, Phil," Veronica told her feathered baby.

He raised his head, top feathers waving at me.

"Good-bye, Phil," he squawked.

"That's a gorgeous bird," Mari commented in the truck as we headed back to the animal hospital.

"But a lot of work." My stethoscope hanging off the rearview mirror swayed in time to the windshield wipers. Light snow was falling to welcome the month of November. "Cockatoos need plenty of attention, an enriched environment so they don't get bored, and space to spread their wings."

"Phil's a lucky bird in that respect. He's got a whole room to himself and his own dog for company." Mari finished updating Veronica's chart before closing down our laptop.

"Warm enough?" Our old F-150 truck had plenty of dings and scratches inside and out, but one heck of a heating system.

"Sweltering." She fiddled with the controls and adjusted her vents. "I hope we can go to the Halloween celebration again next year, maybe with Jeremy?"

I knew Mari was fishing for an update on my love life but the Kate Turner stream of gossip was dammed up for tonight. She'd have to settle for an ambiguous grunt.

Back at my garage apartment, conveniently connected to the animal hospital, I poured a cold glass of white wine, my dog Buddy sprawled across my feet. As a veterinarian I'd been trained to have an analytical mind, but regarding my boyfriend, Jeremy, I'd been reacting with my heart, not my brain. We'd had an intense short relationship in college, followed by a lengthy friendship. After losing track of each other he'd bounded back into my life, a newer and improved version of his old self. After a passionate beginning we'd settled into a comfortable long-distance relationship, but I already felt our closeness fading due to our separate lives and goals.

Buddy twitched in his sleep, probably chasing squirrels in his dreams across a fragrant green meadow as the snow piled up outside.

Maybe this arrangement with Jeremy was enough for now.

Or maybe it was time to push for more.

Chapter Three

The rest of the week passed quickly. Our workload had dropped off a bit as the inclement winter weather forced pets and their owners to stay inside and stay out of trouble.

"Your last client is in exam room two," our receptionist, Cindy, informed me. Ever-efficient, she had already begun straightening up the entryway and correlating the daily receipts in anticipation of closing the office for the day.

"Thanks."

She caught me before I could make my getaway. "Any weekend plans?"

Rats, trapped again. "Not yet."

"Jeremy can't make it up here?"

I plucked a tuft of black hair off my white coat. "We're working on it. Maybe next Saturday." With a smile I tossed the fur into her wastepaper basket, then bolted for the safety of exam room two.

I knocked on the door and surprised a young couple passionately kissing. On the floor sat a brand new cat carrier with the price tag still on it.

"Hi, I'm Dr. Kate Turner. What can I do for you today?"

Still clinging to each other they introduced themselves. "Ben and Holly Doston, like Boston but with a D," Holly said. "We're newlyweds." She held up a sparkling ring set for me to see, then gave her husband's muscular arm a squeeze.

"Congratulations," I replied.

There was a quick knock on the door and Mari stuck her head in. "Need any help in here?"

"Sure. This is Mari, my veterinary technician. Mari, these are the Dostons."

"We're newlyweds." Holly's face beamed with delight as she lifted her left hand to show Mari the ring.

"Congrats." With a quick move Mari lifted the cat carrier on the stainless-steel exam table and swung open the wire door. The little silver cat inside didn't budge.

"Let's leave her be for now." From the paperwork I knew the cat's name was Lady Jane Grey but there was no age written down. Instead, Cindy had written in pen "stray cat" at the bottom of the page.

"When did you find this kitty?"

"Almost a week ago. We named her Lady Jane Grey. Did you know she almost was the Queen of England?"

"They never would have let her rule," her husband interrupted, an intense look on his face. "Mary and Elizabeth were direct descendents of Henry the Eighth, although their legitimacy had been…"

"What's wrong with your cat?" This time it was Mari who interrupted.

"Well…" Holly's pretty face turned serious. "…she's in agony."

"Yes," her husband agreed, "terrible pain. We found her behind The Grill restaurant."

His tone assumed we'd figure out the diagnosis from that statement.

"We Googled her symptoms and we're pretty sure she has food poisoning and abdominal cramps." They solemnly nodded to each. Holly gazed at her hunky husband and blew him a kiss.

At the sound of Dr. Google's name, Mari rolled her eyes.

Just then Lady Jane Grey let out a pitiful unladylike yowl.

Mari and I looked at each other. I had a pretty good idea

what was wrong with Lady without even getting her out of the box. After taking a brief medical history, I prepared to meet my furry patient.

As soon as I touched the young female cat's rear end, it shot way up in the air. This move was followed by seductive stretching and rolling on the table accompanied by loud purring. A quick glance at her teeth told me she was young, maybe eight or nine months old.

"Is this your first kitty?" I asked the couple.

"Yes."

"The most obvious thing I observed is, she's in heat."

They stared at each other, then me, puzzled. "I didn't think the house was that hot, did you, honey?" Holly asked.

"No, but we aren't running around the house in a fur coat like she is," Ben answered thoughtfully. "Do we need to turn the thermostat down?"

Exasperated, Mari said, "She's not hot. She's got the hots."

I bit my lip. "Lady Jane is in estrus."

More bewilderment.

"She wants a boyfriend," I told them, making it as straightforward as possible.

"Really, really bad," my assistant bluntly added.

"Oh." The couple nodded their heads. Mari and I joined in for the fun of it.

Holly's eyes widened then she smiled knowingly at her cat. "Well, honey. I don't blame you."

Lady Jane yowled in agreement.

"So, this is what I am going to recommend..." I moved over to the computer terminal and sat down. "I'd like to test Lady Jane today for the two bad infectious viruses cats can carry—feline leukemia and feline immunodeficiency virus. If those are negative, we can go ahead and schedule her for her vaccinations and spay surgery."

"Okay."

"Let me work up an estimate for you and we can get things rolling. I'm going to have Mari go over general cat care with you and give you our new cat owner packet of information."

The newlyweds listened carefully while they comforted their new pet.

"By the way," I said, "you did a wonderful thing by rescuing her and bringing her in to see me. With winter coming, you probably saved her life."

Tears sprang into Holly's eyes.

"Uh, Dr. Turner. Just one question." Ben held up his phone to show me some kind of app.

"Yes?"

"Do I still have to turn the thermostat down?"

The intense emotionality of Lady Jane Grey and her newlywed owners felt like an itch I didn't have. Not feeling such passion in my current relationship troubled me, but I put it down to the constant stress I was under.

Following my regular routine after the long hours at work I pulled on my sweats and hunkered down on the sofa for another solitary night of eating dinner in front of the television. My stomach rumbled, reminding me I'd skipped lunch again. Comfortable but definitely hungry, I contemplated heating up a can of chili when my doorbell rang.

Buddy growled and charged over to the door. Then, he started wagging his tail. When I looked out the window I knew why.

"Long time, no see," I told Luke Gianetti, who stomped the snow off his boots before slipping past me, a familiar takeout bag in his hand.

"Took a chance you were home with nothing in the refrigerator, as usual." His jacket and dark curly hair glistened with snow. "Want me to put everything in the kitchen?"

"Sure."

"Jeremy here?"

"You're a police officer. You tell me." Since my apartment consisted of only one room, unless Jeremy was sequestered in the bathroom, he wasn't here. My snarky comment slipped out because Luke for some reason still thought he could pop up anytime with Chinese takeout.

He unloaded the food and ignored me.

Annoyed lost out to starving. Luke tipped the scales by reminding me he'd brought all my favorite dishes from Lucky Garden.

My surrender complete, I joined him in the kitchen.

"Okay," he admitted, "I should have texted you. My bad. I was getting something for myself and just thought about you. See, I ordered extra in case Jeremy made it up for the weekend." He lifted two containers in the air to justify his statement, a sweet smile on his lying face.

From that falsely innocent look, I knew he knew I was alone tonight. I wondered which one of my staffers ratted me out. My suspicion fixed on Cindy, via her brother-in-law, Police Chief Bobby Garcia, currently Luke's boss.

"Come on. Don't be mad, Kate." The next smile made his eyes crinkle at the corners, a killer move. His face was more interesting than handsome, guaranteed to get better with age.

"I see a quart of wonton soup, so all is forgiven." Delicious smells of sesame oil and ginger rising from the kitchen counter captured all of my attention. For a few minutes the only two sounds in the room were gentle soup slurping and pesky dog panting. Even though I told him a million times not to do it, Luke always slipped Buddy something under the table, which is why my dog currently stared adoringly at him. Sure enough, I noticed a suspicious move, a morsel of chicken palmed in my guest's hand.

"Luke."

"Just this one piece, I promise."

Both guys stared at me with their big brown eyes. They knew what a sucker I was for that. To change the subject, I asked him how things were going.

He finished a piece of orange chicken before answering. "Pretty good. I'll be able to take my law school exams in June."

"That's exciting. With your background I'm sure you'll have no problems." Luke had been hard at work taking night school courses for the last year to finish all the prerequisites for law school. During the daytime he still worked full-time as a police officer for the town of Oak Falls. His courses included a mix of regular and online classes. For a semester he had a Tuesday night class at the local community college and had gotten in the habit of dropping by on his way home, cementing our friendship/flirtation with eggrolls and fried rice.

"Thanks for the vote of confidence." His chopsticks expertly picked up a stray shrimp.

In a preemptive strike, I secured the last remaining crustacean. "So, anything new with the Oak Falls Police Department? Has your boss forgiven me yet?" Thanks to a strange knack for solving murders and almost getting myself killed in the process, I'd had a few unpleasant run-ins with the chief.

Luke opened his mouth then thought better of it, camouflaging the move with another helping of fried rice.

I gave him my best Meryl Streep-look-a-like stare.

After a few moments he caved. "Well, there is an interesting case. You probably read about it in the papers or heard it on television."

"If it wasn't on HGTV, I doubt it."

Our eyes held a second too long and I wish I could say I didn't feel a little something unsettling. Where the heck was Jeremy when I needed him?

"An elderly lady was killed during a burglary. Strangled. The guy took off with some of her things. He probably thought that because we are up here in the boonies, he could get away with it."

That interested me. "Did you find anything?"

"Not us. The pathologist. We've got a really smart doctor doing our autopsies. He used to work in the city, got fed up with the pressure and moved his family to Rhinebeck."

A strong gust of wind and snow rattled the kitchen window.

"Storm's kicking up," he said. "I probably should get going."

"Not before you tell me what the pathologist found." I hated stories with loose ends, plus all aspects of medicine fascinated me, human included.

"Well, the body looked very natural, obviously hadn't been moved. She died in her bed. But on autopsy he found tiny petechiae on the conjunctiva of both eyes which indicated…"

"She was strangled." A no-brainer if you were a murder junkie like I was. "You already said that."

"Right. Now we just have to find the creep who would do this to a sweet old lady. A shame, because she'd just moved up here to be with her niece."

My stomach clenched. "Do you remember her name?"

He waved his chopstick in the air. "Yes, I do. A very famous name, as a matter of fact."

My stomach clenched again.

"LaGuardia. Gloria LaGuardia."

• • ● • •

"I'm so sorry, Kate," Luke said again. "I didn't know you knew her." He'd cleared all the food off the kitchen table except my tea and his coffee.

Did I know her? Thirty minutes of conversation between us added up to an infinitesimally tiny piece of a long life. Still, her murder stunned me.

"Has forensics found anything?" Part of me wanted to change the subject but the other part craved more details. So far, the curious part was winning.

Reluctance to answer my question wafted off Luke like odor

from a skunk. Would he tell me any more? I gave myself sixty-to-forty odds. His frown made me think I'd lost my internal bet, but then he surprised me for the second time that night.

"Promise me you won't ask anything else." He narrowed his eyes in concentration across the table.

"I promise."

"Alright." The wind rattled the kitchen window again, this time splattering snow against the pane. "All this was in the news story, so I'm not revealing anything confidential."

"Okay."

"Gloria's niece, Irene, arrived at her apartment around eight-thirty in the morning to pick up her aunt. When no one answered the bell she opened the door with her duplicate key. The place was a mess. Worried now, she checked the bedroom, found her aunt's body, and called 911. The victim's apartment showed signs of a break-in. The front door had been jimmied and her valuables were missing. Mostly jewelry. From the lack of fingerprints it looks like the perp wore gloves."

"Poor Gloria." I shook my head in frustration over such a senseless crime, like so many others. There had been no need for violence against a frail elderly woman.

Sensing how upset I was, Luke waited a bit before continuing the disturbing story. "After the forensic team finished up, we had the EMT unit come in and transport the victim to Kingston Hospital."

I poured myself more tea to keep my hands occupied. A stray branch slapped the windowpane, dark stems scratching at the glass.

Luke noticed and commented. "Storm's coming in fast. Might as well stay for a while."

"Might as well," I echoed. The teacup radiated warmth, while the aromatic Earl Grey eased my stomach a bit. Then I remembered he'd mentioned something about his smart pathologist. "So, Luke, what else did your doctor find that intrigued the investigators?"

He vacillated on telling me, but ultimately decided I'd find out anyway. "Alright. One interesting piece of evidence came from our very thorough pathologist."

My teacup poised in mid-air.

"He combed a stray tuft of white hair from her head."

I didn't get it and told him so. If I remembered correctly Gloria's hair was white. "What was so important about an extra bit of hair?"

Then Luke explained. "It was cat hair."

"Cat hair?"

"Yes, white cat hair, and nobody in Gloria's family owns a cat."

After discussing Gloria's murder it proved almost impossible to convince Luke to leave. Regretting his previous candor, he started going all "you need to come down to the station and give a statement" on me, even though she passed away a full week after our brief thirty-minute encounter. Naturally, he demanded to know everything. I relayed to him her odd statement that someone evil was in town and also explained how foggy her thinking could get. How she imagined she recognized so many strangers. At one point, I recalled, she didn't remember who I was. My observations after being with her for approximately a half hour were only vague impressions, nothing more.

It turned out the Oak Falls Police Department first interviewed Gloria's niece, Irene, at length. She lucked out as far as an alibi for the night of the murder was concerned because her son, Peter, sneaking home way after curfew, tried to jump the backyard fence, but slipped on the ice, and broke his ankle. Their late-night trip to the emergency room, and lengthy wait for an orthopedic doctor to supervise casting the teenager's leg, more than covered the estimated time of death for her aunt.

I got the impression from Luke that the authorities had no suspects and no more clues. For now the crime was classified as an attempted robbery gone horribly bad. They hypothesized that Gloria woke up and surprised the burglar, perhaps calling out in terror, and whoever strangled her, merely tried to stop her from screaming. Whether he meant to kill her or just quiet her down remained unclear.

After an hour of increasingly heated discussion, Luke finally left, reminding me again as I started to shut the door to let the professionals handle criminal investigations.

After waiting an hour for a call back from Jeremy I finally took out my phone and dialed his number again. After six rings voicemail picked up.

Although I sat home alone most nights after work, clearly he didn't. A frantic battle broke out between my common sense and my wicked imagination. Since it wasn't getting me anywhere I called it a draw and decided to start the laundry. I scooped up my dirty scrubs and spot-cleaned them, then abruptly tossed everything into the washing machine.

Saturday night and I couldn't reach my boyfriend. What could I do to distract myself until the next load?

I went back into the hospital and took a moment to check the office database for the email address of Gloria's niece, Irene Zeidman. In the quiet I composed a letter of condolence, focusing on how much I enjoyed my brief meeting with her aunt. After sending it I scrolled through my messages and emails.

Fifteen minutes later I glanced at my cell. No calls and no messages from Jeremy.

Frustrated, I returned to the apartment, now focused on the bathroom. Thankfully, the cell phone ringing delayed that plan. Not bothering to check the caller ID, I expected to hear my boyfriend's voice. Instead, a recorded message offered me a three-day time-share vacation in sunny Florida.

The ringtone woke Buddy, who asked for a quick bathroom break. We dashed outside into the cold and wind then hurried back into the warmth. After a noisy lapping of water and a few circles, my dog eagerly sacked out once more in his fluffy doggy bed. I ended up stretched out on the sofa, with a plush new blanket and HGTV softly playing in the background. Six hours later I woke up with a start, my neck stuck in a weird position. Wind whistled behind me as the storm raged on.

Half asleep I checked my phone. No texts, missed calls, or emails from Jeremy.

Chapter Four

The next day when I got around to checking my email, a message from Irene Zeidman popped up. She thanked me for my note and apologetically extended a last-minute invite to Gloria's funeral, being held this Sunday afternoon at one-thirty. Unenthused, I sat in my office contemplating whether or not to go, when my cell phone rang.

"Good morning, sugar."

My watch said eleven-thirty—barely qualifying for morning—but I wasn't about to quibble. I mentally vetoed my first reply, the one that began with why didn't you call me, and simply said, "Good morning to you too, sugar."

"Sorry I didn't get back to you last night," Jeremy explained, "but I went to a late night showing of a documentary on endangered historical sites in the Middle East. Afterward, a bunch of us stayed up talking and I lost track of the time." He sounded contrite.

I closed my eyes and imagined the *please forgive me* look on his face. That image surprisingly annoyed the heck out of me. On the spur of the moment I decided to cut our conversation short and try to make Gloria's funeral service.

"Hey, no problem," I replied sweetly. "But you got me at a bad time. I've got to run. Call you later." It sounded like a brush-off but it was the truth. I had less than two hours to shower, finish getting dressed, walk the dog, grab some lunch, clean the snow and ice off the truck, and head into town. I'd be lucky to arrive on time.

After scrambling to get ready I scraped the last bit of snow off the windshield and climbed into the truck. The shining sun felt extra bright as it so often does after a snowstorm. Crisp shadows outlined the white drifts. On the sides of the road, pine tree limbs bent low, heavy with added snow now starting to melt. All the rusty cars, spare tires, and discarded appliances at the junkyard I passed on the way to the funeral parlor were temporarily hidden from view, transformed for a brief moment into frozen sculptures waiting to be revealed once again.

At fifteen minutes after one, I guided the truck into Franklin Brother's Funeral Parlor parking lot. Only a few vehicles lined the walkway. I questioned for a moment going in, since I'd only met Gloria once, but I did want to pay my respects.

An employee in a black suit directed me to a large room off to the right. The sign at the door read *Gloria LaGuardia, family and friends*. Soft music played unobtrusively in the background. Subdued lighting softly lit the room, with a discrete spotlight focused on a silver urn with scrollwork decorating its rim, resting in a glass case. On display was a large photograph of a youthful Gloria, her arms joyfully wrapped around a man standing next to a young woman in a cap and gown. Although there must have been fifty chairs set up, I saw only seven or eight people quietly talking among themselves. In the first row sat Irene, her daughter to her right. The girl's head hung down, as if studiously avoiding looking at the urn. On her left, his leg in a cast and support boot, fidgeted her teen-aged son.

Three rows back I noted an elderly woman accompanied by a look-alike daughter. Behind them, a woman in her forties settled in, a purple scrub top peeking out from under a heavy winter coat.

In the last row sat a lone red-haired man, scribbling something on a small green notepad. A reporter? Since when did our local newspaper cover funerals? Gloria's niece Irene turned around at that moment and shot him a nasty look.

The funeral director who'd greeted me at the entrance silently appeared and carefully closed the door. I slipped into the closest chair. My watch read exactly one-thirty.

"Please take your seats," he intoned in a practiced solemn voice. "Out of respect for the family, please turn off all electronic devices." Tall and thin, the man settled his face into a professional mask. Irene, who'd stood up to chat with some of the mourners, hurriedly reclaimed her place.

I felt someone's eyes on me and snuck a backward glance. The red-haired guy's unabashed stare met my questioning look. After a brief pause he turned back to his notepad. *Very curious*, I thought. *Was he catching up on work or taking notes?*

The lights dimmed a bit, then a subtle glow lit the polished urn. I couldn't help but recall Halloween night and the last thing Gloria said, those final frightened words. "Someone evil is here."

A subtle tap on the microphone drew our attention to the front of the room.

"We are gathered today to celebrate the life of Gloria LaGuardia," the funeral director recited. As he continued reading from his notes, my mind flashed back to the funeral of my mother and younger brother. I'd sat in the church pew, a stunned fifteen-year-old, barely comprehending anything. One minute my mom and Jimmy had gone out for ice cream, and the next minute they were both gone, killed by a drunk driver. The priest officiating that day hadn't known them and spoke from impromptu notes, just as this funeral director had no idea who Gloria was.

The sudden stillness in the room brought me back to the present.

"I'd like to invite anyone with a remembrance they would like to share, to come to the podium at this time." He gestured toward the front row.

Gloria's niece stood up and prodded her teenagers, who reluctantly followed. As she made her way to the oak podium, Irene removed a folded sheet of paper from her jacket pocket. After clearing her throat she began.

"I'd like to thank everyone for coming to help me say good-bye to my sweet Aunt Gloria. Her husband and daughter, my uncle Danny and cousin Rachael passed, before her," she gestured to the picture. "I'm certain she's happily reunited with them now in heaven." After a deep breath Irene continued with a brief history of her aunt's life as an art teacher and recalled how she came to live with them, helping take care of her sister, Irene's mother, who had been diagnosed with breast cancer. In the years that followed, Gloria became like a second mother to Irene and her family.

As she continued with family history, I casually turned in my chair. The little red-haired guy in a suit and tie continued taking notes. What could be that important about Gloria's life? As Irene recounted the death of Gloria's husband from a heart attack, the woman in purple scrubs snuck a quick peek at her watch.

"Our family is going to miss you, Aunt Gloria. Rest in peace." Irene raised her eyebrows at her kids, questioning if they wanted to add anything, but suddenly shy, both put their heads down and started back to their seats. After lightly resting a hand on the glass case displaying the urn, Irene sat down.

"Would anyone else care to share with us tonight?" The director's solemn gaze efficiently swept the room.

Slowly, the elderly woman I'd noticed in the third row stood up, supported by her daughter. She walked with the help of a three-pronged cane. Once at the podium her knuckles turned white while trying to grip the sides of the smooth, wooden edge. Unshed tears shone in her eyes.

"Gloria was my friend," she stated simply in a surprisingly firm voice. The overhead lights emphasized a prominent nose and pair of strong, high cheekbones. "I didn't know her for that long, but it was long enough for me to appreciate her. Over the last few months we spent most of our days together. Gloria gave me art lessons in exchange for crocheting tips from me. She'd almost finished a lovely shawl for you, Irene. A surprise Christmas present." A slight smile acknowledged her friend's niece in the front row. "I'm going to miss her very much."

Finished, the woman turned to her daughter and the two carefully made their way back to their seats, the cane clicking on the wooden floor.

"Thank you. Anyone else?" To my surprise the funeral parlor representative expectantly looked in my direction. Embarrassed, I immediately broke his gaze and stared at my boots. Then a chair squeaked slightly. Someone behind me got up, and began making their way to the front of the room.

When I looked up, I saw to my surprise the red-haired fellow who had been scribbling notes stood at the podium. Now that I got a good look at him, I revised my estimate of his age to probably around twenty-six or twenty-seven, about five-six, very pale, with light blue eyes that didn't miss a thing. He'd left his long woolen coat draped on the chair next to him to reveal a cream-colored button-down shirt set off with a famous GG-patterned Gucci tie. The black suit jacket he wore screamed designer. Was he a weekender neighbor or the wealthy black sheep of the La Guardia family?

He cleared his throat and cast a quick look at Irene, Gloria's niece, who didn't look too happy, judging from her frown and pursed lips. For a second I thought she was going to order him to sit down and be quiet.

"Ah," he began, "I met Gloria about four years ago. The first time I visited her at her condo in New Jersey she invited me to stay for dinner. I ate too much fast food, she told me, and insisted that I needed a home-cooked meal, which was true. For some reason she took a liking to me, and decided to help me research my book." He cleared his throat again. "She was a sweet, sweet person who didn't deserve to die like this. I owe her a lot."

That very personal account got my attention. Finished speaking he quickly retreated to the back of the room.

No one else volunteered to speak. The service ground to a halt. We were invited by the staff to sign the memory book before we left.

The immediate family stood in a receiving line at the exit, thanking everyone who came to say good-bye. Irene deliberately turned away from the mysterious red-haired mourner, who awkwardly waited in front of her for a moment before silently leaving for the exit.

I quickly paid my condolences then followed him outside. The cold was a shock after the stuffy funeral parlor.

"Excuse me," I said when I caught up to him. "Do you have a moment to talk?"

Unsurprised blue eyes caught mine. "Dr. Kate Turner, I presume. Sure, but can we go somewhere warm?" He pulled his long coat tightly around him trying to block the wind.

"Well, I'm not sure…"

"Meet you at Judy's Place on Main Street in town," he suggested. "I had a great breakfast there this morning."

Before I could agree he pulled out some keys and unlocked a car in the parking lot with a clicker.

"But who are…?"

He'd already started to walk in the direction of the beep. "See you. I'll wait by the front door."

With no more explanation he left me standing in the parking lot. I made it halfway back to my truck before I questioned how this stranger knew my name.

Curiosity forced me to keep our date. For some odd reason, I found plenty of parking spaces in town this afternoon. Through my windshield I glimpsed the red-haired writer waiting outside of Judy's Place, sleek leather briefcase in hand. His clothing definitely looked out of place for our winter weather. I felt sorry for him standing in icy slush on the sidewalk in expensive suede loafers. He'd have a hard time getting the salt and water stains out of them. An unruly mop of red hair cut in British schoolboy style framed a young pale face. Pleasantly doughy were the adjectives I'd use to describe him—like an innocent prisoner locked away from the sun in solitary confinement for several years. Again I questioned if Gloria's death was the only reason he'd shown up in Oak Falls.

"Hello again, Dr. Turner." The hand extended to me in greeting felt soft and pudgy.

"Please call me Kate."

"I'm Tucker. Tucker Weinstein."

"Shall we go in?" I moved to open the door but he beat me to it.

"After you, Kate."

I had an uncomfortable feeling he'd done a fashion assessment of me in those few seconds, from my scuffed waterproof boots to the pompom on the top of my warm unfashionable knit hat.

Once we settled ourselves at a table, I got right down to it. "Tucker. How do you know who I am?"

He took a quick look around the room before pulling out his briefcase. "Instead of telling you, let me show you exactly who I am. I find it eliminates most worries my sources have."

A source? A source of what?

The folder he put in front of me contained copies of newspaper articles with his byline. "I'm a writer," he explained, proudly, "and a journalist." Next he placed a hardcover book published by a major publishing company, on the table; it was titled *Murder and Mayhem in America, A Personal Perspective*. The book jacket featured an extremely flattering picture of Tucker along with a short bio.

"That's just in case you need further proof that I am who I say I am." He scooped up the articles and returned them to his briefcase. "With things the way they are in the news biz today, you never know. But, believe me, I'm no fake."

A waitress interrupted us. We both ordered coffee and a dessert.

When she came back with our orders, he tore open five packets of sugar and poured them into his steaming stoneware mug.

When he added a sixth packet, I winced.

Tucker's leg jerked up and down underneath the table. "Yeah, I know it's not good for me but I figure I'll be dead before diabetes gets me, so why not enjoy myself? Plus it keeps me awake."

"That's a pessimistic attitude," I countered, kicking into doctor mode. Of course I conveniently forgot the excessive amounts of pie and sweets I'd been known to put away, especially when stressed. Which was most of the time.

"Probably." He sipped his coffee and started on a large piece of chocolate cake. "Anyway, let me tell you why I attended the memorial service. I'm trying to contact local people who talked to Gloria in these last few weeks."

"How did you learn about me?"

"Irene told me you helped her out on Halloween. I heard all about what Gloria said to you, that someone evil was there in the crowd. We talked for almost an hour before she kicked me out."

"So this conversation is okay with Gloria's niece?"

"Absolutely. The problem is, she's so focused on her crazy kids, I don't think she'd notice if an alien spaceship landed on her front lawn." He chuckled at the image. "I'm counting on you to be more observant."

I shifted uncomfortably in my chair.

"Let me explain. I've got a nonfiction book deal about men who kill their families," Tucker said. "This focuses in-depth on three specific cases. One guy's in prison, one is dead, and the other man is still out there somewhere."

"What the heck does that have to do with Gloria?" I felt more confused by the minute.

"You don't know?"

"Know what?"

Tucker lowered his voice. "Twenty-one years ago, the family living across the street from Gloria was murdered.

Shocked, I listened to the gruesome story of Carl Wolf, still a fugitive on the FBI's most wanted list after so many years.

"Carl was a computer guy, did online trading in the stock market and ran a private investment club. Married, with twins, he and his wife lived in the suburbs of Tom's River, New Jersey. The guy liked to hunt and fish, went camping a lot—definitely an outdoors person. His wife, Anita, worked in the hospital as a pediatric nurse. According to her family, Carl became more and more of a control freak, although authorities never uncovered any documented evidence of physical abuse. Mental abuse, yes. Their marriage started unraveling, though, after seven years, and in late summer Anita confessed to her mother that she wanted to leave him. Carl had been unfaithful to her numerous times over the years. He'd also run up their credit cards to the maximum without telling her and took out a second mortgage on their house. Fed up with everything, Anita planned to confront him, file for a divorce, and demand full custody of the kids."

So far it didn't sound that different from plenty of stories I'd heard, my own father's included.

Tucker's fingers nervously drummed the table. "Gloria LaGuardia lived across the street from Carl and Anita Wolf. She was newly widowed, went to the same church, and sometimes babysat the twins. Anita sort of took her under her wing, and became like another daughter. If anything in Gloria's house needed fixing, Anita would send Carl across the street to help. Over the years he changed the air filters, repaired a leaking faucet, mowed the grass. She remembered him as a very capable handyman, definitely not afraid to get his hands dirty."

My mind's eye pictured a quiet tree-lined street, green lawns, kids riding bikes. Gloria must have been about sixty years old.

"This next part is a little hard for me." He returned the book to the briefcase, an angry expression on his face. "Anita told Carl on the night of August 18th that she wanted a divorce. It was hot. Most people had their windows open. Multiple neighbors heard a loud argument between the couple. The next morning residents woke to the smell of smoke. A fast-moving fire swiftly engulfed the Wolf home as they watched, threatening nearby neighbors' houses. When the fire department finally put out the blaze, they found three bodies inside the home, Anita and the twins." The lock on his briefcase clicked shut. "Carl had fled in his SUV. They discovered the family dog sitting in Gloria's front yard. He wouldn't budge until Anita's mother arrived."

"Wolf killed his children but spared the dog?"

"No one knows." Tucker stared out the window as a family walked by, bundled up against the snow, laughing at the antics of the youngest trying to catch stray snowflakes on her tongue. "There are other mysterious deaths in his past. Carl's high school sweetheart vanished without a trace one weekend. Rumor had it she wanted to break up with him. Police classified her as a runaway, but her mother never believed it."

Something told me Tucker hadn't finished his story.

"Between taking college classes, Wolf worked a variety of part-time jobs—pizza delivery, veterinary technician, even took a few acting roles in a couple of community theatre productions—before he found his true calling. Working on computers."

My nod must have satisfied him that I was listening because he continued. "Here's another odd thing from his past. One of his college roommates owed him money, couldn't pay him. They argued, and Wolf moved out. A week later the guy overdosed in his car. Several friends and family told the police that despite the evidence they found, he didn't do IV drugs. The coroner ruled it an accident. Wolf came up with a signed agreement from the roommate, promising to return the money he'd borrowed. Long story short, the parents ended up paying it in full, plus interest, in their son's name."

I didn't like what I heard.

"Getting back to his former girlfriend, I think Nancy was her name. Blond, tall, looked a little like you. The cops named him a person of interest but his new girlfriend gave him an alibi for the night in question."

Too many coincidences. Too many people dead or missing.

"Carl Wolf gets mad if you cross him or try to leave. He's very careful, plans things out. The FBI profiler I spoke to stated that Wolf is a chameleon, he might appear arrogant, or a charming fellow, or fade into the woodwork. He also suspects Wolf won't make a move unless the odds are stacked in his favor. Not a risk-taker, by any means."

Tucker continued to stare out the window. I wondered which family he saw reflected in the glass.

I cleared my throat to get his attention. "Tucker, how did he kill them?"

Reluctantly, he recited the details. "Investigators who reconstructed the scene believe he gave the twins sedatives first, then strangled them. He may also have given a smaller dose to his wife and made her witness their murders—before he killed her."

"How horrible." The last sip of coffee did little to mask the bitter taste in my mouth.

Tucker's next statement stunned me. "I believe Gloria saw Carl Wolf here in Oak Falls, on Halloween night."

"What?" Several people turned our way. I lowered my voice. "But the Gloria I met showed signs of mild cognitive impairment." I described how the elderly woman's focus and interpretation of what she saw changed from one moment to another. "It would be more likely she noticed someone who reminded her of Carl in some way, but even that is pretty far-fetched."

His fingers rapped another staccato beat on the table. "I'm certain I'm right."

"How do you know?"

He leaned in toward me. "Because Gloria's been murdered, strangled, according to my sources, just like the twins."

It sounded crazy and yet…

"My gut tells me this was no coincidence. No gun evidence for this guy. He likes to get his hands dirty."

We sat together in silence for a while, the noise from the crowded café a temporary diversion. Tucker's revelations confused me.

"Can you answer a question?" I raised my voice over the din. "Why do you put so much faith into what Gloria said that night?"

He pushed his chair closer, his voice careful. "Because I was Gloria's friend. I'd already interviewed her multiple times for this new book." The table rocked slightly from the nervous tapping of his foot. "Did you know she started out as a teacher but after getting a PhD in art history, she became a professor at New York University?"

All this was news to me.

"Gloria had another, very important skill." His sly smile dared me to figure it out.

Too tired I said, "Okay, I give up. What was it?"

The drumming of his fingers quickened. "You know those trials that don't allow cameras in? Gloria worked as courtroom sketch artist. She drew pen-and-ink sketches of the jury, judge, lawyers, and the defendants that were broadcast on television and published in leading newspapers. These were the good old days before the Internet. I think her most famous trial must be the Son of Sam, with that creepy David Berkowitz. Her portraits from that era are pretty well known."

I began to understand.

"If Gloria LaGuardia said she saw an evil man in Oak Falls on Halloween night," Tucker said, his fingers dramatically mimicking a drum roll, "I'd bet the bank on it."

Chapter Five

Like a bad dream, when I woke the following morning I immediately recalled that strange meeting with Tucker. It's not fun to be barely awake with murder on your mind.

Monday had arrived too quickly. When the alarm rang, all I wanted to do was throw the covers over my head and go back to sleep. The buzzing, though, always set off a cascade of events starting with my dog, Buddy. Unlike me he wakes up refreshed, happy and eager to go outside each day. His twirling dance, yips, and ecstatic licks to my hand eventually serve to propel me out of bed. The cold air outside finishes the wake-up process. Upright and committed to the day, now technology takes over. As soon as I'm dressed I check my email, check my phone messages, check the lab tests that came in overnight, all while sipping a first cup of automatically brewed coffee.

Surprise. I'd already heard from Tucker, who'd made sure before we left Judy's that I entered all his contact numbers into my phone. His early morning text reminded me to let him know ASAP if I remembered anything new or heard something interesting about Gloria's murder from any of my clients or staff. Over the next two days he intended to gather as much information as possible about Gloria's short time in Oak Falls. The more background and local color he provided in the book, the more authentic he felt it would read.

Persistent as he was, I didn't need another reminder from the writer, so I deleted the message. My morning routine finished, I took a breather before going over the day's schedule.

"You've got a very serious look on your face." Mari wandered into my office with Mr. Katt, our hospital cat, in her arms. "Everything okay?"

"Everything's fine. Just thinking." I stretched my hands and rolled my shoulders before logging out of the computer. I'd been searching recent reports of sightings of Carl Wolf. According to the Internet, eyewitnesses swore to the FBI that they've seen him in California, Mexico, and even strolling the beaches of Rio de Janeiro in a Speedo, all during the same timeframe. I stood up and searched for the cold remains of my coffee buried somewhere on my desk.

"Got a minute?"

"Of course. Something wrong with our big guy?"

"I'm not sure. I caught him running around like a maniac, dragging his tail." Mr. Katt wiggled vigorously in her arms in a vain attempt to get down.

Our hospital cat had a stubborn feline mind of his own, and disliked being examined. Even though he lived in an animal hospital, he wasn't the most cooperative of patients.

"Let me take a look." I ran my hand over his back and along his fluffy tail and quickly discovered the problem. "Hold on tight," I warned Mari before I snipped a five-inch piece of scotch tape off his fur.

That did it. Mr. Katt hurled himself from her arms and made a beeline for the top of the treatment cabinets. Out of our reach, he glared down in disdain before delicately concentrating on grooming himself, tail first.

"I bet he's been diving into Cindy's garbage again." Our receptionist sometimes ate lunch at her desk and threw the remains into her trashcan. Ever resourceful, Mr. Katt had been known to wait for an opportune moment before jumping into the basket, hoping to score some food. This time a piece of discarded tape had been his sticky reward.

"Think he's learned his lesson?" Mari asked me.

"No." I turned off the overhead light and followed her into the treatment room. "Unlike some of us, he's a committed optimist."

Optimism was in short supply at our next house call to Sun Meadow Farm. Jane and Lorraine, identical twin sisters, kept sheep, alpaca, llamas, and now goats on their small farm for milk, cheese-making, and wool. The mixed herds normally got along fine, but their rented Nubian stud goat was causing problems. The one-hundred-and-eighty-pound newcomer lowered his impressive horns and went after everyone, including their prized Jacob ram. Although the sheep was larger, that didn't stop this determined billy goat from trying to be king of the world. He'd even attacked the gate between the pens, putting a dent in the metal.

"Billy's a gorgeous Nubian, and comes from a fantastic milk line, but I don't know…" Jane's voice trailed off. "We're getting pretty discouraged." For now they had isolated the bearded troublemaker in his own pen. I noticed some extra metal fencing material for repairs stacked up against the wall.

I had to agree with the gorgeous part. With a heart-shaped white blaze on his head, and long pale gray ears, the well-muscled and experienced stud goat was physically a stunner.

"This is rutting season," I explained. "His behavior is absolutely normal and probably not going to change until the girls are out of heat. Some male goats are more aggressive than others. Just don't turn your back on him."

I spoke from experience. On a trip to a famous goat cheese farm while a student in veterinary school, I'd been warned not to turn my back on the alpha male of the herd. For our class assignment we were expected to observe all aspects of the operation. Several of the female does had given birth so I decided to take a shortcut through an empty pen and check them out. A group of classmates waved to me from the door of the maternity barn. I waved back, eyes focused on avoiding the piles of waste and getting to the other side. That turned out to be my fatal mistake.

Halfway across the pen a vicious head-butt slammed into my back. The sudden shove of hard horns pushed me off balance and I fell smack into all the muck. Everything—my hands, face, and the entire front of my green coveralls was smeared with a combination of mud, hay, and goat turds. Two classmates ran to my aid, pulling me up while laughing uncontrollably. Someone whipped out a cell phone and my predicament became immortalized. That picture ended up being posted repeatedly on our student bulletin board for the rest of the year.

I never forgot that lesson.

"He's over here," said Jane or Lorraine. The sisters wanted me to make sure their handsome Jacob ram, a rare breed from England that sometimes grows four horns, wasn't injured from his encounter with Billy the Goat. A special color called piebald, the Jacob's coat naturally produced both black and white fleece. Hand-spinners, his owners mentioned proudly, love the texture and oil content of this particular breed. Approaching the docile ram proved no problem. All three women helped keep him steady while I palpated his chest and front legs. I came to the conclusion that the goat had probably hurt the big sheep's pride more than anything else.

"That's a relief," one of the twins said. "Do you have time to go over some things with us? This is our first year with the goats."

"Sure," I answered, dusting off my pants.

"Why did you decide to add goats?' Mari asked.

"Our trip to France, and the amazing varieties of goat cheeses we tasted. Just heavenly."

I thought it was Lorraine who answered the question but wasn't one hundred percent sure. As mirror image twins, the two appeared almost identical, but actually were like opposite pages of a book—although they often finished each other's sentences and dressed in the same outfits.

"Well, don't be upset at Billy. You'll find that Nubians are generally very friendly and gentle."

We happily spent some time talking about doe fertility, their five-month pregnancies, the frequency of twins and even triplet kids, and the importance of keeping breeding records. I had to give them credit. They had done their research. Since inheriting the farmhouse and fields from their parents, the twins had been busy becoming certified organic. They'd also reached out to their farming neighbors and joined an active artisan cooperative here in the Hudson Valley.

Once we finished, Jane and Lorraine followed Mari and me back to the truck, chatting the entire time.

Before I left I thought of another good piece of advice. "Make friends with Billy the Goat by giving him special treats when you handle him. Get him used to you, but remember that head-butting is a natural behavior. Keep track of those females who are bred and I strongly suggest a separate goat-only area for Billy until his hormones calm down."

"Right."

"It's also normal for him to become extremely stinky."

That got a laugh, since the odor of a rutting intact male goat was hard to ignore.

"There's always artificial insemination available, to give you some genetic diversity in the future," I reminded them.

"Did you hear that, Billy?" one of them said. "The handwriting is on the wall for you."

As Mari and I packed up to go, I joked, "Ever since you two retired you've been busier than ever." The twins had worked together at a big ad agency in New York City, coordinating advertising print spreads, approving layouts, and generally making things run smoothly for the firm. They'd been involved in some famous ad campaigns. Reminders of that career hung in their home office.

The mention of retirement elicited a groan of agreement from one twin. "It's true. But our stress level is different now. Checking to see if your cheese is maturing is much better than working insane hours in an advertising firm trying to meet an impossible deadline."

"With impossible people," the other twin added.

After a few questions from Mari about naturally dyed yarns for knitting we hopped into the truck and drove down their long, twisting driveway.

"That was nice," Mari commented. Despite the bumpy road she began to update my notes in our laptop computer. "Shoot. I'm not getting a Wi-Fi signal here."

"We'll get one in a minute." I slowed down as we headed down a steep dip. *This must be murder when it ices over*, I thought.

Mari glanced out the window. "These ladies need to get this road leveled out." A branch from a dead tree leaning precariously in our direction scraped the roof.

"What is that, scratch number thirty?" Our truck routinely got beat up on these house calls. "I'll admit, Sun Meadow Farm is one of my favorite places to visit. I'm intrigued with that French goat cheese project. It will be interesting to see what happens in the next few years."

My assistant turned to me. "Do you realize you're starting to talk about staying past your one-year commitment?"

"I guess I am." Sometimes I forgot I had a one-year contract to run the Oak Falls Animal Hospital for the owner, Doc Anderson, while he enjoyed his round-the-world cruise. He and his sister, who was celebrating her remission from cancer, had impulsively bought two deeply discounted tickets for the trip of a lifetime. All of us, staff and clients alike, followed their exotic adventures on a special Facebook page linked to the animal hospital website.

A few remaining red and yellow leaves swirled and danced at the base of the driveway. I looked both ways before pulling out onto isolated Mountain Shadow Road, on my way to the highway. Mari was right. I'd settled into my garage apartment at the hospital, enjoyed a busy job and clients, and had started to feel at home in Oak Falls. The prospect of staying put felt right.

And then I remembered Jeremy.

That night in the apartment, with a cold glass of white wine, I brooded over my love life. After being dumped by my veterinarian boyfriend/boss at my last job, I'd jumped at the chance to get away and move to Oak Falls. With an absentee owner I had full responsibility for the hospital and house call clients. I'd become a workaholic pie-eating professional woman with no love life. The only man who ever stopped by, police officer Luke Gianetti, was in a complicated on/off relationship with his high school sweetheart. Our whatever-it-was friendship remained completely platonic.

After a few months of moping around, my grandfather gently nudged me into jumping back in the dating soup, but I resisted—until an old college boyfriend appeared, ready for a second chance. Jeremy had improved with time, like a fine wine. We began a relationship, a comfortable relationship—no crazy highs and lows—just a steady middle ground. He had his work and I had mine. Our jobs forced us into a long-distance romance that I—naively, perhaps—expected to work with few problems. After all, we were two intelligent adults.

Now I had my doubts.

It's a bad omen to forget you have a boyfriend.

When I'm restless or upset, I dream. It's been like this since I was a pre-teen, and tonight was no exception. All I remembered when I woke up was Gloria drawing me a picture of a man, half-human and half-goat. Jeremy didn't look too bad with golden eyes and curved horns springing from his head.

Chapter Six

Buzz.

My cell phone, set to vibrate while I saw clients and examined patients, gave me a jolt. The staff knew if they needed me they could leave a short text and I would respond as soon as possible. Tucker Weinstein hadn't gotten that memo. Tuesday morning and this was his fourth text in three hours.

Buzz. Each one simply said, "Call me when you get a minute."

I didn't have a minute. Cindy, our receptionist had been squeezing in extra appointments for clients whose animals needed to be seen right away. Our office and staff hated to turn anyone away but it sure wreaked havoc on my schedule. Instead of an allotted twenty minutes with each patient, I ended up falling further and further behind.

"You've got another drop-off," Mari told me in the hallway on my way to exam room two.

"What is it?"

"Cat urinating out of the box. Now he's sitting in the litter box straining to go."

"Male?"

"Yes."

I made a 360, asked Mari to come with me and zipped into the treatment room. "Is this the guy?" In one of the top cages a handsome black-and-white cat stared at us, before stretching his paw out between the cage bars as though asking for a high-five.

"That's Jordan. He does that paw maneuver at home too. Hubby thinks it looks like a free-throw."

I opened the cage, gave his sleek coat a pet, and palpated his lower abdomen to check his bladder. If it was big and hard, we were in trouble.

"U/O?"

"No, thank goodness. Set up a urine collection and put his owner on my call list. You can catch me up to speed on everyone with your triage notes at lunch…if we get to take a lunch."

Veterinarians, like human doctors, use shortcut phrases to describe common medical issues. Mari and I were no exception. A U/O was a urinary obstruction, most commonly seen in male cats and a medical emergency. Usually the obstruction is in the urethra, the very thin tube that lets urine flow from the kitty into the litter box. Crystals or stones that form can plug up the system. With nowhere to go, the urine swells up the bladder and in the worse-case scenario, may rupture.

Jordan had escaped that problem for now, and happily returned to the cage free-throw line. As soon as I had a moment, I would go over the history the owners told Mari, then call them up and take a repeat history of my own.

History-taking, one of the internal medicine professors once told our class, is eighty percent of diagnosis. I agreed. It occurred to me that my murder investigation "hobby" was actually another type of history-taking—but a "hobby" that had proved infinitely more dangerous.

Buzz.

The noise woke me up. It was eight p.m. and I had fallen asleep at my office computer. By some miracle my nose and face had gradually dropped to gently rest on the keyboard typing in a lovely run of nonsense letters into tomorrow's treatment notes. I doubted Mari could give anyone a kkkkkkkkkllllllllllll.

After deleting the nose typing and fixing the treatment orders for the morning, I glanced at the text. Not Tucker this time but Jeremy.

Missing u. Coming up Fri nite.
Want 2 go to NYC for wkend?

I texted back

Absolutely. See you soon xxxxx

The prospect of getting away for the weekend and adding a visit to my Gramps in the mix helped my mental fog evaporate. One thing about Jeremy, he loved to make travel plans and always was open to suggestions.

Id like to have brunch with Gramps on Sunday.

Great idea. Still in Brooklyn?

Yes.

K

It occurred to me that our texting shorthand language was a distant cousin to my medical abbreviations. Would future generations forget how to spell?

I logged out and left those heavy thoughts for another day.

By nine o'clock, with all the medical records updated, I stretched out on the sofa, in my sweats, ready to relax. I'd checked on all the patients in the hospital, including Jordan, walked and fed my dog Buddy, and called every client back who'd dropped off their animals. Since I wanted to see my Gramps this weekend, I needed to give him a heads-up. As a handsome widower in assisted living, he enjoyed a very demanding social life.

After five rings I was ready to give up and leave a voice mail when I heard his familiar, "Hello."

"Hi, Gramps. Hope I'm not intruding." He sounded mildly out of breath.

"Of course not, Katie. You come first in my book. Everyone and everything else has to get in line behind you."

Hearing his voice always made me happy. It occurred to me that he was the only person left in this world who ever called me Katie.

I scrunched into a corner of the sofa and wrapped a blanket around my shoulders. "I might be going into the city this weekend. Want to do brunch?"

"Brunch, it is. Am I going to meet your new fellow? What's his name…Julian?"

"Jeremy."

"Right."

"You met him my freshman year in college, but he's changed a lot since then."

That set my Gramps thinking. "Skinny guy, glasses—really big on anthropology?"

"That's him. I'm surprised you remember." Actually, I was stunned. Gramps only saw him once, if I recalled correctly.

"Nice kid back then."

"Still is."

I was pleased to hear no harshness in my Gramps' breathing. After a long career in the New York City Fire Department he'd suffered fire-induced lung damage. He retired from his position as an arson investigator after finding he needed oxygen to climb stairs. COPD had caught up with him.

"Text me when and where you want to meet, honey. And make sure you bring your new beau with you."

"Sure thing." Gramps had recently purchased an iPhone and was very proud of his texting ability, last time including a smiley face emoji in his message. He'd also figured out how to forward pictures with some help from a friend.

"Don't forget."

Gramps sounded suspiciously excited about our brunch date, I suspected he couldn't wait to check out Jeremy. My grandfather felt very protective of me. He'd hated my old boyfriend, Jared, on first sight and always referred to him as "Dr. Perfect" or "that doctor who thinks he's perfect." I didn't listen, of course, but it turned out he knew what he was talking about. Striving to live up to that expectation of perfection all the time had proved to be exhausting—and impossible for me.

"Anything new? Win any money this week?" Craps, blackjack, poker—it didn't matter what the game, my grandfather played it.

His chuckle started out high and ended up a grumble, punctuated with a cough. "Cleaned the guys out again. I'm going to have to find some more competition."

"Gramps…"

"Hey, it's not my fault they can't bluff without me knowing. Dean has the worst tell—he scratches his nose. Believe me, they'd destroy him in Vegas."

His voice became raspy and I started hearing individual breaths. Time to get off the phone and let him rest.

"Sorry, got to run. Goodnight, you old card shark. See you on Sunday."

"Sunday it is, Katie. Remember. Text me."

"Yes, sir. Love you, Gramps."

"Love you back, in spades," he paused, "with a couple of diamonds, clubs, and hearts thrown in."

Buzz.

When I shut the door after bringing Buddy in from his nighttime bathroom break I heard my phone again. I prayed it wasn't Jeremy canceling on the weekend, now that I'd already called Gramps and set everything up.

Buzz.

"Hello." I sounded a little breathless after making a dive across the sofa arm to answer it.

"Kate?"

The male voice on the other end didn't sound familiar. "Who is this, please?" I hoped the answering service hadn't made a mistake and forwarded an emergency call to my personal phone.

"It's Tucker."

Oh, no. I glanced at my watch—just shy of eleven o'clock. I'd forgotten to text him back. "It's late, Tucker." My tone of voice implied no nonsense.

"Sorry. Why are you so mad?" his voice incredulous.

"If this is some kind of late night…"

"Wait a minute. First of all, you aren't my type, and second, this is strictly business."

"Okay." Still wary, I waited for an explanation.

"I'm leaving the day after tomorrow and hoped to talk to you one last time. Plus," he sounded a bit embarrassed, "I hate to eat dinner alone. Last night I ate takeout in my hotel room and now the whole place smells like barbeque and Mountain Dew."

Pathetic but endearing somehow. A visual image of chewed ribs on a Styrofoam plate next to a pile of greasy napkins popped into my head.

"Okay. Chinese or Italian?"

"Chinese, I guess."

"Alright. Meet me at the Lucky Garden restaurant at the south end of town at seven-thirty tomorrow. If you can't make it, call me and cancel."

"Will do."

"Sorry about not getting back to you. We were really busy." I tried to remember when he'd contacted me last but I was too tired to think.

"Ah, the reason I texted you so many times is because I gave an interview to the *Kingston News* about my new book, and Wolf's possible connection to Gloria and the Hudson Valley."

"What's that got to do with me?"

A slightly uncomfortable silence was followed by an unpleasant disclosure. "Well, I sort of mentioned you as an animal expert and one of the last people to talk to Gloria."

"What?" If I could have grabbed him through the phone line, I would have.

"The reporter needed a local angle. You were the first person I thought about. Hey, it will probably be good publicity. I really talked you up as an expert on the human/pet bond. Also mentioned that you were helping me do important research for the book."

He sounded very proud of himself. The problem was I didn't know Carl Wolf from a hole in the wall and my human/animal bond knowledge consisted of basic training in behavior and some continuing education classes. An expert, I wasn't.

"Oh, don't worry," he blithely said after I complained. "You can just wing it."

"Wing it?"

"Now you're getting it," he replied. "See you tomorrow."

I was fuming. Veterinarians don't take being called an expert lightly. My only hope was that this story might get lost or overlooked with Thanksgiving looming and Christmas close behind. But, I vowed that the next time I got a text from Tucker, I would answer it more promptly. Unsupervised, who knew what kind of trouble he could get us both into?

After I hung up I thought about the half-hour I'd spent with Gloria on Halloween night. It had become the longest half-hour of my life. I couldn't imagine Tucker would learn anything more from me. But I intended to learn a lot more about him.

Chapter Seven

"Kate, look here," Cindy called out the next day when I walked into the animal hospital break room. "You're famous."

Her enthusiastic smile did not harmonize with my scowl. I hated having to deal with anything first thing in the morning until I'd had at least one cup of coffee. Not sure what she was talking about, I poured myself a mug, grabbed a granola bar, and sat down.

Last night's resolution to get up early, do some yoga, and have a healthy breakfast cooked at home had already flown out the window.

The ups and downs in my personal life weren't helping.

A cell phone abruptly materialized in front of me. On the screen flashed the online version of our local paper. A quick scan of the article revealed three names that popped out; Carl Wolf, Tucker Weinstein, and Dr. Kate Turner.

"What the heck?" I still hadn't processed the information.

"I know. It's fantastic publicity." Cindy smiled and scrolled to a different page. "See, they even mention the address of the animal hospital at the end."

All I could do was shake my head and pour another cup of coffee. Instead of a nice pliable granola bar in my hand, this one felt stiff and stale, despite the unopened wrapper. I tossed it in the trash.

It was going to be another long day.

● ● ● ● ●

That afternoon after collecting the mail, Cindy handed me two medical journals and a small envelope.

"Looks like an invitation," she commented. "Go ahead, open it."

Keeping any secrets from my staff was futile. I lifted the flap and slid out a cream-colored card edged in black. "Another memorial service," I commented after reading the notice.

"Anyone I know?"

"You may have met him. They called him 'D'." I slid the announcement back into the envelope. "His liver cancer had metastasized, so this really isn't unexpected."

"Oh, I remember. Older man, really thin, rode a huge Harley?"

"That's right. By the time we met, though, his bad-ass days were over."

Cindy paged through the rest of the mail, throwing the advertising circulars directly into her recycle pail. "He'd reinvented himself, I guess."

"That's the truth, reinvented himself completely." The Diabolo I knew had lost thirty pounds, shaved off his beard, slicked his hair back, and taken a job as a welder. The only reminders of his former life he couldn't conceal were the prison tattoos on his knuckles.

By ten-fifteen I'd already received two calls from clients congratulating me on the book and helping solve Gloria's murder with Tucker as a trusty sidekick. That article successfully tied me to the investigation publicly as well as privately.

I hated to admit it but it started me thinking about Carl Wolf, and reinventing yourself. What did he neglect to change, I wondered, that his former neighbor, Gloria LaGuardia recognized?

A lull in our appointments allowed me the luxury of putting my feet up in the office and reading a few veterinary journals. I was deep into learning a new surgical technique when Mari stuck her head in the door.

"What kind of pizza do you want?"

Pizza orders meant only one thing. We were having an office meeting.

"What gives?" I asked, my feet still resting on the desk. "I'm pretty sure it's not Friday yet."

"It's Wednesday," Mari confirmed, "but Cindy's taking Friday off. Her sister is scheduled for a C-section on Friday."

Our receptionist was the sister-in-law of Oak Falls Police Chief Bobby Garcia. I vaguely remembered they were expecting their second child, but didn't realize when the due date was.

"Everything alright with the baby?"

"As far as I know. I think her OB-GYN is going on vacation."

"What's a vacation?" I quipped.

"An illusion," Mari countered. "Just an illusion."

Forty minutes later I slid a barely warm slice of mushroom and cheese pizza onto a paper plate, while Cindy updated us on the latest OSHA requirements. The government agency's many regulations were designed to help keep medical facilities safer for both consumers and employees. As she began reviewing some guideline changes, she was interrupted.

"Do we have time to talk about our new uniforms?" Mari piped up. "Because I'm still not convinced that the one-hundred-percent-cotton fabric is right for us. Too wrinkly."

I groaned, signaling all eyes to turn my way. "Sorry. I thought this was settled last month."

"We chose the color, not the fabric," Cindy reminded me.

It seemed as though the staff had been arguing about new uniforms since I'd arrived. As the only doctor at the moment, my choices stayed simple on purpose. I wore whatever the heck I had that was clean, topped with a three-quarter-length white jacket. From working at several different hospitals, before and after school, I owned a colorful array of wildly different scrubs. The only common denominator in my work wardrobe was the cargo style of my pants, which I'd recently been told were out of fashion.

Today I wore a bright turquoise scrub set, leftover from a summer job I took during veterinary school.

"Alright, everyone, here they are." Cindy turned and gestured like Vanna White, presenting the two final choices like they were vowels on the big board. On the right was the comfy cotton blend that might need some ironing, and on the left the standard wrinkle-free but non-breathing polyester—truly a world-shattering decision.

"Anyone want to place a bet on which fabric wins?"

Our college student technician Nick's joke was ignored. "By the end of the day I'd like everyone to sign this list," Cindy held up a clipboard. "After the weekend staff votes I'll tally everything up and we can finally put this uniform matter to rest."

After a resounding cheer from kennel help, Nick, who Mari was convinced only came to the meetings to scarf up pizza, was zapped with my trusty assistant's evil eye.

Not stopping a beat, Cindy presented her latest holiday idea. "For Christmas I'd like us all to tie red ribbons around the cat and dog food samples as cute gifts for our clients." To demonstrate she held up a plastic envelope of dry food with a thin ribbon bow tied around the middle.

"Cute," muttered Mari. "As if we don't have enough to do."

"Sorry," I spoke up. "I'll have to veto that idea."

Our usually chipper receptionist gave me a scowl.

"Ribbons can become surgical foreign bodies," I commented. "Those are the perfect length for kitties to swallow, especially with the odor of cat food on them." I'd lifted too many cat tongues to see ribbons or tinsel that weren't meant to be in their gastrointestinal systems stuck on their way in or out.

Cindy slapped her hand to her forehead. "What was I thinking?"

"No harm done," I consoled her. "You just tried to get us into the holiday spirit. Let's brainstorm something else."

"Red yarn," Nick offered.

"No," the entire rest of the staff yelled.

"Ditto with the rubber bands and hair ties." I stood up, eyeing the last slice of mushroom pizza. As I strode forward to claim it, my foot caught the foot of the chair next to me, which sent me crashing into Mari.

Startled, Mr. Katt hurtled onto the treatment table, slid across the stainless-steel surface and scattered pizza boxes and cheesy slices all over the floor—cheese-side-down, thus effectively ending the meeting.

When I arrived that night to meet with Tucker at the Lucky Garden Chinese restaurant he'd already been seated at one of my favorite tables overlooking the river. I noticed he wore the same clothes from Gloria's funeral, which made me wonder if he'd intended to stay this long in Oak Falls.

Our waitress came by and put a wonton soup in front of him. "Sorry," he explained. "I'm starving, so I ordered an appetizer."

"No problem. Go ahead and start. Mu shu shrimp for me." I handed her back the menu.

"Could I get the shrimp in black bean sauce entrée and an order of steamed dumplings, also?" he added.

"Would you like something to drink?" Our young blond waitress picked up the menus as she spoke.

"Great idea. How about a pot of jasmine tea?" Nothing like sipping hot tea inside while watching the snow fall. Outside the window, random fluffy flakes floated into the fast-moving current to be quickly swallowed up by the cold black water.

My attention drifted back. "When are you going home?" I asked my dinner companion.

"Tonight." His spoon snagged a wonton bobbing in chicken broth.

"Tonight? You need to drive carefully," I warned.

His pale blue eyes rose to stare into mine. "You're too young to be my mother. Don't worry. The weather report predicts only flurries. Besides, the traffic going into the city will be light this time of night and I've got to get this car back before my room-mate comes home tomorrow."

After that pronouncement Tucker returned to attacking the soup.

"You have a roommate?" I questioned him, getting hungrier by the second.

"Of course—two, in fact. I don't make any money. I'm a writer. The only people who are poorer than writers are actors. One night I calculated all the hours I put into my last book and how much I made, minus the cash off the top that my agent and publisher took. I would have been better off working at McDonalds."

Somehow I couldn't picture Tucker flipping burgers.

When the rest of our food arrived, we both dove in with no pretense.

"Now, your situation, Dr. Kate, is different. As a veterinarian you've got to be raking it in," he said through a mouthful of dumpling.

"Wrong. I've got one hundred and fifty thousand dollars' worth of student loans to pay back. Plus, I made the mistake of accepting my current job at a straight salary. So, even if I work over forty hours, which I do, I don't get paid extra for it."

"Me, either."

"So we must love our jobs…"

"…or we're both crazy," he said loudly.

A few heads turned to look at us. One older woman simply shrugged her shoulders, as if she'd seen it all. Another guy sitting alone wearing a baseball cap and earbud headphones, concentrated on his food, too engrossed to look up.

"Do you mind if I record you?" Tucker asked, placing a small tape recorder on the table. Under the table his knee started jerking.

"No problem."

I'd forgotten he'd wanted a final interview with dinner.

"I'd like you to go through everything that happened Halloween night again, but this time with your eyes closed. Try not to leave anything out, even if you think it's unimportant."

Slightly annoyed I cleared my throat, shut my eyes, and thought back once again to the night I met Gloria. My memories were organized, scene after scene, like a movie played to an audience of one. Dutifully, I recited everything. When Tucker clicked off the recorder, I opened my eyes.

"Congratulations, you're an excellent observer, Kate. But that must be part of your veterinary training. Now, if you uncover anything related to the Big Bad Wolf, email me."

"Big Bad Wolf?"

"That's my nickname for Carl Wolf...the Big Bad Wolf. Since you've been so helpful I'll be sure to give you credit on the Acknowledgments page."

"Seriously?"

"Seriously." He reached into the pocket of his coat, which was lying on the spare chair next to him, and took out a small notebook.

The bright green cover caught my attention. "Weren't you writing in that at the memorial service?"

"Caught red-handed." He seemed a little embarrassed. "Very old school. Can't seem to get rid of the habit. Just like the tape recorder. It started when I was a reporter for the school newspaper in high school."

"No kidding? I wrote stories for my high school newspaper freshman year too, but then...things changed." There was no point going into my lousy teen years, although I suspected Tucker's weren't much more fun than mine.

He smiled at me, looking like a little boy dressed up in grown-up clothes. "We have something in common."

"Any brothers or sisters?" I asked him.

"Nope. You?"

"Not anymore."

If he found my answer an odd one, he didn't follow up. It made me think Tucker had done his homework before talking to me after the funeral. There were no secrets in the digital age.

Almost finished with my dinner, I rolled up my final pancake with the remaining mu shu, took a satisfying bite, and stared out at the snow.

"Want my last dumpling?"

"No thanks." Warmed by the tea and stuffed with Chinese food, my world became a happy place. I'd even forgiven my dinner companion for the newspaper interview. "So, what's next for you, Tucker?"

"Well, I hunker down with all my info and source material and start to weave everything together with any final edits. Then I hand it to my agent who sends it to the publisher."

"Do you work from home?"

"Yeah. I've got a tiny desk in the kitchen. None of us guys cook, so my piles of paper don't interfere with anything. The final draft I'm working off of is on my laptop."

"What about this?" I tapped the cover of his notepad.

"Well, after I incorporate these notes into the picture, I tear the corresponding page out and clip it to the printed hard copy. The tape and notes are then placed in my reference files." He slipped the pad back into his inside jacket pocket. "Basically, I keep everything. You might say I have a minor hoarding problem. Our landlady understands and is nice enough to let me store some boxes in her basement."

"That's helpful."

"I share a two-bedroom place in Brooklyn with two other guys," he explained, "so there isn't that much room."

"You're one bedroom short, if my math is correct."

"True. My bedroom is basically the living room sofa and the hall closet."

He responded right away to the sympathetic look on my face.

"It's okay. Except for my paperwork, I don't have much stuff. Obviously, not a lot of clothes." He gestured to his sweater. "This is all second-hand designer stuff I buy from thrift shops. You'd be amazed what you can get at those places."

I couldn't help but smile. "You had me fooled. Here I was thinking you were a clothes-horse, with your fancy labels. If you get famous, you'll have to rent a storage locker."

"First impressions can be crucial," he stirred two extra sugars into his tea with a chopstick. "And, correction, it's not *if* I get famous, but *when* I get famous."

His round face struck me as very determined. "Sorry, *when* you get famous…"

"I'll buy a storage locker…and I'll get one for you, too."

We sat and chatted comfortably about our lives long after the bill came. His family in Ohio didn't approve of his lifestyle or his move to New York City, since coming out of a completely different kind of closet. His candid confessions made it easier to admit to the estrangement from my father. Tucker, like me, had enjoyed a close relationship with his maternal grandparents while growing up. He'd been devastated by their deaths. I joked that I'd loan him my Gramps for the day. After settling up the bill and putting our coats and gloves back on, I reminded him to keep in touch.

"Definitely. It's been a pleasure, Kate."

"Hey, let's take a selfie. I can say I knew you when."

We both stood up, Tucker being a good head shorter than me.

I lifted up my phone and realized the fellow in the baseball cap behind us definitely didn't want to be in the picture. He'd hunkered down in the booth, effectively hiding out of sight.

Our meeting now captured in my photo library, I gave Tucker a hug good-bye, surprised at how close I felt to this baby-faced writer from the Midwest after such a short time. His obvious affection for Gloria and unrelenting work ethic struck a responsive chord in me. Perhaps on one of my trips to New York City to visit Gramps I'd invite Tucker to join us for lunch.

When we made our way past the other diners I noticed the patron in the baseball cap and oversized winter coat hustling out the front door.

I wasn't the only one to notice. Tucker stopped next to me and stood silently staring at the man's back before it vanished into the parking lot, an odd look on his face.

It occurred to me when I got home that I hadn't actually read the whole article that mentioned my name, so I turned on my computer and pulled up Tucker's interview with the *Kingston Tribune*. A handwritten note lay under the mouse. Several reporters had called the front desk to Cindy's delight, asking for phone interviews. One tried to pitch an article titled, "Veterinarian Ferrets out Clues" which obviously someone thought was a funny play on words.

A quick search revealed Tucker had been a busy guy. Repeats of the article ricocheted all over the Internet. Once I finished reading, I understood why. Basically, the article enthusiastically promoted his upcoming book, hinted that Carl Wolf was alive and well and living in the Hudson Valley, and that I had come up with several clever and unusual ideas on how to search for him, ideas ignored by the FBI. He touched on Gloria, her past connection with Wolf and hypothesized she'd recognized her killer on Halloween night, with me by her side. A brief summary of the former investigations I'd been associated with ended the piece, along with the address and phone number of the Oak Falls Animal Hospital. I felt like a destination on a map, brightly highlighted, underlined with a Sharpie—and with a big red target drawn on my face.

What possessed Tucker to drag me into this?

It was long past damage-control time. If I commented on Carl Wolf and the FBI's most wanted list it would only add fuel to the fire. Better to say nothing and let the flames die down by themselves. Hopefully, another sensational story would grab the headlines tomorrow and this story would be forgotten.

Maybe the FBI had a sense of humor about these types of articles, but I doubted it.

Wishful thinking.

If Tucker were here I'd be tempted to kill him myself.

Chapter Eight

The rest of the week flew by in a whirl of appointments, house calls, and late-night emergencies. When Friday arrived I was more than ready to see Jeremy and escape to New York City for a few days of rest and relaxation. Or so I hoped.

Cindy and I had started closing up the hospital when my boyfriend arrived, carrying two large grocery bags from the super expensive specialty deli in town.

Jeremy surprised Cindy with a cheek kiss and hug before turning his enthusiastic attentions to me. The spicy scent of his aftershave plus his eager lips on mine fired up my engines. As usual his enthusiasm energized the room.

"I brought a picnic dinner, a few bottles of wine, and a quiche for breakfast," he confided to us, "since I'm unfortunately familiar with the usual contents of your refrigerator, Kate."

About to protest I remembered my near-empty fridge held a half can of dog food, some dried-up sliced turkey, and a few plastic containers with suspicious-looking stuff growing inside. "Great idea, honey." I turned back to my receptionist. "Anything else you can think of before we lock up?"

Cindy whipped out her phone and checked her notes. "No, looks like we're good to go. I'll put on the answering service. Enjoy yourselves this weekend and say hi to your Gramps for me."

"Will do." Gramps and Cindy had a lively text message relationship going on. After I suffered a nasty injury to the back of my knees trying to solve a cold-case murder, Cindy took it upon herself to keep my worried Gramps in the loop, knowing I'd simply sugarcoat my recovery so he wouldn't worry. Those exchanges had morphed into a buddy connection, with frequent advice from him on how to handle her rebellious teen son. My grandfather's genuine concern and interest in other people often resulted in surprising friendships over the years. It was one of the many things I envied about him.

We said good-bye and escaped to my converted garage apartment. "What have you planned for this weekend?" He immediately uncorked one of the fancy bottles of wine and poured out two glasses while I put the food away. I'd been so busy lately he'd offered to handle all the arrangements. Mari had Buddy for the weekend. The only thing left to do was pack some clothes and slide into his Mercedes.

"A toast," he said. "To surprises." A mischievous grin punctuated his statement.

"Perfect." Not needing to make decisions for a few days was the height of luxury for me. Jeremy removed his battered leather jacket, which gave him an Indiana Jones sort of thing. A trained anthropologist in real life, I swore he played his slight resemblance to the Jones character to the max, but hey, you do what works.

And it definitely worked for me.

The smell of coffee woke me up. Daylight streamed through the curtains. No dog to walk, no clients to see. Ahead stretched two blissful lazy days.

"Don't get up yet," a voice said from the kitchen.

Jeremy surprised me with a kiss, plus a breakfast tray loaded with strawberries and quiche. When he was around, he certainly knew how to make an impact.

When he was around.

We'd planned on getting an early start, but due to my sleeping in, plus amorous inclinations on both our parts, we didn't set off until late morning. By eleven-thirty we were on the New York State Thruway headed for the Big Apple. Although it was a cold November day, the sun rose high in the sky, warming our faces through the car windows before we were enveloped in darkening clouds.

"I hope this weather holds off until we get there," Jeremy said as the big car smoothly hugged the road. Trees and icy meadows gave way to more and more concrete the closer we came to the city. When we saw the skyline in the distance I got energized. Our boutique hotel was located in Greenwich Village, so we zipped down the West Side Highway before cutting across lower Manhattan.

By two-thirty we were checked in and strolling along famous McDougal Street in New York's West Village. The threatening clouds blew off to the south and had been replaced by cold, but sunny, skies—a treat for this time of year. Somehow Jeremy had wrangled us tickets to one of the most popular plays on Broadway, and booked a dinner before the show at a well-known eatery, Joe Allen's Restaurant, in the theatre district.

"How did you manage all this?" I asked as we passed Abingdon Square and ambled down tree-lined West Twelfth Street. Picturesque brownstones with iron fire escapes lined the sidewalk which was bustling with residents scurrying along carrying shopping bags as well as with slower-paced tourists enjoying the scenery. My shoulders began to relax and loosen up, a reminder of how stressed I'd been over the last few weeks.

Holding Jeremy's arm, I stopped to browse in a shop window. He leaned in and whispered in my ear. "Confession time. I cheated."

"What?"

He seemed surprised.

The angry look on my face finally registered with him.

"No, I didn't cheat like that, Kate. I hired a travel planning company. They create a weekend-in-the-city package and take care of all the reservations and details for you. So far, I'm impressed."

"Very enterprising. The white roses in the hotel room…"

"Included. I left the flower choice up to them."

"Nice touch." My mild touch of sarcasm was lost on him.

We continued down the street, our arms still linked together. It made a certain amount of sense to let the professionals handle everything, especially if money wasn't a concern. It didn't feel very personal, though.

The next morning I had to admit it—we'd had a wonderful time. A great table at Joe Allen's was followed by a delightful show, followed by sophisticated cocktails served at a small table in the wood-paneled bar at our hotel. Afterwards, we'd moved into the small lounge, sat in soft leather chairs and listened to a fantastic jazz piano player. The booking company even sent a limo both ways and picked us up outside the theatre.

My bones felt like mush—total relaxation mode.

Wrapped in the hotel-provided bathrobes, I'd opted for a light Sunday breakfast served in our room in front of the window overlooking the cityscape, before our brunch date with Gramps. I indulged myself by picking a second chocolate croissant off the pastry plate and paired it with a cup of Earl Grey tea.

"Great, isn't it?" Jeremy looked up from his phone. "No classes to run to, no assignments to finish…"

"No trudging through messy sheep pens, no dogs peeing on my shoes…"

"You're kidding, right?" My boyfriend sat opposite me, a bit horrified.

"Sorry. It's a little too early in the morning for veterinary humor." The last bite of croissant crumbled as flakes of dough drifted across the terrycloth robe.

He took a sip of coffee and buttered a sesame seed bagel.

"Actually, that's the part of my job I'm happy to leave behind. All the bugs and junk at the dig sites was getting old."

"But it's real life."

"This is real life, too. Why not enjoy it?" His extended arms took in our expensive hotel room and fabulous breakfast.

"Not all the time. I think I'd get bored. But for a weekend, it's wonderful." Part of me felt guilty because Jeremy wouldn't let me contribute any money to our getaway. Given that his monthly income from the family trust was probably ten times what I make in a year, it made economic if not emotional sense, so I decided to stop worrying about it and go with the flow.

My fiercely won independence took an uneasy breather.

We were meeting Gramps for brunch at one-thirty at the River Café in Brooklyn, a place I remember going when I was little. Until then it was window-shopping, limos, and living the high life.

The River Café is situated almost under the Brooklyn Bridge and sits right on the East River overlooking the Lower Manhattan skyline. Views are spectacular, because it's right on the water. Unfortunately, that proximity proved catastrophic when Hurricane Sandy hit in 2012.

Gramps sat opposite us, sipping his hot tea, and telling us of the devastation the storm had caused. As soon as they could safely manage it, he and a few of his retired fire department buddies waded through the old neighborhood, helping as best they could. He'd headed over to the café to see if it was still there.

"Your grandmother and I celebrated many an anniversary here," he recalled, looking out at the water. "That's why it was a sad thing to see the place flooded and closed for so long."

I vaguely remembered a party here with my family, and being told ahead of time to be on my best behavior. Mom had bought me a new dress for the occasion. Those memories when they came were a mix of happy and sad—happy they took place and sad they ended too soon.

"But these renovations," my Gramps continued, "they've made the old girl look better than ever."

"Cheers." I lifted my water glass to Gramps.

"Cheers," added Jeremy.

The waiter came by with an ice bucket and a bottle of champagne.

"I'm sorry. We didn't order champagne," Jeremy told him.

Three elegant flutes were placed in front of us. "Compliments of the house."

Two of the three of us were puzzled.

"Tell them many thanks," Gramps said. The cork popped loudly and the bubbly flowed.

"To happy days." He made a point of clinking both our glasses. "Are we celebrating anything in particular?"

"Just being alive," my boyfriend said.

"Well, I'll drink to that," Gramps laughed and subtly checked out my ring finger.

That's when I realized my grandfather might have thought this was an engagement celebration. I'd been seeing Jeremy for several months now, first as a long-distance Skype relationship, then when his dig in Africa closed down we'd transitioned into an up close and personal affair. That changed when he moved away to receive additional training at the University of Pennsylvania. Now we were back to square one.

"I didn't know you knew anyone here, Gramps." My grandfather constantly surprised me. Modest to a fault, he never bragged about the many famous people he knew.

"We're fishing buddies," he told me, then nodded toward a tall, white-haired gentleman fishing off the deck of the restaurant.

"I'm impressed," Jeremy said.

Gramps waved it off. "Kate tells me you're going back to school."

"That's right," my guy admitted. "Even though I have a doctorate, I've found the focus of anthropology has shifted. Technology has made tremendous strides in DNA mapping. That's where all the excitement and new discoveries are. Universities can now afford extensive testing on specimens they've collected over the years. Some artifacts have been sitting forgotten in storage rooms since the beginning of the century."

"Technology is fantastic," I agreed. "As long as it's working."

"If it isn't, that's when you've got to go old school," Gramps laughed. "Like me."

That old school remark reminded me of Tucker and his little green notepad. I had a feeling that my writer friend and my grandfather might have something in common.

Our delicious waterside brunch turned out to be a success. Gramps and Jeremy got along much better than I'd anticipated, especially when my boyfriend revealed one of his great-great-grandmothers had been born in County Mayo, Ireland. The two guys talked about fishing, poker, and traveling. Jeremy had us laughing as he regaled us with more crazy stories from his various digs around the world.

However, things ground to a halt when he mentioned Tucker, his book deal, and Gloria LaGuardia. I kicked him under the table but by then it was too late.

"Katie." Gramps' expression turned serious. "You're not going to start investigating things again, are you?"

At a loss, my boyfriend made everything worse by trying to help. "I'm sure she's just curious. Right, honey? After she got injured by that maniac with a baseball bat, I'm certain she learned her lesson." He finished his statement by draining his wineglass and kissing my cheek.

"Young man," my grandfather rebutted in an iron tone, "you've got a lot to learn. If you think a little thing like that would stop my granddaughter, then you don't know her as well as you think you do."

Although I turned an innocent face to Jeremy, my Gramps was right. Jeremy remembered the girl I'd been in college more than he knew the woman and doctor I'd become. Every day I made life and death decisions for my patients and clients—and accepted the consequences of my actions. Being in charge had toughened me up.

Why did I want to find Gloria's murderer? The driver of the car that killed my mom and brother got away. Maybe that event prodded me to find justice for victims when police investigations into their deaths stalled.

"Okay, Gramps. I'll make you a deal this time."

His bright blue eyes held mine. Even the thick white hair on his head stood at attention. "I'm listening."

"Let's do this together. You do research on Carl Wolf's case and I'll make a list of people Gloria had contact with in Oak Falls. Then we'll turn everything over to Tucker and let him win a Pulitzer Prize."

No delighted smile appeared on either guys' face.

Jeremy spoke first.

"Oh, come on. The FBI has been searching for this guy for twenty-one years. What's the likelihood you're going to find him?" I noticed a little more than a hint of sarcasm in his question.

Gramps gave him a long hard look before he commented, "Tell me, Mr. Anthropologist. Do you play poker?"

The following morning, reality set in. No breakfast in bed, no delicious chocolate croissant calling to me. No boyfriend to fool around with. Instead, a doggie tongue slurped my hand and woke me an hour before my alarm was scheduled to ring. Yipping a high-pitched squeal and dancing around, he obviously needed to go out.

With eyes glued half-shut I sensed the beginning of a headache even before my feet hit the ground. Wrapped in a less-than-luxurious bathrobe and fuzzy bedroom slippers, I opened the apartment's front door.

Overnight, the parking lot had gone from dry and cold to four or five inches of snow. Even Buddy was reluctant to put his paws into the slippery mess. Each dog foot cracked the thin crust of glazed-over ice on top, as though the parking lot had magically turned into a giant crème brûlée. Still groggy I tried to help him, but my weight broke completely through the snow. Now standing in two holes in the snow I felt the freezing powder slide down my legs and fill up my slippers. With six sets of frozen toes, we both retreated inside.

That luxurious life I'd sunk into with Jeremy seemed like bliss.

Awake and grumpy, I dried my dog's feet, hung the matted slippers up to dry and decided I was too cold to take a shower. Hoping to get a jump on the morning, I stalked off to brew some coffee. The can was empty. So was the fridge. Jeremy's feast had long since disappeared.

Unless I wanted to eat old dog food, I'd have to scrounge up my breakfast.

Buzz.

I glanced toward my phone on the nightstand. Someone was texting me at five-forty-five a.m.? My irritation escalated to a slow boil until I noticed the caller ID. The message and the sender momentarily baffled me. Why would Gramps text me so early and tell me to check my personal email?

Mumbling to myself I pulled on my scrubs and went into the animal hospital break room, started a pot of coffee, and found a slightly stale sesame bagel in the communal refrigerator. I mounded some cream cheese onto the top so it looked like a snowcapped mountain and headed for my office. With the first bite most of the cream cheese slid down my chin like an avalanche to come to a halt on the front of my scrub top.

Needless to say it was going to be another long, long day.

Distracted by some important lab tests that arrived overnight, it was an hour before I got around to reading Gramps' email. When I opened it I noticed there were five separate attachments.

After another gulp of coffee I braced myself for the contents. The depth of information and structure of his reports on Carl Wolf and the murders he committed astonished me. Had I underestimated how much time Gramps had on his hands—or what an excellent investigator he was? Maybe he got a kick out of getting back into a harness for a day. Tucker probably had all this stuff already, but what the heck? If it gave Gramps and me a project to do together, what was the harm? My contribution would be pretty limited. Gloria's niece, Irene, was a much more important source of information than I was. Halloween night would be a small piece of a huge puzzle.

That reminded me of the interview Tucker gave the newspaper. I suppose it made sense for a writer to drum up some publicity for his book, but I wish he'd left me out of it. On my desk were three more requests for interviews from reporters, some second requests, referencing Tucker's story in the local paper and its online edition. Much to Cindy's dismay, I had no intention of speaking to them.

Before he went back to the city, Tucker assured me his writing objective was to stir things up, make the public aware of the decades-old investigation, and sell a zillion books—not to unmask the killer. That job was best left up to the FBI.

Where I fit in to that scenario, I had no clue. Part of me, I suppose, thought it would be fun to contribute to a book. After quickly printing up the attachments I emailed Gramps back, reminded him I was at work, and promised to read everything in detail later tonight.

Before I started seeing appointments I texted Tucker to say hello, and tell him I'd be sure to keep him updated on anything I found here in Oak Falls. His quick response came as a surprise.

My cell phone rang immediately. After briefly catching up, my writer friend zeroed back on his favorite subject, the Big Bad Wolf.

"Fascinating history, isn't it? You have to admit, Kate, the guy is smart. He got into computers and eventually writing code really early and worked from home way before most other people. During my research I tried to contact his old firm, but they'd merged with another tech company that doesn't exist anymore."

Obviously he'd done tons of background research. "What about his hobbies? Didn't you say he was a real outdoors kind of guy?"

Tucker went into overdrive, his voice speeding up while he reeled off a list. "Hunting, fishing, camping, you name it, he probably did it. Always bought himself the best equipment, too, which was one of the sore points with his wife."

Knowing several people like that, I easily visualized his away-from-home life. "Did he include his family in his trips?"

A rude sound came from Tucker. "You've got to be kidding. Except for a few local camping things with the wife and kids, he spent most of his free time alone, with the dog. There were a few guys he met up with at campgrounds and fishing spots that he'd mention, according to his mother-in-law. Otherwise, he kept to himself. When I searched for any of those contacts, I hit a dead end."

"How far did you go back?"

"All the way." He paused, before continuing. "Abusive father, family moved around a lot. Wolf was popular, though, in high school. Smart student, starred in the senior play, but several hints of trouble even then."

That brought up an interesting point. "Did you share all of this with the FBI?" Tucker didn't seem like the kind of kid that shared his toys, or his sources.

This time his reply came more slowly and carefully thought out. "The FBI is very aware of my book and all the research I've put into it. Believe me, if I knew where the Big Bad Wolf was,

I'd tell them in a heartbeat. Not only would I get the reward, but the publicity might translate into millions of extra book sales."

My friend always had an angle. "In that interview you mentioned your suspicions regarding Gloria's murder, right?"

"Right."

"So you informed the FBI?"

"Sort of," he admitted. "I'm working on a few things."

Knowing Tucker I doubted he would tell me, but I asked anyway. "Want to share?"

His silence told it all.

"Anything that's public knowledge," he explained, "I'll be happy to rehash with anyone, but I keep my research private. The only way to know what I'm working on is to steal my laptop, and this baby is practically glued to me at all times."

"Builds the tension, I suppose."

"You got it. Even my agent is in the dark about a few things, which annoys her. But, hey, it's fun to keep agents on their toes. The publisher is another story altogether. They take no prisoners and have zero sense of humor."

"What about the other two murderers in your book? Aren't you busy with them, too?"

"Nope." His tone was matter of fact. "One of them is dead, so that's pretty easy. I've got plenty of stuff on him. The other guy is incarcerated and recently found Jesus. He doesn't want to talk crime anymore, he wants to save my soul. We've been bartering back and forth for the last two years."

"Funny."

"What he doesn't know is that to be on the *NY Times'* Best Seller List and get picked up for a movie option by Hollywood, I'd sell that sucker in a second."

The idea of Tucker and the Devil making a deal over his immortal soul for a movie of the week amused me. My writer friend sounded like he could go on and on about his favorite subject but I needed to get back to work.

After we hung up I realized I'd forgotten to ask him an important question, one that had been bothering me.

Of all the murderers in the United States, why did he pick Carl Wolf?

Chapter Nine

Drama raised its head in the exam room the next day, when two local residents dressed in jeans and flannel shirts had reluctantly brought their dog in to see me.

"I told you not to do it." With that, Lydia DeVries gave her husband, Amos, a hard whack, knocking his bifocal glasses to the floor. He squinted at Mari and me before placing them back on.

"It's not like you had any better idea," he retaliated. The spouses glared at each other over the patient, a Labrador retriever lying on my exam table.

Lydia was built like a linebacker, with thinning brown hair and a stern face, frown lines deeply embedded in the skin around her mouth and forehead. Amos, on the other hand, resembled a Chia pet gone wild, with a scraggly beard, unruly hair, and a pot belly that hung over his belt. Bifocals gave him gigantic googly Coke-bottle eyes.

I immediately smelled the faint but rank aroma of singed dog hair in the room.

The unlikely couple continued to argue, each one insistent on making their point.

Mari rolled her eyes.

"Sam will be just fine..." I started to say.

Lydia interrupted with both barrels. "What idiot uses a match to kill a tick? You could have set our dog on fire and burned down the house."

"I blew out the flame before I squished it," Amos countered.

This time I swear the dog rolled his eyes.

"He should have put Vaseline on it. Right, Doc?" the wife continued. "That would have smothered it to death."

"Not really." My mild comment was lost in the noise.

Sam's deep brown doggie eyes followed back and forth between his screaming owners. Luckily, he didn't seem the type to hold a grudge.

Mari appeared to be dying to say something but I beat her to it.

"Where do you think he picked up the ticks?" I asked. I counted eight red burn marks around the dog's neck. As I spoke I ran my hands through the thick fur on his back and discovered another spot.

"Hunting," Amos told me. "Sam followed me into the woods out back on our property."

"My family's property, dumbbell."

Amos frowned but didn't say anything.

"Labs are usually used for birds," I questioned him. "This is deer season."

"Yep. But he whines whenever he smells a deer nearby." The dog lifted his head, exposing one of the oozing sores. Lydia made a groaning sound while Amos tried to make amends. "I'm sorry, Sam," he told the dog. "I was just trying to help."

People sometimes don't think things through.

"Baby doll, don't be mad." He reached a hand out to his wife.

"It's okay, honey," Lydia moved toward her husband and hugged him, her basketball player-sized hands resting on his shoulders. All had been forgiven. "The doc's gonna fix him up real good, right, Doc?"

Poor Amos now stared at me, his own eyes unconsciously mimicking the dog. "There's no lasting harm done," I reassured the humiliated owner. "We're going to take Sam into the treatment area for a little while, and scrub up those infected spots.

Mari will print you out some wound instructions and the receptionist will set you up with a recheck appointment with me."

Everyone nodded, even the dog.

"Oh, by the way. I'm going to recommend testing Sam for Lyme disease. Then he needs to start taking an anti-tick and flea medication. Dogs get tick-borne diseases just like people do."

"That reminds me," Lydia said. "Amos, show the doc that thing on your you-know."

Amos' face fell. "What? Now?"

"Sure, she's a doctor, dummy."

I wasn't sure what part of Amos I was about to see.

His wife turned back to me. "He's got this fungus thing. Come on, sweetie, show her."

With a sigh Amos unbuckled his belt and pulled down his jeans. Lydia walked over and lifted his red plaid shirt up so I got a full view.

"It's ringworm, right?" His wife pointed to a large fading lesion on his upper butt cheek. Meanwhile her husband clutched his boxers, flying at half-mast, for dear life.

"I've been putting that Vagisil cream on it every day," she said earnestly.

A snort exploded from Mari.

Although incredibly amusing, I needed to put a stop to the fun. "Have you shown this to your doctor?"

"Oh, we don't believe in going to doctors, no offense."

Normally, I don't encourage my human clients to drop their clothes, although in the exam room I've been shown surgery scars, skin rashes, moles, lumps, and bumps—you name it. But this time I was very glad for the show because that large bull's-eye lesion could be a marker for Lyme disease.

"Lydia," I said. "Why don't you take a picture of this with your phone and show it to your physician?"

"Okay." She thought about it for a second, then gestured for me to switch places with her, so I could hold up her husband's shirt. Mari stood behind us, almost bent over from trying not to laugh. It took Lydia forever to dig her cell phone out of her purse.

"Move a little closer. Now smile."

Amos turned his head toward the camera with a big grin and darned if I didn't smile too.

Mari didn't miss a beat. "Can I get a copy of that?"

In the privacy of the treatment room, with only the dog as a witness, my assistant burst out laughing. I was carefully shaving the fur around the burns, getting ready to clean and medicate the wounds. Sam the Labrador also had a grin on his face.

"This has got to go on our web page."

"That's a definite no," I emphatically told her.

"But you should have seen your face. It's so funny. Plus those bifocals made Amos look like he had four eyes."

"Still no."

With that, Mari couldn't hold it in and buried her head in the lab's side to stifle her giggles.

"Okay," I admitted. "It was pretty funny from my end, too."

That turned out to be a poor choice of words. Mari completely lost it—and Sam joined in with a couple of woofs.

It took about forty-five minutes before Sam the Labrador, was ready to go home. The couple spent their time in the waiting room, yakking with my staff. It turned out that Lydia and our receptionist, Cindy, used the same hairdresser in town. A major scandal had erupted when said hairdresser had divorced her husband and then begun dating the salon's female owner. Plenty of juicy gossip was exchanged while Mari loaded Amos down with information on Lyme disease and demonstrated how to handle Sam's wounds. My chatty employees made the couple promise to see their human doctor. Mari particularly impressed Amos by telling a horror story of a cousin who was now on intravenous antibiotics to treat an advanced case of Lyme's.

Of course, Lydia shared that exam room picture of her husband with everyone in the waiting room, which soon echoed with peals of laughter from clients and staff. I made them promise not to post it on social media.

Another photo I hoped wouldn't show up at my veterinary class reunion.

At the end of the day Cindy gave me my callback list and reviewed tomorrow's appointment schedule.

"Thanks for everything, by the way." I mentioned to her. "You know Amos needs to get to his doctor ASAP. Those lesions can fade pretty quickly, which is why I asked Lydia to document it."

"Oh, it's documented, all right," she said.

I diplomatically chose to ignore her joke.

"I even sent it to the newspapers…just kidding."

"I hope so." Knowing the temptation of social media, it was anyone's guess where that silly image might end up.

"Alright, I'm done." Cindy put on her serious face. "I'll ask Lydia when I call to confirm Sam's recheck appointment. She wears the pants in the family."

I nodded, agreeing with her observation.

"That DeVries family is one of the oldest in the Hudson Valley, and one of the most eccentric. Her younger brother hoarded everything and never let anyone into his side of the house. There were rumors he kept all his toenail and fingernail clippings in glass jars in the pantry."

"Yuck."

"Lydia hated this place and took off as soon as she hit eighteen. She must have had a hard life, because my mom said she hardly recognized her when she came back for her parents' funeral."

Once again I was reminded that small towns had long memories.

"Everyone was stunned when she met Amos and married him."

As interesting as all this local gossip was, I needed to interrupt. "I was thinking it would be a good idea to put some guidelines on how to remove ticks on our website. Also, I'll send you a link to a YouTube video put out by one of the veterinary organizations that is pretty good."

She made a note in the computer.

Before she started up with strange tales from the Hudson Valley again I took off for the quiet of my office, then turned and added one more thought. "When you disturb an embedded tick, like Amos did, that tick can react by releasing even more bacteria and viruses into their host's bloodstream. Another reason to remove it gently."

Her "yuck" bounced off the walls of the empty waiting room.

My comfortable desk chair turned out to be occupied by someone who did not intend to move. Mr. Katt deliberately avoided looking at me, instead concentrated on grooming various parts of his anatomy. I countered by sliding onto my chair, inch by inch, effectively gaining half of the disputed territory. Our hospital cat now served as a living kitty heating pad for my back.

Once settled, I pulled up my callback list. Most were medical cases I wanted to touch base with. Another client was waiting for a biopsy report to come back from the lab.

It took over an hour to finish everything, since I ended up speaking to the pathologist about the tissue sample I had sent. Then I consulted an oncologist friend and formulated a chemotherapy protocol for my middle-aged dog patient.

As soon as I stood up, Mr. Katt expanded back into the chair like a balloon, somehow covering up every inch and more, his fluffy tail hanging defiantly over the edge.

An hour later my phone chimed. This time I'd sprawled out on my tummy, catching up on the latest copy of the American Veterinary Medical Association journal.

"Hi, Tucker. How is everything?" I wondered if he was calling about the photo release form I had to sign, which sat unopened in my email.

"Hey, Kate."

"Listen, I've been so busy I haven't gotten around to signing that photo release but…"

He interrupted what would have been a long drawn-out explanation. "That's not why I'm calling. Is everything okay up there—no weird things happening to you?"

My internal alarm bells went off. "Define weird."

"Oh, I don't know. I'm a little on edge because...I've got this feeling I'm being followed."I could hear his nervous fingers drumming away.

"Are you sure about that?"

"No, that's the thing. I might be imagining it, but have you ever felt someone behind you staring—but when you turn around there's no one there?"

His voice revealed a rising fear. I barely knew Tucker. What should I say to him? He sounded upset, so I decided to approach it in a rational manner. "Listen, I think most people have had that happen to them. It's certainly happened to me. Is there something you are doing to call attention to yourself? Something you're wearing, maybe, or carrying?"

"Not a chance. I'm not the greatest-looking guy on the planet, in case you didn't notice. Most of the time people look right past me on the street, or ignore me."

"That's not true."

"Yes, it is. Even in the bars I barely get noticed. Of course, I'm usually sitting in a corner working. You know I only got this book deal by working twice as hard as everyone else." Tucker paused for a second, then continued. "Listen, sorry for bothering you. Maybe I'm getting a little paranoid. I've been fighting with my agent over this last Wolf chapter and I'm so revved up on sugar and coffee, I barely average four hours of sleep at night." His voice trailed off.

"Who do you think is following you?"

"Who do you think? It's got to be the Big Bad Wolf."

The old nursery story popped into my head before I remembered that nickname. "You're talking about Carl Wolf?"

"Yeah. My agent thinks I'm crazy. She told me to take some Xanax."

His story began to worry me. "Have you called Gloria's niece, Irene, and asked her if she's experienced anything out of the ordinary?"

More fingers sounded louder, busily drumming in the background. "Of course I called her. She hung up on me. Like I said, it's probably my imagination."

His nervous energy almost shot out of the phone at me. "I think you're putting too much into what Gloria said, Tucker. She must have thought she recognized ten or twenty people that night."

"What can I say? All this stress is driving me nuts."

Our conversation kept going around in circles. I tried a different approach. "If you're really concerned, I suggest you contact the police."

An uneasy silence followed. I was about to reiterate my advice to him when Tucker confessed something.

"I can't go to the police. About six months ago I thought some guy was following me, a really tall, skinny dude, with blond hair. He started showing up outside my apartment building, sitting in his car at night, looking up at my window…it totally freaked me. I called the cops on him."

"What happened?"

"Turns out he wasn't looking at my apartment, he was keeping an eye on the apartment above me—checking to make sure his sister was okay. Her old boyfriend threatened her and the brother wanted to have a little talk with him, using a baseball bat for punctuation."

"Well, you couldn't have known that."

More drumming sounded, even faster than before.

"When he found out I'd complained the brother started yelling at me, and I yelled back. Then the cops tried to intervene. I told them they were public servants who actually worked for me and they should arrest the guy. That didn't go over too well. Before long the sister comes down and starts in and it went south from there. I'm pretty sure telling everyone I was a journalist didn't help either." He paused for a breath. "Long story short, the girl's brother threatened to file a false complaint report against me and one thing led to another until we both were hauled down to the station."

"Tucker…"

"The whole incident got written up and I received a warning. Look, the local cops have me pegged as a troublemaker. Why would they believe me this time?"

Chapter Ten

As the next week went by Tucker dropped off the face of my little part of the universe, and Gramps' enthusiasm for Internet searches featuring the Big Bad Wolf waned. Our emails ground to a halt. I suspected the red-haired writer felt he revealed too much in our lengthy conversation. Each text I sent received a one- or two-word answer. "No" he hadn't called the police and "Yes" everything was back to normal. I decided to give it a rest.

On the animal front, reports were that Sam the Labrador had begun healing up nicely from his tick burns. Cindy told me that his frugal owner, Lydia DeVries, was so grateful she actually paid her bill.

Jeremy and I tried to keep up the momentum of seeing each other every weekend, but that didn't last very long. An emergency foreign body surgery on Friday made it impossible for me to travel anytime on Saturday while the dog was recovering from eating a yellow rubber ducky. Then Jeremy had a colleague from Africa drop by and they made plans to fly to New Mexico for a few days to visit an active dig site run by another mutual friend. Of course Jeremy offered me a half-hearted invitation to join them, but I would have spent the entire weekend traveling. We did, however, have frequent texting and late evening phone calls, which filled in some of the gaps of our relationship. With Oak Falls in the grip of a particularly ferocious upstate New

York winter it was easier to put off any decisions involving my personal life. Instead, I took to hibernating in my apartment after work. Crawling into sweats or pajamas, and cuddling with a soft blanket, a cold glass of wine and HGTV became the comforting nightly cave I retreated to.

On Thursday night, I was watching another episode of *House Hunters* when the phone rang. I lowered the television volume, but kept the picture on as the commercials played. I'd made myself a bet the young married couple was going to choose house number two for their first home.

"Hello," I said, my eyes on the screen and not the caller ID.

"Hello, yourself. I'm betting it's going to be house number three. No doubt about it."

"Hi, Gramps. This time you're going to lose. My money's on the second one, that ranch with the view. How could they pass that up?" As I spoke, the program resumed.

The couple chose house number three.

I sat up on the sofa. "Lucky guess?"

He laughed. "It's a rerun, Katie. But you're right, they should have gone for the view."

When I was on my veterinary school breaks, Gramps and I spent many a night watching HGTV together. Because of his background first as a firefighter, then as an arson investigator for the city of New York, he disliked watching crime shows, while I found many of the popular medical shows implausible. He liked the History Channel while I watched animal videos. What we could both agree on was HGTV. It had now become a stress-free addiction we both enjoyed.

"Everything okay?" Gramps and I usually talked every Sunday. If he called during the week a tiny fear always jangled in the back of my mind that something was wrong. COPD, chronic obstructive pulmonary disease, was something this formerly robust man lived with every day. It worried me more than it worried him.

"Never felt better," he assured me. "Each month Kitty, our

recreation lady here, posts museum exhibits and shows going on in the city on our bulletin board. And guess what?"

I had no idea where he was going with this. "I'll bite. What?"

"There's a retrospective exhibit of courtroom sketch artists at some museum on Seventy-seventh Street, just off the park. Gloria LaGuardia's drawing of the Son of Sam is on their poster."

"How'd you find that out?" Buddy lifted his head from his dog bed, realized my question wasn't for him, and with a grunt went back to sleep.

"From Kitty and the museum website." Gramps' voice reflected a degree of satisfaction. After initially rejecting our galloping electronic technology, he now had embraced it, proudly mastering each weekly computer lesson given at his independent living complex.

"I thought you and I could go together this weekend. Then afterwards we can head back to the old neighborhood and eat at Roberto's. Remember? We had your graduation celebration there."

"Of course I remember."

The memory of that night was a highlight in my life. I had finally graduated from veterinary school and Gramps booked the whole restaurant for the night. All our neighbors, his friends from the firehouse—everyone I'd ever known, it seemed, had been invited to Roberto's. Before dinner began, my grandfather, as proud as he could be, made me come up to the front of the room, and he introduced me to the crowd as Doctor Katherine Turner.

My father, an orthopedic surgeon, remarried with a second, much younger family, sent his regrets and a check.

I glanced around my studio apartment, the safe little cocoon I'd constructed around myself. Time to break out.

"You're on, Gramps. I'll meet you at your place on Saturday morning." Already I felt more energized.

"Bring Jeremy along, too," he added.

"I'm flying solo this weekend. Jeremy's at a dig in New Mexico with a buddy of his."

When I sensed the disapproval on the end of the line, I added, "It's business."

"Then I'll have you all to myself." Gramps wisely decided not to comment any further on the subject. "You can stay in the spare bedroom."

"Sounds perfect." I'd slept over in his large two-bedroom apartment before. Gramps had installed one of those pull-down wall beds for guests, but mostly used the space for his office.

"Blueberry pancakes and bacon in the morning?"

"Of course." Another memory of my big burly Gramps was of him flipping pancakes on Sunday for his chronically pissed off teenage granddaughter. I had a lot to be grateful for.

"Love you, Gramps," I said.

"Back at you, sweetie."

Friday morning dawned cold but overcast. My first appointment was with a family and their elderly dog, Polly, a border collie mix, a thirteen-year-old senior with no obvious health issues. Her problem? Memory loss.

"How has her behavior changed?" I asked the owner, Doris Koliti, who stood next to the exam table. Polly lay on the floor being cuddled by a young boy named Junior with fear in his eyes.

"Well, she's barking at night for no reason, and she never did that before. And when we let her out to go to the bathroom, she wanders around like she's lost," Doris explained, a look of bewilderment on her face. "Then she comes in and pees in the house."

"Polly won't play fetch with me anymore," added the voice from below. "I throw the ball but she only stands there."

I got down on the floor and did a limited neurological exam on the cooperative dog under the watchful eyes of her young master. Her reflexes appeared slightly slow, but well within the normal range for her age. Cranial nerves were fine. Her pretty doggie face appeared symmetrical, no droop or tics. Eye exam revealed early cataract formations in both eyes, with both retinas otherwise normal.

"Well," I said, getting to my feet, "I'd like to run some blood tests and take an X-ray of Polly's head and neck to rule out any…" I hesitated, not wanting to alarm the boy at my feet, or his mother next to me by saying tumor. "To rule out any abnormalities," I continued. "Can you leave her with us for a few hours?"

The mom nodded yes and then bent down to pet her dog and comfort her son. I knelt down on the floor again.

"We'll take good care of her," I told them. "What kind of ball does she like to chase? A tennis ball?"

Junior said, "Yes."

"My dog Buddy likes those, too."

A knock on the door meant Mari had arrived to admit our patient.

"This is Mari, my veterinary technician. She's going to take Polly for her tests. You should be able to pick Polly up around four-thirty today so she'll be home in time for her dinner."

That seemed to reassume Junior a bit.

I left the rest of the admission process to Mari and Cindy. A possible diagnosis had already formed in my mind, a diagnosis, oddly enough, that reminded me of Gloria LaGuardia.

• • ● • •

By four-thirty I'd accumulated quite a bit of information for Doris Koliti and her family. A brain tumor, which is pretty rare in dogs, was ruled out by X-ray, as well as any abnormality caused by parasites, abscess, or cysts. Thanks to our sophisticated in-house laboratory equipment, I had all Polly's results an hour after I admitted her to the hospital. The blood counts and blood chemistry tests were in normal ranges for a senior dog, and her kidney function was excellent. The border collie had been a wonderful patient, sweet and well mannered. I gave her a kiss on the top of her head before I brought her back to her loved ones.

The reunion in the exam room was exuberant on both the dog and human side. After things died down to a dull bark, I brought Polly's digital X-rays up on the computer.

"All her tests look very good. I had a brief consultation with a veterinary neurologist who also looked at her films via email, and given her symptoms, we agreed on a tentative diagnosis."

"What's that?" Her owner sounded apprehensive.

"We think Polly is showing signs of cognitive dysfunction."

Before I could continue with my explanation, Doris shook her head and said, "Can you say that in simple words?"

"Of course. Polly's brain is aging and she is having some recognition issues such as fetching the ball and becoming confused at nighttime."

"Like doggie Alzheimer's?" Doris blurted out.

Junior wrapped his arms around the border collie's neck and stroked her black and white fur. Halloween night Irene had stroked her aunt's hair, in the same loving manner.

"They aren't the same thing, but some of the symptoms can overlap. The good news is there is medication I can recommend to help Polly. I've personally seen it make a big difference in cases like hers. I have to warn you, though, it doesn't work for all individuals."

My warning put a damper on the initial enthusiasm.

The boy and his mom sat in silence as I went over the treatment plan. "Do you have any problems giving her a pill?"

"That's easy. We put it in cream cheese."

"Great. Now you may not see any changes for at least two weeks."

"Okay."

"And, I'd like you to do some behavior modification work. For example, take Polly out at night on a leash and guide her to her bathroom area. Let her sniff around and encourage her to go.

Stay outside with her until she does her business, then give her a treat, and go right back into the house. Establishing a routine and sticking to it is important. Also, work on basic commands like sit and stay at least three times a day. More often would be better. What you are trying to do is reinforce her learned patterns through repetition."

I saw nods from the son and mom, but I knew from experience that the shock of a diagnosis like this often causes minds to go blank. Anticipating that, I'd prepared a typed summary of cognitive dysfunction, the pill schedule, and my behavior reinforcement suggestions, which would be given to them at check-out.

"I've written everything down in your discharge orders. You have my email at the bottom of the page and on my card. Feel free to contact me with any questions." I handed Doris my business card and gave her son one as well. "This medication is well tolerated, but if you think she's having a reaction to it, let me know immediately."

No one spoke. I'd texted Mari already and could hear her coming down the hallway. I was about to open the door when a small voice asked a difficult question.

"Will she ever play fetch with me again?" Junior asked.

"Polly's been playing fetch with him since he was two," his mom added. Both looked over at me as though expecting a miracle.

"I hope so," I answered truthfully.

The boy hugged his dog tightly, partially hiding his face. "I'm going to hope so too."

Chapter Eleven

Finally, an entire weekend off with plans. After dropping Buddy at Mari's house for a weekend playdate with his Rottweiler friends, I headed toward New York City via the New York State Thruway to see Gramps. Predictions promised no new snow and with a dry road in front of me, I was a happy camper. As the fields and hills covered by patches of snow rolled past I thought of how many times I'd carpooled with college friends, taking this same path to the city. It's funny to look back on those days now. Back then all I could think of was graduating from vet school. Being in school, studying for endless exams felt like the most stressful thing in the world.

Now school seemed like the last carefree time in my life.

Traffic increased the closer I got to the city, until finally it was bumper to bumper. The culprit turned out to be a stalled car in the middle of the George Washington Bridge. As soon as I cleared that it was smooth sailing down Manhattan's west side, through the Brooklyn Battery tunnel to the Brooklyn Queens Expressway. With any luck I'd be only a half hour behind schedule, practically on time, given the distance and convoluted combination of roads, bridges, and tunnels necessary to get me to my destination.

Gramps had reserved a visitor spot in his complex's parking garage for me. Waiting in front of the elevator, I texted him. He texted me back, to go straight up to his place. As always I was initially impressed by his independent living facility, noting many active seniors socializing in groups in the luxurious surroundings. Closer observation revealed more frail residents, shuffling along with walkers or navigating in motorized carts. My grandfather took it all in stride as a part of life. I got off in the lobby then walked to the separate elevator to his floor.

"Is that you, Kate?"

I searched around for the person attached to the voice. A trim white-haired lady in full makeup broke off from her group of friends and headed my way. Her face appeared familiar from a previous visit, but I didn't remember her name.

"Hi. Nice to see you," I stammered out.

Her face crinkled up in a smile showing a full mouth of perfect teeth. "It's Frannie, dear. Frannie Rhetland. Mick's friend."

"Of course. How are you?" Now I remembered. She was one of several "lady friends" my grandfather admitted to.

"Still vertical." She laughed at the popular joke, then patted my arm and gave me a little hug. "Your grandfather is looking forward to seeing you again. He told me all about having brunch at the River Café and your very handsome date."

To my surprise she gave me a cartoon-style wink.

"Get it while you can, dear," she said. "I certainly am."

On the elevator ride up I wondered if I should mention meeting Frannie to my Gramps. For some reason her candor shocked me a little. I wasn't used to that kind of frankness coming from a senior citizen that I barely knew. Especially if it involved my grandfather.

Once the doors opened I was enveloped in a big hug. Gramps always smelled like a comfortable blend of Old Spice aftershave and Ivory soap.

"You made good time," he commented as he took my backpack from me, walked me across the hall and ushered me into the apartment.

My first impression was that something had changed since

the last time I'd been there. I noticed a vase of artificial flowers, and some throw pillows on the sofa.

Gramps hated throw pillows.

I sat down on the sofa and lifted a jaunty blue-and-white-striped square in the air. "Anything new you want to tell me? Dear?"

"You've met Frannie, I take it." His cheeks turned a deeper pink than usual. "She helped me decorate a little."

"It looks nice." I waited for a further explanation but none came. Instead he clapped his hands together and stood up.

"Let's get going. Ready, Katie?"

"Ready, Mick."

Then I winked at him.

We took the subway into the city, along with a few thousand other people. Gramps was a master of the underground system. I followed as he skillfully switched trains and changed stations. Many of the cars were newer versions of the old clunkers I remembered from my high school days, but they still screeched to a halt.

Our destination was the New York Historical Society Museum, on Seventy-seventh-Street and Central Park West. The special exhibit concentrated on famous trials held in New York, and the courtroom sketch artists who provided an inside look when cameras were barred by the judge.

The gray stone building with Greek columns held a multitude of artifacts, traveling and permanent exhibits as well as special presentations, like the one we were viewing. Sure enough, a sketch of Son of Sam by Gloria LaGuardia was prominently displayed. Several other sketches of the lead lawyers, judge, and a surviving victim drawn by fellow artists surrounded her most famous pen-and-ink drawing. Her realistic style not only captured a likeness but it conveyed an emotional edge that gave an inkling of the personality of the subject. Quickly penned line strokes managed to give a feeling of movement to what could have been a static picture.

"Very impressive," Gramps commented. "I remember David Berkowitz and this trial. He said he received messages from his neighbor's dog."

"That's spooky. I'd forgotten that."

We meandered through the displays, through different eras and trials with different artists, showing vastly individual styles, from ultra realistic to almost cartoon-like colored pencil sketches.

"I wonder if Tucker knows about this?" I asked my grandfather as he gazed into a glass display case of doodles and handwritten notes to lawyers from their killer clients.

"Probably," he answered. "From what you told me, I think he's a pretty savvy guy."

My eye wandered to an old photo of a scrawled message from a murderer written on a wall. Standing next to it, for size comparison sake, I guess, stood a very uncomfortable-looking cop, captured for all eternity by the photographer.

"Tucker told me he was hunkering down at home, so it's possible he hasn't heard about the exhibit. I think I'll text him, anyway." I took a photo of the exhibit poster and forwarded it to his phone with a brief explanation. "The worst he can do," I said to Gramps, "is ignore me."

To my surprise I received an immediate unexpected response.

Who is this?

Our trip back to Brooklyn became a somber one. The mysterious person on the phone turned out to be Tucker's photographer roommate, Dimitri Petrov. Tucker was in New York Presbyterian Hospital's ICU. He'd been beaten up outside a gay bar, a victim of a hate crime. We were meeting his friend in the ICU waiting room.

"Been in this elevator too many times," Gramps mumbled when the door opened.

"Sorry to put you through this," I said. "I can meet you later, if you want."

He shook his head. "A lot of memories here for me. Most of them bad ones."

I realized this hospital might be the designated trauma center for fire victims and injured police and firefighters. Gramps must have at least forty years of memories haunting him. Meanwhile the elevator bell chimed.

A distraught Russian-looking man with a large camera bag sat at the far end of the waiting room texting, even though a sign outside the elevator asked that you refrain from using your cell phone. He didn't look up until I called his name.

"You must be Kate Turner. Sorry to meet this way." He looked past me to my grandfather, his black eyebrows raised in question across a handsome Slavic face.

After the introductions, he got down to what happened. Dimitri obviously felt guilty for dragging Tucker out of their apartment on Friday night. Both night owls, they didn't get to their preferred bar, The Trolley, until ten-thirty. Instead of social-izing, Tucker hid himself in a booth taking notes on something, while Dimitri met up with friends. Annoyed at his anti-social roommate, he joined a group of guys headed for a different club a few blocks away.

Two hours later the police called him. Tucker had been jumped and attacked in an alleyway only a block down from The Trolley bar. The writer's cries for help had been heard by patrons standing outside the front door, smoking cigarettes. Their quick intervention saved his life. A drag queen gave chase, following the assailant halfway up the alley, but was hampered by his gown and extremely high heels. The only description the witnesses remembered after a night of drinking was seeing a man in a black coat and black ski mask. No one agreed on race or age.

So far, Dimitri told us, there were no suspects. It was the third case of gay-bashing in that neighborhood in the last six months.

"Does his family know?" I remembered Tucker mentioning growing up in Ohio.

"He's estranged from them since he came out," Dimitri disclosed in a matter-of-fact manner. "They'll think he got what he deserved."

A doctor stuck his head out of the automatic door and gestured to a middle-aged couple sitting quietly in the corner. It was obvious the wife had been crying. "You can visit him now," was all he said.

That left the three of us. After a few minutes, Dimitri spoke once more.

"I found a medical power of attorney in his files. He put my name on it."

Gramps and I exchanged glances.

The photographer seemed overwhelmed. "Tucker is crazy efficient. I just wish he'd asked me before he did it."

That appeared to be a recurring theme in the writer's life. "Tucker told me he kept a lot of files." I remembered joking with him only a few weeks ago about storage lockers and saving every scrap of paper. On my phone I still had the goofy selfie photo of the two of us taken at the Lucky Garden when he bragged about how famous he intended to be.

"Do you want to see him? I think I'm the only visitor he's had so far." Dimitri walked over to a button next to the automatic doors and pushed it. He spoke briefly into a monitor, and the doors swung open.

"If they ask, tell them you're a cousin," he whispered. "They don't check."

Gramps took my arm before I went through the doors. "Meet you out here," he whispered. "I'm going to check on something."

I had just enough time to step inside before the doors began to close behind me.

The person in the bed could have been anyone. The only feature I recognized was a lock of red hair that had slipped out of the thick bandage wrapped around his head. Puffy blackened eyes were swollen shut. Plastic tubes delivered oxygen through a severely broken nose. Dark stitches, like train tracks, ran across his lower lip and chin. Bruises in shades of yellow, brown, and purple ringed his throat.

A nurse stood next to him changing out a bag of intravenous fluids. A red label fixed to the bag signaled they'd added in a powerful antibiotic.

"How's he doing?" Obviously upset, Dimitri veered his gaze away from the hospital bed.

"About the same." The nurse's bright pink scrubs were a blast of color in the white and beige space. She efficiently checked the vital signs displayed digitally behind the bed and made a note in her records. "You need to speak up," she advised us. "It's good for him to hear familiar voices."

I moved a chair to the far side of the bed and picked up Tucker's hand. Broken nails and bruised knuckles attested to the self-described tough nerd not giving up without a fight.

"Good for you, Tucker," I told the silent body on the bed. "Good for you."

The two of us sat by Tucker's side for at least a half-hour while Dimitri relayed all the information given to him by the bar owner, witnesses, police, and medical staff. Whoever had beaten him up had worn thin gloves and a black ski mask. The witnesses saw Tucker on the ground kicking and punching, a man bending over him, hands around his throat. They yelled and the perp took off running down the alley before disappearing down another darkened city street.

By the time the EMTs and cops arrived the assailant was long gone.

Our visiting time over, the two of us went back out into the starkly bright waiting room.

"Has Tucker said anything about that night?" I asked. We were standing in front of a vending machine, Dimitri getting his second Diet Coke since I'd been there and a bag of potato chips.

"The nurses told me he's been incoherent. Mostly he says no and mumbles stuff that doesn't make much sense."

"Like what?"

"Let me think a minute."

He ripped open the bag of chips and took a sip of soda before he answered. "Tucker says jumbled sentences and kid stuff, like nursery rhymes. The MRI showed brain trauma from blows to the head, so that's expected, I suppose." Dimitri paused to chug more Diet Coke.

"Nursery rhymes?"

"That's what they told me. Something about the Big Bad Wolf."

I sat alone in the waiting room, processing what Dimitri innocently revealed. Tucker called Carl Wolf, who he suspected of killing Gloria LaGuardia, the Big Bad Wolf. Was he trying to tell us who attacked him?

Who else was at risk from the Big Bad Wolf?

My thoughts jumped back to that stupid newspaper interview Tucker did, calling me an animal behavior expert who would be helping with research for his book.

Had Tucker unknowingly put me at risk too?

I'd been vacillating back and forth about Tucker's suspicions, based only on an elderly woman's scrambled memory, nothing more. But now two people connected to this old case had been attacked, one killed and the other one alive only by luck. The sight of Tucker lying silently in the hospital bed, bruises circling his throat, was still vivid in my brain.

In my estimation Wolf had made a big mistake if he was the one who attacked Tucker. By coming out of hiding he'd called attention to himself and possibly refocused the ongoing FBI investigation into his whereabouts. Deep in thought, I startled when a large shadow suddenly loomed over me.

"Sorry," Gramps said, "I thought you heard me come in." He sat in the adjacent seat and put an arm around my shoulders. "It's always hard to see anyone in the hospital. Even worse if he's a friend."

His words and warmth comforted me in the sterile waiting room whose harsh fluorescent lights made us both appear haggard. The light paint and bland pictures on the walls did little to relax anyone. "By the way," I asked, finally pulling away, "where did you go?"

"Oh, I made a few phone calls to some old friends in the department. The police have got nothing so far."

"That's what Dimitri said."

"This kind of beating has happened close to that bar before, one in the same alleyway. The cops think someone is specifically targeting gays in this area."

Another example of hate crimes you read about in the newspapers. The stories don't become immediate until it happens to someone you know. Now I wasn't sure what to think.

"Gramps," I confessed, "I hate to leave him here alone in this condition. He's got no family nearby, no close friends to look after him. I need to be back to work in the morning and Dimitri leaves for China on a photo shoot tomorrow night."

"Where's that third roommate?"

"Somewhere in Montana. He's an actor traveling for nine months with a cross-country theatre tour."

Silence settled on us, as we both realized the extent of Tucker's predicament.

"You know, I can stop by here once a day and check up on the little guy," Gramps volunteered.

"Why would you do that? You don't even know him." My grandfather's generosity overwhelmed me.

"Why not? Extra brownie points in heaven." His ruddy face became serious.

"You've got plenty of brownie points, Gramps. I hear St. Peter already has you booked for the express lane."

"Funny." He bent his head toward his knees, voice barely audible. "Listen, Katie, nobody should be alone in this place. Your grandmother died here in this hospital. Seeing her slip away every day was…very hard." He rubbed his eyes with the back of his hands. "I'll bring some paperwork, a pack of cards. Maybe I'll convince some of these nurses to relax and organize a game or two on their breaks. Who knows?"

I couldn't tell if he was kidding or not.

"You're going to play blackjack with the medical staff?"

"Sure, why not? I figure Tucker will be awake in a few days. Then they'll transfer him to a live-in rehab facility for a month or so. Once he's there he won't be alone, he'll be surrounded by people."

My grandfather deliberately downplayed the seriousness of Tucker's injuries, probably to make me feel better. I knew my friend might be in for a long recovery.

"I don't know…"

"Give me the phone number of that Russian fellow and I'll set the whole thing up. He'll have to add me to the visitor list—and I'll need all of Tucker's family contacts."

I realized Gramps had everything under control. At least Tucker would be safe in the hospital. Until I knew more, I wasn't planning on sharing any information about him or Carl Wolf with anyone. As far as the world and the Internet were concerned, Tucker Weinstein had been beaten up during an anti-gay hate crime, Gloria LaGuardia was just the unfortunate victim of a bungled burglary, and Carl Wolf only a forgotten name on an old FBI poster.

Maybe Tucker thinking he was being followed hadn't been crazy.

We all needed to lay very low on the assumption that Wolf might be out there. Watching. Waiting.

Let the Big Bad Wolf think he got away with everything. He'd have no idea that Little Red Riding Hood and her Gramps were hot on his trail.

Chapter Twelve

Each day Tucker made small improvements, but his doctors were worried about the lingering brain swelling they saw on their tests. He'd been transferred out of ICU to the neurology ward, but there was still no date when he would be released. True to his word, Gramps managed to spend some time every day by his side. During a brief period of consciousness, he'd introduced himself to the red-haired writer and received a blink acknowledging Tucker understood. For the most part the medical staff kept him under sedation to allow his brain to heal.

Meanwhile, I went back to work, and found I had precious little time to devote to finding Carl Wolf. I needed to come up with an alternative plan.

When Luke stopped by one night with our now customary Chinese takeout, I found my opportunity.

"How's school going?" We sandwiched our conversation between bites of food. As usual we sat at my kitchen table, stacks of takeout containers surrounding us. This time we ate off of the pretty blue-and-white china plates Jeremy had bought the last time he was here. He'd been horrified by the strange assortment of chipped plates in the apartment.

"School's good." Luke skillfully used his chopsticks to pick a piece of chicken from the chicken fried rice. "Finals are coming up soon for this semester. I'm glad I took a leave of absence from the force, though. I can't imagine studying for the LSATs and finals while working full time."

"I don't blame you. When I studied for my boards I became a hermit. Gramps practically slid my meals under the door." Luke reached for the soy sauce, but I detected an illegal move on his part when he slipped Buddy some food under the table. "Hey, I saw that."

"Saw what?" He smiled his lopsided smile at me, confident the evidence had disappeared. My supposed anger was a big bluff. He knew I'd been known to share snacks with my dog.

"No wonder he likes you." Sure enough, Buddy stood at his feet, gazing up at Luke in adoration and licking his chops.

"How's Jeremy?" my dinner companion asked, suddenly very involved with his shrimp in black bean sauce.

"How's Dina?" I countered. Last time I heard he was on the outs with his on-again, off-again high school sweetheart. Their relationship was difficult to keep track of, like an endless tennis match—back and forth and back and forth again.

From under the kitchen table came the thump, thump, thump of Buddy's wagging tail.

"I'm not in that much contact with her anymore," he confessed. "You?"

"Most of the time Jeremy's at the University of Pennsylvania working, but we did manage a beautiful weekend in the city a few weeks ago." To emphasize my point, I smiled and popped a wonton in my mouth. What did "not that much contact" with Dina really mean?

"So it's going good for you two?" His downward gazing eyes were impossible to read.

"Well, a long distance relationship is difficult…" My voice trailed off. I wasn't in the mood to share secrets with Luke. For all I knew he'd be back with Dina by next week. It had happened before and it could certainly happen again. I decided to change the subject.

"Any news in the Gloria LaGuardia murder?"

He scooped out the rest of the fried rice before he answered my question.

"Not really. Why do you ask?"

My mind scrambled around for a benign explanation. "Her niece, Irene, is my client. When she comes in with her cat, I don't want to stick my foot into it." I got up to refill my water glass and escape his suspicious gaze. "You guys are sure it was a robbery gone bad?"

"That's what they say. Last I heard Kingston police recovered a few of the stolen items. A wedding ring, some assorted family pieces. Irene identified the lot." Luke's tone had become clipped, which meant he didn't want to discuss it.

I let it go. A follow-up phone call to Gloria's niece from me about the sketch artist exhibit in New York was in order. I'd casually question her about her aunt's stolen property then. My glass full, I went back to my chair and picked up the chopsticks on my plate.

"The FBI posted a possible sighting of Carl Wolf in Utah two days ago." Luke watched my reaction carefully.

"Makes sense," I agreed with an innocent smile. "He would be crazy to stay here on the East Coast. Anyway, I'm staying out of it."

From the questioning expression on his face I could tell he had his doubts.

Later that night as the wind howled outside I started a new computer file on Carl Wolf. What did I really know about him? Most of the plain facts had come from copies of the news stories and police reports of the murders that Gramps sent. Maybe I could come up with a different way of looking at all those facts, something based on my field of expertise, as Tucker called it.

The Big Bad Wolf professed to be an avid hunter and outdoorsman who often disappeared on weekends on hunting trips. That was one of the complaints his wife had, that and his ever more controlling personality. To the outside world he appeared charming and ingratiating, but behind closed doors was another matter. Everyone in the family jumped when he said jump. According to his mother-in-law, however, he did have a constant loving companion. A companion he lavished attention on.

I decided to start with that loyal companion.

I needed to concentrate on the dog.

The Internet is a great research tool, but I found it hard going when I tried to pull up details about the Wolf family dog. No breed, age, or sex was mentioned in the newspaper reports. Only that the dog had been found wandering the neighborhood in the early morning before the bodies were discovered. Since Carl Wolf enjoyed hunting, I assumed his dog would be one of the sporting breeds, but that left a heck of a lot of different types of canines to choose from.

I felt a little creepy calling Anita Wolf's mother out of the blue, but it had been twenty-one years since her daughter and grandchildren were murdered. On the other hand, some wounds never heal.

The archived newspaper articles contained several interviews with Anita's mother, Andrea Bradshaw. She and her husband, Fred, lived only fifteen minutes away, and smelled the smoke on that August morning her beautiful family had been wiped off the face of the Earth. My guess is she'd remember every detail.

I took a chance she still had a landline phone. It paid off. After finding the name "A. Bradshaw" in the directory, I breathed a deep calming breath and dialed.

The female voice that answered the phone registered strong and clear.

"Mrs. Bradshaw. I'm Kate Turner, and I've been working with Tucker Weinstein who is writing a book that includes the Wolf family murders."

"Yes. I know Tucker very well. What can I do for you?"

Bingo, the right Bradshaw. No anger, or hysteria, an altogether successful step one.

"I'm so sorry for your loss, and I regret asking you to relive your pain." I had an inkling of what she was going through. The car accident that killed my mother and brother when I was fifteen always lurked at the edge of my consciousness.

Her sharp sigh said more than any words. "Every day I live with pain, Ms. Turner, but I try to balance that by celebrating their lives. Some days are better than others."

"I understand." Emotion made me hesitate and gather my thoughts. "I'd like to ask you some questions about Carl and Anita's dog."

"Werner?"

"I beg your pardon?"

She laughed. "That was his name. Werner Von Braun. I just called him Brownie."

Now I understood. Someone named the dog after that famous German rocket scientist. "So, you knew the dog, correct?"

"Who do you think took the poor thing in after...after that monster killed my babies?" Real anger fueled her words. Twenty-one years had passed but time hadn't dimmed the pain.

"Do you mind me asking what kind of dog he was?"

An uneasy suspicion could be felt on the other end. "Did you say you worked with Tucker? Why are you asking me all this? I thought he had it in his records."

Thinking quickly I said, "I'm confirming some notes he made. You know, for accuracy. Editors these days usually demand every source be verified by at least two people."

"Oh," Andrea replied. "Of course. I didn't think of that." She cleared her throat and excused herself. "Sorry. I've got a cold. Let's see, you wanted to know about Brownie. He was a purebred German shepherd. Had papers and everything."

I was surprised. German shepherds weren't specifically hunting dogs, like the Labradors and pointers. They were valued most for their sense of protection. That's why police often used them. "Who picked that breed?" I asked her.

Anger surfaced again. "Who do you think? Carl did. If he

had his way, Brownie would have ripped everyone's throat out on command."

"Carl Wolf trained his dog to attack?" None of the newspaper articles had mentioned this.

"Yes. There was some kind of secret signal he could give Brownie. He used to brag that having a guard dog was better than having a gun because dogs were legal in every state."

"I see." I tucked the phone between my shoulder and left ear and kept scribbling. "Anything else? Was there something he always wanted to accomplish, a life goal?"

"Well, he always talked about wanting to join the FBI, but he said he couldn't because he had the kids and a wife and responsibilities…bla bla blah. Made it sound like Anita's fault. Personally, I doubt he would have passed the psychological testing, but you never know. He fooled a lot of people."

"Fooled them how?"

"He pretended to be human." She sniffed again, before blowing her nose. "Excuse me. Is there anything else?"

I could sense her becoming restless. Time to wrap things up and get back to the dog. "Did he do Brownie's training himself, or were there classes…?"

"Honestly, I don't remember. But they had an argument about how much the dog cost, I know that." She paused and I could hear her sipping something in the background. "Brownie turned out to be a great comfort for me. A wonderful watchdog if someone came to the door, but with the people he knew he always became a sweet and gentle boy. He lived to be almost thirteen years old, which is old for a German shepherd, Doctor Holtzer told me."

"Doctor Holtzer?"

"Sure. He was Brownie's veterinarian."

Bingo.

My curiosity now ran at a faster pace. I searched my notes for any mention of Brownie or his veterinarian. Did Tucker purposely leave them out or had they been pushed to the periphery of the story?

It had been twenty-one years ago since Carl Wolf owned his dog. The odds were pretty good his veterinarian wouldn't remember events from back then. That is, if he was still around.

I looked up Dr. Ethan Holtzer in my American Veterinary Medical Association directory. Surprise. His name popped up as a member, but retired from practice.

With Andrea Bradshaw it had been easier to ask questions, posing as Tucker's assistant. I couldn't think of any way to explain this call from out of the blue by a stranger. It took a long pep talk with myself to dial his number. While it rang I paced back and forth, trying to focus my thoughts and present my case.

"Hello?" An elderly voice on the other end spoke loudly into the phone.

"Dr. Holtzer? I'm Dr. Kate Turner, a veterinarian at Oak Falls Animal Hospital in upstate New York."

"Are you sure you have the right number? You do realize, Dr. Turner, that I'm retired from practice." His response to me had been quick and to the point.

I kept pacing back and forth, still a bit anxious to be calling a stranger. "Sir, I got your name from Andrea Bradshaw. I'm helping an author named Tucker Weinstein research a book about Carl Wolf. He murdered his family twenty-some-odd years ago in your town. I'd like to ask if you remember anything about him and his dog, a German shepherd named Werner Von Braun."

Nothing.

"Wolf named him after the Nazi rocket scientist, but Andrea called him Brownie. You were his veterinarian. I understand if you don't remember. It was a long time ago."

Still only silence.

I was about to apologize and hang up, when Dr. Holtzer spoke. "Well," he said, "it's about time."

Once he began to speak, he didn't stop. It seems that Dr.

Holtzer was surprised that the FBI had never interviewed him during their lengthy investigation. He had taken the unusual step of contacting the lead agent and offering to give his impression of Carl Wolf as a client and dog owner, but had been quickly rebuffed.

He never offered again.

I briefly explained my curiosity about the only aspect of Wolf's life that no one had investigated. "There might be a pattern here," I explained, "that could be repeated."

"I agree," he said. "Carl Wolf originally presented to me as just another dog owner, albeit, of a very valuable animal."

"What do you mean?"

"Brownie was a purebred Schutzhund-certified German shepherd imported from Germany. He probably cost upwards of five thousand dollars, and that was twenty-some years ago."

Astonished, I had to ask, "Did he plan on breeding the dog?"

"No. Wolf just wanted the best. He also was a big proponent of the way the Nazis trained their military dogs."

That struck no chord in my memory. "I'm sorry. I don't understand."

"The Nazi command and the Gestapo used German shepherds as police dogs and then to control prisoners in concentration camps. Disgusting use of dogs, in my opinion. I'm not sure why, but during one of Brownie's exams, Wolf let down his guard for a moment and revealed a personal philosophy of life, so to speak."

"Which was…?"

"His politics were completely out-of-the-ballpark. Does the term white supremacist ring a bell?"

A half an hour later Dr. Ethan Holtzer and I were on a first-name basis. Most people don't realize that the veterinary community is relatively small. Within a few minutes of talking shop, we discovered several mutual friends. One of my professors at Cornell had been Ethan's lab partner in vet school.

Now that he'd warmed up to me, his recollections became

more detailed. Since observation is a huge part of our training, most vets find it difficult to turn off. Even out of the office our brains keep watching and cataloguing the world around us. Ethan was no exception. While he examined Carl Wolf's dog, he was also visually examining the owner. And what he picked up was disturbing.

"I only met his wife once," he told me. "Petite, very sweet person, but she clearly was under his spell. Now, I saw Wolf a couple of times with Brownie. Initially, his manner with me was casual, very friendly, just a regular guy. But after conversing with him over time you got a hint of his arrogance, the sharpened steel under the surface. His way or the highway—and that went for the dog, too. He demanded an unusually high degree of control from that German shepherd. In fact, I think that's one of the reasons I remember him so well."

Clients, I knew, rarely thought their veterinarians might be making assessments of them as well as of their pet.

"Did they have a cat?" I thought back to the cat hair the pathologist found in Gloria's hair.

"No, definitely, a dog person, that I'm sure of. Didn't have much use for cats."

I nodded on the other side of the line, scribbling notes as we went along.

"Did you ever feel intimidated, or threatened by him?"

A deep laugh spilled out of the phone. "I'm an old horse vet," he said. "Started working with small animals after a back injury. It takes a lot more than attitude to intimidate me."

"Same here," I agreed, the huge jaws of a pissed off iguana snapping at my arm freshly embedded in my mind.

I knew exactly what he meant. While helping to tranquilize a horse in vet school, I'd been pinned to a wall when the sleepy Palomino gelding decided to lean in my direction. Since he outweighed me by about a thousand pounds, I scooted under his belly and out the other side. That same day an annoyed cow attempted to kick me during a pregnancy exam, but I jumped out of side-kicking range as soon as I saw her hoof come off the ground. All those challenges honed my observation skills as well as forced me to develop quick reflexes. Karate lessons all during high school came in handy too.

Background noise muffled out Ethan's response, before I heard him say, "I'll be there in a minute."

"I'm sorry, I've probably kept you from your dinner." I'd lost track of the time. "You've been so gracious to speak with me and…"

"Nonsense," he interrupted. "Whatever I can do to help. This guy needs to be put away."

"My thoughts exactly. It's an insight into his mindset, I think, being this involved with his dog."

"I wonder," Ethan continued, "if enough time has passed that he'd feel comfortable going back to his first love, German shepherds. He was very into having an attack dog, by the way. All his voice commands, I remember, were spoken in German. The guy bragged about it to me."

"Really? That's taking it a bit far, don't you think?" I hadn't given much thought to commands other than the usual sit, stay, and down.

"Not in this case. If I remember, and it's been a while, Brownie was trained in Germany and imported by Wolf as a young adult dog into the United States."

More background noise and what sounded like the word dinner.

I felt as though I had taken up enough of Dr. Holtzer's time. "You've been invaluable, Ethan. I can't tell you how much I appreciate all this information. I'll be sure to pass it on to Tucker."

"You're very welcome, Kate. Take care of yourself, now. Don't start digging a deep pit for yourself."

I laughed in spite of myself. "You sound just like my grandfather."

"We old codgers give some good advice." More noise erupted in the background, with someone calling his name again. "Okay, sorry, got to go."

"Thanks again," I said. But before I could hang up, he had one more thing to say.

"Rottweiler or Doberman maybe."

"What?"

"Wolf is a real smart guy. The FBI probably knows he had a trained German shepherd. If I were Wolf, I'd choose another German breed and fly under their radar. Definitely not a Dachshund," he joked, "but I can see him thumbing his nose at the Bureau by owning a Rottweiler or a Doberman."

By the time I finished transcribing my disjointed notes, my eyes were tired and itchy. Sleep beaconed and felt long overdue. After I walked Buddy, we both made beelines for our beds. My poor brain refused to shut down, though, as it tried to process today's information overload.

When I did fall asleep, I dreamt I was a judge at a dog show. But these were no beautifully pampered and groomed entries. Lined up in front of me stood a bevy of snarling dogs dressed in Halloween costumes, their jaws snapping and biting again and again as each handler took turns signaling their dog to lunge at me.

Chapter Thirteen

As the week passed, my life fell into a routine. Work, sleep, get up, and work some more. Gramps continued his updates on Tucker's condition. They didn't change that much from day to day. The neurologists had decided to induce a coma, since he'd become restless, and tried to climb out of the bed. My grandfather settled into his own routine predicated on when doctors did their rounds. On the neurology/stroke ward rounds were scheduled around ten in the morning. Right at nine-thirty he'd be sitting by the writer's bedside with a large coffee and buttered roll. By the end of the first week, he told me, he knew everyone, from the phlebotomist who loved his job to the angry curly haired nurse dumped by one of the second-year residents for a different curly haired nurse in orthopedics. Upset with having to see her former boyfriend five days a week, her chronically cranky mood hovered over the ward like a black cloud whenever she was on duty.

I reminded Gramps that patients tended to forget that what was life or death to them was just another day at the office for the hospital employees.

Through his fire department and police contacts, Gramps confirmed there were no new developments in the assault case on Tucker. Hate crimes were more common than the general public thought. The forensic team found the alleyway where the attack took place a swamp of DNA containing multiple sources, having been used by bums, prostitutes, and drug addicts for months, if not years. The pawnshop located next door periodically hosed it down to get the urine odor out, but that was it. No city services ventured there.

Tucker had put up a ferocious fight. Defensive wounds showed on both arms and hands. Broken fingers and toes indicated how hard he tried to protect himself. When knocked down, the writer crawled his way through the alley, clawing and kicking his attacker in a heroic attempt to get away, but at the same time covering his clothes and body with a potpourri of random DNA and fibers. No identifiable DNA was recovered from under his fingernails. With a vague eyewitness description and no coherent statement from the victim, the crime remained unsolved and probably would stay that way. Each day meant new victims in the Big Apple.

That night, after work, I tried to expand on Dr. Holtzer's dog-owning theory, but immediately became bogged down.

After doing a computer search of the Oak Falls Animal Hospital files, I discovered over one hundred-fifty German shepherd or German shepherd mixes over the years who had been patients. This was assuming the breed data had been entered correctly. Our office was one of fifteen veterinary hospitals in the Greater Kingston/Saugerties/High Falls and Woodstock area. I didn't even bother to add in Rhinebeck and the outlying counties. To make matters more complicated, there were two AKC registered German shepherd breeders in our immediate area, as well as the famous monks of New Skete up north in Cambridge, New York.

Tracking down owners of German shepherds using all this data was an impossible task, not to mention the fact that the Big Bad Wolf might have switched breeds. For all I knew, Carl Wolf now owned a pit bull.

Everything changed later that evening when Gramps finally called with good news about Tucker. The brain swelling had resolved and his weakened arm had gained some strength. But the best news was that our redhead patient was walking the halls without help, talking about his writing, and loudly complaining. His docs expressed cautious optimism for a full recovery.

With our patient mostly out of the woods, Gramps and I reviewed Tucker's allegations, trying to decide whether to take these claims to the FBI.

First: Gloria herself never said she saw Wolf, only someone evil. Tucker alone jumped to that conclusion. Second: Any truth to his suspicion of being followed? There was no evidence to support that. Third: Had Carl Wolf come out of hiding and assaulted him? Tucker, in his delirium, probably mumbled the last thing on his mind, the Big Bad Wolf, a pivotal part of his new book. With no memory of the event, that was another supposition.

Logically, nothing clearly pointed to a killer hiding in our midst. The FBI had plenty of real threats to deal with. If we brought our concerns to them at this point they'd most likely assign it a low priority. In fact, when I went back over our list of "clues" I had to admit many could be chalked up to an overactive imagination. After our conversation, Gramps diplomatically recommended we both cease our amateur investigating, at least until Tucker could make the decision to go to the FBI for himself.

Reluctantly, I agreed.

A huge feeling of disappointment settled in. I kept seeing Gloria's face. If Tucker was right, but no one believed him, Wolf would win again.

Chapter Fourteen

"Can you squeeze in one more house call?" Cindy yelled to Mari and me as we were halfway out the hospital back door. Although we'd been ready to leave early this Monday morning, we already had been delayed twenty minutes, thanks to a severely iced up windshield.

"Text us the info and explain to the clients about the weather." Outside a sneaky winter storm made visibility a little iffy. Dressed in just about everything warm I owned, I listened as snowplows rumbled by. Ready to back up the truck, I noted that our parking lot had an additional fine layer of new snow since it had been cleared a few hours ago. Before we inched our way onto the road, I was encouraged to see several other cars and trucks drive by.

"Well, that's a good omen," Mari commented. Her hand clutched a metal thermos of hot coffee like it was the Holy Grail.

I'd armed myself with a cup of hot chocolate, having already gulped down two cups of coffee. My nerves should start to jangle in about fifteen minutes, I figured.

"Please tell me our first call isn't up in the mountains somewhere." I steered the truck with its new set of winter tires Cindy had insisted on buying, onto the main road. The snowplow had created a three-foot-high shoulder of dirty snow on both sides of the road. A thin strip of grayish white leftover slush ran down the middle, covering the dotted line in the asphalt.

Mari didn't answer right away. She was struggling with her puffy down coat, maneuvering it unsuccessfully past the seat belt straps. The excellent heater in our F-150 had kicked in and created a steam bath-like effect inside the cab, which made us unbelievably uncomfortable. Since the defroster needed to be up on full blast for a while, the only solution became stripping off some of our layers of clothes.

"I guess I can't exactly ride around in my underwear," she quipped, finally peeling off her massive coat and squishing it into the backseat.

"Did you do some kind of magician trick?" I asked. "I was sure you were going to have to unbuckle your seat belt to get that thing off."

"Persistence," she answered, "and a certain amount of practice in my truck."

The sky had that weird gray reflected light glow we sometimes saw in storms. Only a few minutes earlier, when we started out, snowflakes were gently falling. Now Mother Nature had stepped up her game to create a major accumulation. Even with the snowplows scraping and salting the roads, I started to worry.

"Can you call Cindy and find out who absolutely needs to be seen today?" As I slowed for a traffic light, I felt the tires slip and slide before coming to a stop.

A lifelong resident of the Hudson Valley, Mari didn't seem that concerned.

Past most of the homes now and in the country, I noticed the open fields on either side of the road. Long expanses of white were outlined with stacked bluestone walls, their grayish capstones topped with glittering sugary snow.

While my assistant chatted about the weather with our receptionist, I sensed movement off to the left from the corner of my eye. Suddenly, a young deer darted out in front of us. My foot slammed on the brakes, slowing us just enough to miss the feet flying past. My close-up view of sharp hooves directly in front of my eyes felt surreal. Unfortunately, trying to avoid the animal set us into a spin, then a sideward slide across the road.

"Oh, no, oh no." A litany of "oh no's" flowed from Mari's mouth. I could vaguely hear Cindy asking, "What's wrong" while I steered into the turn trying to control the truck.

"Hold on," I yelled as I prepared for impact. But luck was with us. The front fender took a slight hit into the snowbank, which slowed us down. We sort of ricocheted back onto the road until I gently pumped the brakes. That didn't do what it was supposed to do. Instead, it sent us into another spin and we headed back toward danger. I set the parking brake, which helped, but failed to keep the truck from inching toward a particularly high mound of snow on the right side of the road. In slow-motion Mari and I braced for the inevitable crash.

The jolt, when it came, wasn't too bad. Thankfully, no other cars were in sight.

Shoulders aching from tension, hands cramped from gripping the steering wheel with all my strength, I said, "You okay?"

"Yeah." Mari still held her cell phone in her hand. On speaker-phone, we both heard Cindy demanding to know what just happened.

"We're okay." I told her. "A deer jumped in front of us. When I hit the brakes we skidded into a drift on the side of the road. I'm going to back out and then I'll check for damage."

Despite having the truck's front end stuck in the snow, the heater was working, as were the windshield wipers. I flipped on the flashing hazard lights and zipped up my coat.

"Cindy wants to know if we need her to call her husband for a tow."

"I'm not sure. Tell her we'll call her back." That would give our receptionist a few moments to calm down. Her imagination probably painted a much worse picture than our actual situation.

I rolled down the window and leaned my head outside. The truck's front grillwork was hidden in the snow, but the hood and tires didn't seem damaged. Satisfied we were okay for the moment, I threw the transmission into reverse and began trying to rock us back and forth.

To my surprise, we didn't budge. Instead, the tires just spun uselessly on the ice.

"Do we have any cat litter in the back?" That had been one of the tricks they'd used at Cornell when our veterinary school vehicles got stuck on farm calls.

"No, it's on our order list. I remember because I did the inventory on Friday."

"What about paper, or cardboard, or anything that would give us some traction?" Like Mari, my mind zipped through what we usually carried in the truck.

She laughed. "Only some stray tools. I guess I picked a bad time to clean out the backseat."

I knew exactly what she meant. We usually had an assortment of empty takeout bags, newspapers, old packing boxes, and rock salt.

"Even the salt?"

"Used the last bit on the walkway this morning, while you were on the computer."

Not giving up, I revved the engine and went into reverse. All we did was slide sideways, threatening to wedge us further into the massive snowbank.

Not wanting to be cold and stuck in the snow, I rolled the window back up, my hair and jacket sprinkled with melting flakes.

"Well, that didn't work," I muttered. "Maybe you should call…"

Bright lights flashed us. In the rearview mirror I saw a black SUV with a big shiny Mercedes emblem parked behind us.

"Nothing like being rescued in style," Mari said.

The driver got out, keeping close to the two cars, trying to lessen the possibility of someone else hitting that black ice and crashing into all of us.

Our Good Samaritan was all bundled up, hat jammed over his hair, wearing mirrored ski-type sunglasses, and a muffler wrapped loosely around his lower face. He tapped on the glass, big fluffy snowflakes falling on his head and shoulders. In the rearview mirror a blond-haired woman waved from the comfort of the Mercedes' passenger seat.

I rolled down the window.

"What the heck did you do? Seems like you ladies got yourself into a mess." Our Good Samaritan sounded a tad condescending.

"Need some help?" he asked.

"That would be great. What do you need me to do?"

Mari leaned over. "I think we have some chains in the back."

"Thanks, but you ladies sit tight. I've got it under control." He left for a second to take a quick look at the front end of the truck, then came back to the driver's side window. "Damage isn't too bad. You lucked out. When I flash my headlights, put it into neutral."

Before I could agree or introduce myself, he disappeared back into the storm. Meanwhile, Mari turned and waved and smiled at who we presumed was his wife.

The clunk of metal on metal signaled the hooking up of a length of chain between the two vehicles. He waved his hand and waited for my return wave before climbing into the driver's seat. After leaning over and saying something to the woman, he flashed the lights at us.

"Hold on," I warned Mari and slid us into neutral.

As the chain tightened, we felt a jerk and heard a creaking groan. Then, little by little, we were sucked out of the snowbank and pulled onto the main road. Freed from the ice, our big tires hunkered down and gripped the cleared surface. I rolled down the window and waved at our rescuer to signal we were okay.

He left the big Mercedes running, removed the chain, and came back to my driver's side window. "We'll wait and make sure you're okay before we head off."

"Thank you so much," I told him. "You were a lifesaver."

"Next time turn into the skid."

"I did."

Our rescuer turned chatty. "You little ladies work at the animal hospital?"

I'd forgotten our logo and phone number were prominently displayed on both the driver and passenger side doors. Since he'd been so helpful, I decided to let the "little ladies" comment slide.

"Yes, we do. I'm Dr. Kate Turner, and this is my veterinary assistant, Mari. We were on our way to a house call, but had to slam on our brakes to avoid a deer."

"Yeah, those deer will get you every time. Glad to be of help. I'm Jasper..." The rest of his name was obliterated by the noise of a big snowplow rumbling by. He held out a large hand encased in a thick leather glove. Snow blew through the open window, flakes melting as soon as they hit anything inside.

"We should be fine now," I assured him.

"Okay. See if you can get back on the main road. There's a gas station a few miles up ahead with a repair shop. You can have them check for damage."

"Good idea," I told him.

He rubbed his hands together and wiped some snow off his sunglasses without removing them. Their yellow reflective surface distorted my face like a fun-house mirror. "Don't worry, ladies, I'll follow behind till you get there. Try to stay out of trouble if you can."

Although he meant it as a joke, it felt like a put-down.

"I don't get worried," I answered, my tone a bit rough.

In an effort to smooth things over, Mari leaned toward him and loudly added, "Thanks again. You're a lifesaver."

I rolled up my window and waited until he'd gotten back into his truck. "Well, here goes nothing." Putting on my turn signal, I eased out onto the empty road. Our old F-150 did her thing, dug in, and moved along as if nothing had happened.

"Woo hoo," Mari yelled. She glanced down at her phone. "I've got to text Cindy and tell her we're on our way."

"Have her reschedule everyone she can. Let them know we had a minor accident and are checking for damage to the truck." Unfortunately some of our more demanding clients wouldn't consider that a valid reason for being late.

The drive to the gas station was uneventful. After we turned in, the big Mercedes beeped its horn and flashed its lights before continuing down the highway. We caught a brief wave from the blond woman in the passenger seat before they disappeared around a curve.

As soon as I pulled next to one of the gas pumps, thankfully sheltered under an overhang, we both jumped out to check the front end for damage. Thanks to our heavy-duty wrap-around steel grill, there were only scrapes to the paint and minor dents. Given the beat-up condition of our workhorse vehicle, it was nothing that needed immediate repair. Even the front lights worked fine.

"I don't know about you, but I need a bathroom break." Mari peered at the scraped paint, her red puffy coat making her look like a walking apple.

"Race you," I joked.

We had been lucky. If we'd hit the deer or another car, the outcome may have been more serious. I took our accident as a warning sign and made a mental note to buy some extra chains, flashlights, duct tape, a caution sign, and a whole bunch of cat litter.

Late that afternoon, after visiting several clients, we called it quits. The storm got a second wind and roared through the Hudson Valley. Mari and I practically crawled back to the office, arriving sometime after four o'clock, the truck doing no more than twenty miles per hour on the treacherous roads. Lack of visibility from thick snow and blowing winds added up to make driving hazardous.

"Boy, I'm glad this day is over." My assistant struggled to close her door against an unexpected hard gust of wind.

I checked the cab a second time, stuffing anything that needed to go inside the hospital into my pockets or knapsack, before carefully setting my boots down onto the parking lot. Except you wouldn't know it was the parking lot, since it had a good three to four more inches of snow cover. Our neighbor, Pinky, whose winter job was plowing people out of their driveways, had already been to our place early this morning. I doubted he'd get back to us again until the storm was over.

We both trudged into the office, shaking snow off our boots and clothing while Cindy circled around us like a hen with towels and hot drinks.

"I'm calling up tomorrow's office appointments and canceling. Pinky busted his plow on a boulder and no one else is available to plow us out. We can't see appointments if the parking lot is covered with snow." Busy helping Mari get out of her gigantic puffy coat, part of Cindy's sentence came out muffled, but I understood the gist of it.

Once we all sat comfortably in the deserted waiting room getting toasty, Cindy asked the most important question.

"How's the truck?"

"Fine, for now. No sense in doing any cosmetic repairs until after this winter is over." Through the large front windows of the hospital I watched the snow finally start to slow down. If the temperature continued to drop, all that slush from the salting would become ice.

I gestured to my friends, pointing to the road in front of our building. "You two might consider leaving soon, while it's still light out."

Cindy turned to Mari. "Why don't you leave your truck parked here next to mine? The hubby is coming to pick me up with our tow truck. He's hearing too many accident reports to let me drive."

"Well…"

"We can drop you off at your place. I'll call you when Pinky gets the plow going again and clears out the parking lot."

I expected a big argument from my feisty assistant, but to my surprise she simply nodded in agreement. "Thanks. One accident a day is enough for me."

Satisfied I didn't have anyone else to worry about, I breathed a sigh of relief. One more night cuddled up on the sofa all by myself sounded pretty good.

"Doc Anderson had a stroke of genius welding that giant wraparound grill onto the truck bumpers," I said.

A chuckle from Cindy revealed the real story. "That's because of what happened to his old red truck," she explained. "He was working a farm call, back in the day, and drove into what he thought was an empty pasture to park. Unfortunately, the client had just stashed his bull in it. The darn thing rammed the truck a couple of times, dented the whole front end and broke the headlights. Ever since then every truck he bought got that special grill welded on it, front and back. Doc called it his "no bull" protection."

"It did the trick today."

"And he never bought another red truck."

A honk from the parking lot signaled Cindy's husband had arrived. The tow truck bristled with thick chains on all four monster tires.

As they gathered up their things, Cindy asked about the Good Samaritans who stopped to help us.

"I think they were from the city. Not many locals are driving around in a shiny Mercedes SUV."

"What was his name?" Our receptionist prided herself on knowing almost everyone in Oak Falls.

"Jasper something or other," Mari answered. "Interesting guy."

A second honk prompted Cindy to stick her head out the front door and wave. "Let's go," she said, "before my bull has a cow."

We only had one young kitty left in the hospital, a neuter that was boarding overnight until his owner could safely drive over to get him. I moved him to a big cage, added a nice soft blanket, and gave him some extra attention before I strolled through the hospital, turned off the lights, and set the alarm. Mr. Katt ambled along behind me. Cindy had used her free time to clean the countertops and cages so we wouldn't have to. I'd noticed our staff could be counted on to pitch in and help each other with the endless cleaning and disinfecting, regardless of their job description. It was one of the reasons I enjoyed working here and, with my own vet assistant background, I never felt it was beneath me to bend down and clean up poop.

Bored with my same old-same old activity, Mr. Katt dashed off, scaling the cabinets and cages to take his favorite spot over-seeing his domain.

My cell rang while I was letting Buddy back in from his walk. "Just a second," I yelled into the speaker as I dropped it on the couch. My poor dog had ice balls clinging to the hair around his pads. A warm washcloth took care of it, leaving only wet footprints on the floor, which I cleaned with the towel stashed next to the door.

Task completed I collapsed on the sofa, glad to be out of the cold. "Hello."

"Hey, Katie. You sound like you have your hands full." Gramps, on the other hand, sounded very chipper.

"I had to dry off dog feet." After slipping off my boots, I noticed another wet puddle on the floor. A napkin rescued from the coffee table solved the problem.

"I've got more good news. Our boy is starting to remember events around the time of the assault. They're going to have to tie him down to keep him from going back to work."

"Wonderful." The doctors had said we could anticipate some

memory to return, but I hadn't expected it so soon. "Is he making sense?"

"Surprisingly, yes. Complained again about the hospital food to me. Smart kid." I could tell Gramps was amused. When I'd visited him after an emergency appendectomy a few years ago that's all that my grandfather wanted to talk about—the lousy hospital food.

"Does he remember the actual attack?"

"It's patchy for now. I'm under orders not to upset him or ask too many questions."

"Did your neurology poker buddies tell you when he's going to be transferred to rehab?"

"Not yet."

"It's probably up to the insurance companies, number of rehab beds, and paperwork, more than the medical staff." Another reason I preferred vet medicine to human medicine.

"You're right about that." There was a deep chuckle on the other end. "By the way, those doctors might know medicine, but they don't know their cards. Let's say it's been a pretty profitable stay."

Although part of me felt I should chastise my Gramps, the other part of me was laughing my butt off. "Enough about your winnings," I joked, "what about rehab?"

"It's up to the head of neurology. Tucker is the chief witness in an active criminal case that's gotten quite a bit of local publicity. No one wants their medical decisions to be under court scrutiny, so they're doing everything by the book. That bar the kid visited is suing the city for discrimination. Seems they've complained before about harassment and were promised extra police patrols at night, which never happened."

Nothing put the fear into a practitioner like the threat of litigation.

"Well, keep me posted and tell him he's in my thoughts."

"Will do. How's that storm up there? I hear you got the worst of it."

I wasn't about to worry him with the story of our accident. Hopefully, his buddy, Cindy, wouldn't feel like sharing, either.

"Cindy closed down the hospital until the day after tomorrow. Our parking lot isn't even plowed out yet. Anyway, the emergency clinic is taking all our calls, so for now the staff has some paid time off."

"Good idea. I'm happy you'll be confined to your apartment for a while." I knew if he had his way I wouldn't be driving at all in the winter.

"Oh," I caught him just before he hung up. "Did Tucker mention Carl Wolf at all?"

"Negative. He remembers going out with Dimitri, but as far as I can tell, he doesn't recall anything new about who assaulted him."

We talked a little more before saying goodnight. This news about Tucker complicated everything. The writer remained the driving force behind all the conjecture about Wolf. Without him our suspicions would collapse, like the first house the three little pigs built in the familiar children's fable—the house made out of straw.

The Big Bad Wolf had huffed and puffed and blew that house down.

Chapter Fifteen

The next morning, thanks to the storm, I slept in, sliding back under the warm covers after walking Buddy. When I woke, weak sunlight shone through the curtains. At first all the free time was refreshing. I took a nice long shower, painted my toenails, and French-braided my hair. But after six hours of forced relaxation, I started going stir crazy. The hospital stood empty and silent. When I checked my windows and the hospital windows for leaks or storm damage, all I heard were the echo of my footsteps. For a while Mr. Katt joined me but soon tired of the routine. With a dismissive look he turned and jumped to the top of the cabinets.

Even my patient, the little male neuter, stretched his legs then went back to sleep in his bed.

There wasn't much to do in my apartment and I couldn't get ahold of Jeremy because he was still in some remote part of New Mexico. He'd warned me that deep in the canyons, where the excavations were located, Internet and cell phone reception could be pretty sketchy.

Even HGTV had lost its allure.

Pacing up and down didn't get me anywhere either.

The sudden noise of a truck and the scraping sound of a plow outside were a cause for celebration. Our neighbor must have fixed his plow. Back and forth he worked to clean the five inches of snow and the odd drifts off the parking lot and around the entrance to my apartment. It usually took him almost a half an hour to finish, since part of the work included pushing the unwanted snow up against our fence while avoiding the dumpsters.

With my options suddenly brighter, the phone rang.

"Hi, Kate, hope I didn't call at a bad time." Cindy's voice sounded predictably cheery.

"No, just catching up on a few things." I didn't want to admit I'd been twiddling my thumbs.

"Did Pinky get over there and plow you out? Because if he didn't he's in big trouble."

My imagination conjured up an image of a perfectly coiffed Cindy putting her dukes up against our rotund, completely bald neighbor, who had her by at least two hundred pounds. Of course, my money would be on Cindy.

"Kate, are you there?" I jerked out of my reverie. To my surprise when I lifted the window curtain I saw a nicely plowed surface outside. Along the edges huge dirty snowdrifts hid the fencing from view, but Mother Nature would take care of them. With the sun out, the dark asphalt would absorb the rays and help melt whatever snow remained.

"Pinky came through. We're plowed."

"Good. I'm going to call Mari so we can pick up our trucks. We'll put down some rock salt on the front sidewalk and over by your door too."

"Do you want me to stay and help?"

"Nope." I heard her yell to her husband to get the truck ready. "I've got a great idea. Relax today. Get out of the house. Maybe you should go to the mall. You can stay nice and warm and start getting into the Christmas spirit. We're going to have the office Secret Santa drawing soon."

"It isn't even Thanksgiving," I reminded her.

"It's never too early to think about Christmas," she countered.

I had my doubts about that but her other suggestion held

some merit. The Kingston Mall was the only indoor shopping area nearby. At least I'd get some exercise, and check out the sales. Gramps and I usually exchanged funny gifts, but maybe this year I could step it up and get him an electronic something or other. Decision made, I walked the dog, dressed in multiple layers to cover any changes in the weather and headed for the mall experience.

Everyone else in the Hudson Valley had the same idea. By the time I arrived, the only parking spaces were a decent hike from the entrance, through sloppy puddles left by the melting snow. Families hauled their bored teenagers with them, little kids were itching to run around and grandparents marched in, determined to get everything they needed for the holiday early so they wouldn't have to do this again.

The rest of the Valley's residents were probably busy on their computers ordering everything online.

Sure enough, the inevitable Christmas music cheerfully played through zillions of speakers. The mall decorations of giant candy canes were up, fake pine boughs sprouted from the support beams, and lights twinkled everywhere. Most stores joined in but a few decided to wait until after Thanksgiving, and instead had season-appropriate displays of pumpkins and fancy gourds artistically arranged in their front windows. Red and gold banners announcing sales hung everywhere. It had been a while since I'd been mall shopping, so I decided to orient myself by doing a surveillance lap around the place. The wide pedestrian area, normally clear, was clogged up with little pop-up stands selling all kinds of items, from cell phone covers to hair products. Since I didn't need anything, I spent the time browsing, catching up as it were, with all the things the salespeople tried to convince shoppers to buy. Did I really crave a fancy cork for my wine? As I contemplated a particularly attractive blown-glass stopper, I realized all my wine bottles had twist tops, or came in a box that sat on the refrigerator shelf.

That impulse nicely thwarted, I ambled down one side, amazed at the number of stores appealing to teens and pre-teens. Featuring tight trendy clothes, odd earrings, and uncomfortable-looking shoes, many merchants targeted that specific segment of the buying population. All around me clumps of kids, temporarily free of their parents, stood in front of store window displays, giggling, texting, and causing minor traffic jams.

As I approached the more sedate anchor department store at the far end of the mall, things quieted down. Out of habit, I glanced at my watch. I had no appointments and no one waiting at home except Buddy the dog, and I already had his gift covered. My impromptu plan consisted of hitting the men's section and getting some ideas for Gramps and now Jeremy, although Jeremy probably had everything he could possibly need or want.

Undeterred, I maneuvered past glittering cosmetic displays with elegant salesladies dying to sit you in their chair and reinvent your face for you. All that makeup made me think how much easier it was for a man to alter his facial appearance versus a woman. Women can't cover half their features like men can. Guys can grow massive bushy beards, shave their heads, cultivate odd mustaches, or get buzz cuts. Really, the only parts that remained the same, without plastic surgery, were eye shape, ears, and mouths. Noses could be broken and not set and eyebrows encouraged to grow wild and wooly. Contacts altered eye color in a heartbeat, and hair—well, hair was the most easily changed of all. It made me think about the Big Bad Wolf, and what he might look like now.

Basically he could be anybody.

With that thought on hold, I vowed to concentrate on my Christmas presents. Maybe I...my thoughts were interrupted by someone calling my name.

"Hi, Dr. Kate. I thought that was you." A familiar face poked out from behind a mannequin dressed, strangely enough, for the beach.

"Hey, Veronica." It was my client with the sulfur-crested cockatoo. "Doing some holiday shopping?" I noticed several large bags in her hands.

"Just a few things. Some of these sales are irresistible. What about you?" I'm sure she noticed my lack of packages.

I shifted my purse and answered, "Just getting some ideas. The guys in my life are hard to shop for."

"The only guy right now in my life is Phil," my client confided, referring to her cockatoo. "A new toy and some fancy bird treats and he's set. I wish all men were that easy." She rested her packages on the floor and flexed her fingers as though getting ready to carry the bulky packages again.

"Nice seeing you," I said. "Say hi to Phil for me."

"I will…oh, that reminds me."

I figured a veterinary medical question was about to be asked, but she surprised me.

"Phil did very well in his therapy animal training and is receiving his certification next week. When he does, I thought about taking him over to the Oak Falls Community Center. That's where the adult care group I work with is located. They're having a Thanksgiving show and I thought that might be a great opportunity to show him to everyone."

"I'm sure they'd get a kick out of that." I'd seen most of the tricks Phil had mastered and they were pretty amazing. He talked, fetched on command, and could sing and dance. Veronica's patience with the large bird had paid off.

"Maybe you can join us? It's most likely going to be on a Sunday. It would be nice for him to have some familiar faces around, especially the first time he visits a strange place."

Since the only time I saw Phil was to cut his nails, I doubted he would be happy to see me and told her that.

"Absolutely not," Veronica insisted. "He likes you. He's told me a bunch of times."

It was a testament to her relationship with her bird that I

believed that statement. "Well, if you think it will help. I'm a big believer in therapy animals, especially those that visit nursing homes and hospitals." Although not as cuddly as a big golden retriever, Phil had his own special charm and novelty. I was sure he'd be a big hit.

"I'll give you plenty of notice, since I know how busy you are. Should I call Cindy with the date?"

"That's probably best." I didn't want to confess that my diligent receptionist would stay on my case and make sure I put it into my calendar. Heck, she'd probably want to go with me.

Veronica smiled and began juggling her packages again. "I'm so glad I ran into you. Happy shopping." With a quick wave she took off in search of more bargains.

Time drifted by, what with the music and the holiday spirit in the air. I dawdled along, scoring a free sample of fudge from outside one place and a sniff of some cinnamon-scented soap from another. Passing by a catalogue store, I made the mistake of sitting down and getting a demonstration in one of those massage chairs you always see in the mall. After being pummeled and pounded to excess, I explored a few of the crazy gadgets in the store. There were examples of different types of drones, intricate inflatable boats, a sophisticated flashlight that doubled as a club, and all sorts of things I never imagined existed. Wandering around undecided, I took their Christmas catalogue along with their website address. The salesperson assured me that the website had many other gifts, all of them available for quick home delivery. Stocked up with more information than I needed, I patted the massage chair good-bye. That's when I had one of those funny feelings of being stared at, when the hairs on the back of your neck stand up. Expecting another client, I turned toward the store's side exit, directly behind me.

People milled around in and out but none of them appeared interested in me. As I gazed out at the sea of shoppers, primarily women, my eyes drifted past a man in a baseball cap staring into a store window.

Then I came back to him.

First of all, the store he stared into appeared to be one of those places that cater to teens, filled with cropped tops and all manner of fashionably ripped jeans. Japanese street-style outfits inspired by anime cartoon characters filled one display window. If he had a daughter, he'd know you never buy clothes for a teenager. If he didn't, why was he so interested in those clothes? In my experience, fathers waiting for their families usually sat down on benches, and scrolled through their phones, with annoyed expressions on their faces. As I watched, baseball hat dude moved slowly along the row of stores, always with his back to me, head down, profile deliberately averted.

From this far away, all I could verify was a man wearing jeans, work boots, and a mid-length brown winter coat. At least the person dressed like a man. Compared to the other shoppers, he seemed tall but I couldn't tell his build, because the coat and jeans were loose, not tight. From this angle, I saw no reflections of his features in the store windows.

Was I becoming as paranoid as Tucker?

On an impulse, I decided to follow him, maybe get a license plate number when he got into his car, or a quick picture from my cell phone. Eyes fixed on the dude's back, I hurried out the store, and inadvertently slammed into a middle-aged woman heading the opposite direction. Her purse dropped and spilled on the tile floor.

"Why don't you look where you're going?" With an angry gesture she bent down to pick up her stuff. I apologized profusely and stooped to help. When I handed her a pen and some change that had fallen out, her suspicious gaze all but said you better not steal anything.

Finally, with everything accounted for, I stood up, apologized again, and searched the mall for the man in the baseball cap.

In the few minutes I'd been occupied, he'd vanished like a ghost.

Safely back in the apartment, my restlessness increased. Three or four times I peeked out the window at the empty parking lot. Was I overreacting? I certainly couldn't confirm anyone obviously stalked me or followed me. Maybe remembering how Tucker sounded spooked me a little. I didn't believe him then. Now I wasn't sure.

I hoped walking the dog in the cold air would clear my head. It didn't.

Closing the door after I brought Buddy inside, I noticed the end of a muffler poking out from behind his dog bed. Curious, I pulled it out. It belonged to Luke. He must have left it on his last visit, the visit that ended in yet another lecture.

With nothing else to do, I texted him, told him I had his muffler, and I'd leave it at the reception desk, but the office was closed until the morning.

Ten minutes later I received a text:

Finished studying. Will swing by. Are you there?

I hesitated. Did I really want to see him? We were sure to get into some kind of argument. We always did. On the other hand, how many more hours of HGTV could a human watch? Besides, whether I wanted to admit it or not, the experience at the mall spooked me a little. So I wouldn't appear too eager for company I replied with one word:

Yes.

Twenty-five minutes later Buddy barked once, then ran over to the door and whimpered with joy. I hated to disappoint him, but there'd be no handouts under the table for him tonight. With the muffler in my hand, I opened the door.

"Here you are." I basically shoved the muffler toward him.

"Mind if I come in for a while?" Without waiting for an answer, he began taking off his coat, this time hanging it up next to the muffler, then leaned down to pet Buddy.

"Whatever you want." Although trying to appear nonchalant, I was dying for company. Even argumentative, hard-headed Luke.

If Luke sensed anything amiss on my part he gave no hint. Instead, he kept up a steady stream of conversation about the roads, number of accidents in the last few days, and tomorrow's weather report.

As long as he'd decided to stay, I might as well play hostess. "Can I get you some coffee or tea?"

"Hot tea would be great. I've been drinking nothing but burnt coffee for hours. Do you still have that one with the orange peel in it?"

Surprised he remembered, I told him I'd make a pot for us both to share.

We sat down at the kitchen table. Luke had dark circles under his eyes, as though he'd been up all night. When the teakettle boiled, I popped up.

"Tired?" I asked him. With the tea brewing, I put out cups plus a tray of homemade chocolate chip cookies and some lemon pound cake.

"Don't tell me you've taken up baking?" The astonishment in his voice annoyed me.

"I might," I replied, "someday."

"Sure," he replied amicably, before digging in.

"Alright. They're early holiday presents from Henry James." The "Baking Biker" was a good client of mine and a longtime friend of Mari's. He always dropped off cakes or cookies before the holidays for the staff. I'd taken a few for myself and left the rest in the break room, along with a tin of mixed nuts and some homemade fudge. From Thanksgiving to Christmas, thanks to grateful clients, our staff operated on a constant sugar high.

We sat comfortably eating away, Buddy begging at Luke's feet as usual.

"What did you think of the arrest?" he asked, before taking another bite of chocolate chipped goodness.

Since I was mid-swallow, my question came out garbled. "What arrest?"

"Didn't Cindy tell you?" From Luke's low level of excitement, we might as well have been back talking about the weather.

I shifted in my seat. "Cindy's told me about her newborn niece, her sister's episiotomy, how infants get their first vaccination the day they are born, and all kinds of maternity-related subjects. But nothing about an arrest."

"That's funny. All my boss Bobby says is that the baby is cute but paternity leave is harder than work."

We kept getting off track. "What arrest?" I persisted in asking.

Luke took another big bite of cookie before answering. "They made an arrest in the Gloria LaGuardia case. The perp has a long rap sheet that includes burglary and assault with a deadly weapon, not to mention a juvie record."

"Did he confess?"

My cookie-loving companion's face scrunched up. "No. But he's in possession of stolen property from her place. The Kingston police traced him back from the pawn shop where he hocked Gloria's gold wedding ring."

Relief made me take another cookie.

"I heard the guy's on parole for another offense, is unmarried, thirty-one, and lives in his mother's basement." Luke finished up the last chocolate chip cookie and began to eye the pound cake. "Oh," he tapped his temple," I forgot to add something. The suspect's mom owns three cats, two of them black and white."

"Tuxedos," I muttered, glad my suspicions about being followed at the mall turned out to be just that. Unfounded suspicions.

"What?"

"Black and white cats," I explained to him. "We call them tuxedo cats."

He nodded and slipped Buddy a morsel of pound cake under the table.

"Did he say why he killed her?"

"He didn't say anything other than 'I want my lawyer.'"

Frustrated, I got up and put the kettle back on. "I guess it's better than nothing."

"Of course it is." For the first time he looked directly at me. "What's wrong, Kate?"

I debated telling Luke about Tucker and feeling uncomfortable at the mall, but ultimately didn't want to start another argument. My writer friend obviously had been wrong about Carl Wolf being involved in Gloria's death. Wishful thinking on his part—perhaps so there'd be more drama for his book? I had no idea any more what his motives might have been, or why Tucker included my name in that local newspaper story. Maybe he really was a little "creatively" paranoid from lack of sleep and an overactive imagination. The only important thing now was for him to recover from his injuries, and having the police complicate that recovery with more questions wouldn't help matters.

The sympathetic look in Luke's dark brown eyes almost made me spill the beans. Then he spoiled the mood.

"Trouble with Jeremy?" he asked.

"No." I lied. "How's Dina?"

At first I didn't expect him to answer. The last I'd heard, his high school sweetheart and on/off girlfriend, Dina, had abruptly left town for a job in Albany, leaving her loyal boyfriend, Luke, behind.

To my surprise he shared an update with me. "The job isn't what she thought it would be. I think she is considering moving back."

Great. How long before they got back together this time? Luke and I seemed destined to be the steady halves of our separate romantic relationships—Jeremy was off doing his thing, Dina doing hers—while both of us plodded faithfully along, holding down the home forts.

Once upon a time, I thought Luke and I might fall in love. The crazy chemistry certainly was there. But for us, once upon a time turned out to be only a fairy tale.

Chapter Sixteen

As Thanksgiving loomed closer and closer on the radar, our staff began exchanging turkey and stuffing recipes, fostering fierce debates on what to add in, whether to baste or not to baste—the entire topic culminating in the inevitable deep-fried turkey debate. I found nothing remotely appetizing about discussing the merits of stuffing in the bird versus stuffing in the oven over a messy surgery in the operating room.

As I ventured out in the truck for the afternoon house call appointments, the sky appeared clear for once with no snowflakes falling. The nice weather reflected our giddy moods. Mari and I giggled like little kids on the way to our client's house and placed bets. What would Daffy and her dog be dressed like today?

"Let's see," Mari began. "It's past Halloween and not yet Thanksgiving. Maybe some winter sports get-up?"

"We already had the golf outfits, so I'm going to go wild here and bet one dollar on Thanksgiving Pilgrims." I'd based my hunch on the calendar. Our next scheduled visit to cut Little Man's Chihuahua toenails would fall right after turkey day. I was pretty sure Daffy Davidsen wouldn't be able to resist an early celebration of our national holiday.

"You're on," Mari said. "Although I'd love to see that tough little dog dressed up like a turkey."

That idea made us laugh once more. Our eccentric but sweet

client spent much of her free time sewing matching outfits for herself and her Chihuahua. Little Man's expression was usually one of resigned disdain for being dressed in people clothes. With his bulging eyes, huge bat-like ears, and knobby legs, he wasn't the handsomest specimen of his breed. However his elf-like looks had their own endearing qualities. Regardless of Daffy's unique outlook on life and fashion, Mari and I enjoyed our visits. Not to mention she spoiled us afterwards with a lavish spread of cookies, cakes, and refreshments.

We arrived at her cute white-picket-fenced cottage a little before eleven. Her garden, which was glorious in the spring and summer, had been bundled up for the winter, rose bushes tightly wrapped in burlap with window boxes empty and cold.

Only a light drift of snowflakes greeted us when we stepped into the frigid November air. I'd thankfully take this chill over freezing sleet and snow any day. With my stethoscope securely draped around my neck, and Mari stomping her feet next to me, I rang the doorbell. A cheery little doggy chime played loudly inside.

When the door opened, I realized both Mari and I were winners. Dressed as a Pilgrim, complete with white bonnet, Daffy displayed spot-on precision in her period costume. However, tucked under her arm we noticed a strange mix of dog and turkey. Sure enough, Little Man glared at us, then growled, his ears and body from the neck down enclosed in a sweater-like costume, complete with bright red wattles flapping under his chin. A few real feathers both decorated and hid his doggy tail.

"Come in, come in," she said, holding open first the screen door then the front door. Wiping our feet on the doormat, we entered the unique world of Daffy—a world of doilies and tiny china figurines, heavy drapery, and plenty of furniture. We navigated the scrupulously clean but cluttered room and made our way into the kitchen. As always our client had prepared for our visit by spreading heavy layers of newspaper on the island countertop in anticipation of, essentially, her dog's personal health and grooming appointment.

Little Man meant everything to our older client. After a bad anal gland abscess, or as Daffy referred to it his "Down South" problem, she set up regular appointments with us to make sure it never happened again. The entire event proved so traumatic to both dog and owner that the extra money she paid out for house calls was offset by securing her peace of mind.

Besides, I suspected Daffy enjoyed the company.

Mari and I had our exam maneuvers down perfectly, like Olympic pair skaters. My assistant diverted the Chihuahua's attention with jingling keys or jazzy hand movements, allowing me to glide behind Little Man and deftly slip a small gauze muzzle over his pointed snout. With all parties now more comfortable, we quickly trimmed toenails, performed our butt-cleaning ritual, and checked him for any other issues. Since Little Man needed to demonstrate his Chihuahua power over us, he half-heartedly tried to bare his fangs, threatening us with eight pounds of grumpiness. Mari and I acted dutifully impressed, while his owner clucked and chided her baby to "be nice." Mission accomplished, we gathered up all the newspapers, threw in my used exam gloves, and wrapped everything in a garbage bag. After taking quick trips to the bathroom to clean up, my assistant and I looked forward to indulging in a sweet fantasy of treats.

Instead, all we saw on the table were a handful of nuts, a sprinkling of cranberries, and a bowl of what looked like puppy poo.

Daffy fluttered around the table in a ruffled apron, a blue-and-white china pot of tea in her hands.

"This year I decided to be historically accurate in everything having to do with the first Thanksgiving. On the table is authentic corn mush. The nuts and berries would have been gathered by the children for the feast, along with any vegetables that survived the early frosts. Of course, there were many other items at the celebration, such as venison and lobster, but I thought they'd be too heavy for the morning."

"Where is the pumpkin?" I asked.

"Pumpkin is open for debate," Daffy declared primly.

"I'd rather read about it than live it," Mari commented before sitting down. Since she adored eating the big chocolate chip cookies Daffy usually offered us, I felt her pain.

I gamely scooped a few tablespoons of the yellow grainy goop into a bowl.

"Would you like some molasses?"

"No thanks." A tentative forkful tasted, well, like nothing much. Vaguely sweet, it was the gritty texture that left quite a bit to be desired. However, her authentically British black tea tasted hot and delicious.

Mari wisely stuck with the tea. I chewed a few tart cranberries, cracked a couple of walnuts, and laboriously picked the meat out of the shells. With nothing else to eat on the table, we both poured ourselves more tea. The corn mush sat like congealed glue in the center of the table.

"Are you sure the Pilgrims didn't have at least one chocolate chip or raisin-oatmeal cookie on the Thanksgiving table?" The plaintive question fell on unresponsive ears.

"So, Dr. Kate…" Our hostess pulled up a chair, Little Man, back in his turkey costume, tucked under her arm. "I understand you have a steady beau. What is his name…Jeremy?"

Did I mention Daffy liked to gossip? My stomach answered her question first with a low rumble. "Excuse me," I muttered.

"More corn mush? I've got plenty." She gestured to a pot full of the stuff on the stove.

"No thanks," I told her. "I'm fully mushed."

Mari barely stifled a snicker.

Daffy ignored it and kept probing. "Your Jeremy seems quite a…traveler."

Sometimes Mari came to my rescue but today I sensed I faced our hostess on my own.

"Yes, he is quite a traveler."

I gave my assistant a visual high sign to wrap it up so we could get out of there.

"What does he think of you being involved in another murder?" she sweetly asked.

Not knowing exactly what to say, I stalled by taking another sip of tea.

"That story of yours in the newspaper wasn't very clear." Daffy threw her baited line into the deep water as she skillfully fished for details.

"Oh." I kept my tone casual. "That ended up being a tempest in a teapot." Thinking my allusion to our tea party sounded clever, I compounded it by saluting her with my cup.

Daffy's delicately plucked eyebrows arched in surprise. "What do you mean, dear?"

"The police have a suspect, a local man. Obviously, the writer quoted in that piece who speculated that Carl Wolf killed Gloria LaGuardia simply tried to stir up publicity for his new book. Why he mentioned me, I have no idea." I didn't want to go into Tucker's whole story and felt a little bad about throwing him under the bus, but I preferred to stop Daffy's gossip before it went Oak Falls viral.

I smiled all around, Mari smiled back, and we both stood up, ready to go.

"So, you haven't heard?"

The knowing tone in our client's voice meant trouble.

Mari continued packing up our stuff but nervously glanced at us over her shoulder.

"I've been sort of busy." That sounded lame even to me.

"Then let me bring you up to date. The police released Mr. What's His Name this morning, according to the news report I heard. His alibi checked out, as did his story of finding the victim's jewelry in a trash bin outside the mall."

"Where?" I sat back down.

"Outside the Kingston Mall." She leaned in toward me. "A

review of the mall's video footage confirmed his story. Seems our Oak Falls Police Department jumped the gun, as it were." Little Man took that moment to snarl at me, a nightmarish hybrid turkey with teeth. Daffy lowered her voice in a confidential manner. "A little bird told me the chief is fuming. He's on paternity leave, you know, at the moment…such a sweet little baby girl, I hear."

Luke must be out of the loop too, I realized, since he'd recently taken a leave of absence from the police force to study for his LSAT.

Seeing the stunned look on my face, our hostess gracefully changed the subject, and instead prattled on about her latest property taxes, how expensive house and land prices were, and the proposed new luxury housing sure to ruin our rural paradise.

Since I'd heard it before, I just kept nodding. As soon as I had a moment I intended to confirm what Daffy told me, but I'd never known our Chihuahua-loving client to be wrong.

With no suspect, Carl Wolf still might be the terrible answer.

●●●●●

I got my answer straight from the horse's mouth later that night. The horse being Tucker.

"Hi, Kate."

When I answered the phone, I didn't recognize his voice. This person sounded hoarse and frail at the same time. He spoke carefully, searching for words to complete his thoughts. I let him talk, not wanting to interfere with his momentum.

"Thanks, again to you and Gramps."

This was the third or fourth time Tucker said the same thing in exactly the same way. I began to worry.

"You're welcome." I told him. "Dimitri helped, too, especially right after you were admitted to the hospital."

"Who?"

My hope began to fade. "Your roommate." I started to explain but he cut me off.

"Oh, you must have said, Dimitri. Sorry, my eardrum is ruptured on the left side, but I'm so used to holding the phone up to that ear, I forget. Let me switch to the right ear."

After some scraping noises, Tucker came back on. "That should be better."

My Gramps had advised me not to ask too many questions. The inability to recall events made Tucker become agitated. It was better to let him fumble along at his own pace. "So when do they transfer you to rehab?" The last I'd heard he was on the neurology floor waiting for some of the blood tests to improve. They also monitored his brain scans for any bleeds.

"I think the neurologist, that short guy with the gray hair, said in five or six days? I've started to write everything down because I can't always remember. As my head heals and they wean me off some of this medication, my recall should get better."

A sigh punctuated his last sentence. Nothing must be more frustrating than not being able to rely on your brain or memory. It made me think again of Gloria, battling cognitive dysfunction, certainly realizing in the early stages that some of her mental faculties were slipping away. I also recalled the sadness my clients felt when their elderly dog, Polly, forgot how to play fetch with them.

"Kate, are you there?"

"Yes, I'm here." I tried to come up with a light-hearted reason for not answering him. "Sorry, I guess I was daydreaming a little."

That got me a chuckle. "Hey, I'm the one who got hit over the head."

"Right."

"Thanks, again, though. I know I've said it a million times, but I can't tell you how comforting it is to wake up and see your grandfather sitting next to me. I don't feel so alone anymore." His voice wavered, full of emotion. "When he leaves he puts a note on the nightstand next to the bed, and writes down when he'll be back. He's a great guy, Kate. You're so lucky you've got a family that supports you…" This time his voice trailed off to nothing. I suspected he'd covered the speaker with his hand to muffle what he didn't want me to hear.

I continued as though everything was fine. The doctors had cautioned Gramps that after a head injury the patient might be very emotional—from crying or screaming, to throwing things to simply shutting down.

"Now that I know you're feeling better, I'll call you tomorrow," I told him. "I'm sure you get pretty antsy in your hospital room."

"Oh, I get to do laps around the ward now. Slow laps. And they even let me read a little, although I get huge headaches and a little bit of fuzzy vision if I stare at the page too long."

Poor Tucker. I fervently hoped all these post trauma symptoms would resolve in time, but knew each patient recovered in their own way.

"I wish I could remember what happened that night in the alley. All I know is what the detectives told me." His anguish resonated in each word. "I keep thinking there might be something…something I saw that would help the police. But…I've got nothing. Zip."

"Don't worry about it. Time is on your side." In my eagerness to be positive, I stumbled around saying whatever sounded supportive. "Try to rest and do what the doctors recommend," I advised him. "And whatever you do, if you play poker with my Gramps, don't play for money. Believe me, he'll clean you out."

I heard a bit of a commotion, like something falling, before Tucker replied, "Yeah, that's what the night nurse said."

• • ● • •

A few hours later I received a full report on Tucker's condition, courtesy of my Gramps. But before I listened, I chided him about his late-night hospital poker games.

"I can't believe you're running a game in the ICU," I said.

"I wouldn't do that." My Gramps voice became indignant.

"Tucker's on the neurology ward now. Please, honey, give me a little credit."

"Like the credit you're offering the night staff, I suppose."

"No one needs credit. It's just a nickel and dime game. Most of the patients in this place stay in their beds. Besides, the staff only plays cards in their free time or when their shift is over. Hey, they need a little relaxation too."

What had I unleashed on New York Presbyterian Hospital? Oh, well. Tucker was due to be transferred at the end of the week, which would put a crimp in the rolling poker game. Or at least put an end to my Gramps' participation in it.

Too restless to sit, I got up and poured a glass of water. "Have they given you an idea of his ultimate prognosis?"

Gramps lowered his voice. I wasn't sure exactly where he was, hopefully not in earshot of our patient. "Well, Nick says…"

"Who is Nick?"

"Dr. Nickolas, the head of neurology. Anyway…"

I listened while medical terminology filtered through my Gramps and came out the other side. It didn't really make that much of a difference. No one could predict the course of Tucker's recovery. Even with sophisticated treatment it was a wait-and-see proposition. He did have youth on his side, and no critical underlying health issues. With luck he might regain most if not all of his brain functioning—luck and the ability to heal being the most important parts of the equation. Medical science now knew that our complex nervous systems were much more pliable than once thought.

"Tucker told me he's grateful to have you in his corner." I wanted Gramps to know his presence did make a difference. "But don't worry, by the end of next week you'll have your old life back."

A combination of grunt and cough followed my pronouncement. "Well, I've gotten kind of fond of the little guy," he admitted. "I've promised to go visit him at the rehab center."

Again, I was bowled over by his generosity of spirit. With that thought, I forced the picture of Gramps surrounded by neurology nurses and orderlies throwing craps or playing blackjack out of my mind.

Only after we hung up did I realize there'd be a lot more card players to choose from in rehab.

Chapter Seventeen

"I think you're going to be surprised," Mari whispered to me before I went into my next appointment.

"Who is it?" We'd been so busy I hadn't had a chance to check the appointment schedule. I generally worked off a tablet or laptop, pulling my typed medical records up from the hospital veterinary software database. Not only was it more efficient, but the technicians could actually read the treatment orders. Sadly, my cursive handwriting had become indecipherable even to me.

"Let's just say they are very happy clients."

When I opened the door a wagging black and white tail told the whole story. My border collie mix patient, Polly, looked up at me with bright eyes. A smiling Junior stood at her side, a yellow tennis ball in his hand.

"She's so much better," Doris Koliti volunteered before I even said hello. "Almost like her old self."

The elderly dog looked from one member of her family to the other and then focused her eyes on the ball.

"Is she playing fetch again?" From the eager expression on Polly's doggy face, I thought I knew the answer.

"Yes." For a live demonstration Junior tossed the ball in the small exam room, where it ricocheted off the wall, banged into the bottom of the exam table, and started to roll before being expertly scooped up by his pet.

Everyone in the room laughed and Mari broke out in applause.

With the bright yellow ball firmly wedged in her mouth, Polly proudly pranced around for a moment, then brought it over to her young master and gently dropped it in his hand.

If I didn't have to maintain my professional attitude I would have bawled my brains out.

This was one of those moments when you are thankful to live in our modern world and have a sophisticated medication available to help your patient.

The family eagerly shared more stories of their dog's dramatic return to normal. This year would be a truly thankful Thanksgiving for everyone.

Mari and I took Polly to the treatment room for a quick blood draw, checking her kidney and liver functions, in particular, for any adverse reaction to the medication.

"How long will it last?" Mari questioned me as she helped me take the lab sample.

"I'm not sure anyone knows," I answered truthfully. "I'm going to get the latest statistics from the pharmaceutical company and from some of my old professors. We may have diminishing returns down the road, but I'll prepare the family for that eventuality." Our blood draw finished, we returned the elderly dog down to the floor, and watched her twirl like a puppy.

"For now," I said, laughing at her antics. "Let's just celebrate."

● ● ● ● ●

You know how sometimes one theme keeps repeating over and over in your life? That's how I felt when my client, Veronica, invited me that same weekend to her cockatoo's debut performance at the adult daycare center where she worked. There was some kind of pre-holiday celebration going on, although what a cockatoo had to do with Thanksgiving, I had no idea. Hopefully, no one would mistake him for a scrawny turkey.

"Want to come with me?" I asked Mari, after we finished our final appointment.

We were in the treatment room about to soak an abscessed foot on a kitty. Theodore had run out the back door and straight into trouble with the neighborhood bully cat. Why this timid guy made a break from his warm cozy house into the cold snow was a mystery to me. Twelve hours later his pitiful cries woke up his owners. At the time he seemed okay, but three days later they noticed his back foot was swollen.

"Can't," she said. "Rented a cabin with a bunch of my friends. It's going to be a skiing, football, and beer weekend."

"Sounds like fun."

"We could squeeze in one more, if you wanted to join us." Mari and her friends still partied like college kids, crashing on the floor in sleeping bags and playing video game marathons.

"Maybe some other time. Thanks for the invite," I said, diplomatically.

Theo meowed at us, hoping to be returned to his cage. A smart fellow, he figured out his foot got wet while on the treatment table.

"I'm glad he's up-to-date with all his shots," I mentioned to Mari. "There's no way of knowing what this other cat might be carrying." The distance between the tooth marks had pretty much guaranteed the biter was another feline.

Theo held pretty still for his soaks. He'd recovered well from the surgery that opened the entry wounds up wide to let them drain. Now on antibiotics and subcutaneous fluids, Theo would board until Monday, because his owners preferred to avoid the messy wound-handling.

"I'll do treatments this weekend if you want," I told my assistant. "Jeremy had to cancel again. He thinks he's coming down with something."

"Yeah, there's a lot of that going around."

I ignored the sarcasm.

Together we carefully dried Theo's foot, gave him his antibiotic, and put him back in the cage. While Mari opened a can of cat food, I updated my notes, then checked Veronica's email invite again.

"Oh, what the heck," I muttered to no one in particular. "It's not like I have anything else to do this weekend."

If Mari heard me, she was nice enough not to comment this time. "I bet it will be a hoot. Phil can be very entertaining. That place is near the Kingston Hospital, right?"

"Right."

"Cindy told me a new restaurant opened down there that's pretty good. You can switch up your Chinese food menu with Vietnamese food. The place is called Pho Palace. Let me know what you think of it."

"Kate Turner, veterinarian and restaurant critic. I like that." One last look around and I started switching out lights.

I walked Mari to her truck. Surprise, surprise, it was beginning to snow.

Once again I locked up and listened to my footsteps echo down the empty hall. Just before I entered the apartment I thought about dinner, or the lack thereof. Canned soup and some chips, if I was lucky. A supermarket run became high on my to-do list.

At least tomorrow I'd be in the soup one way or another.

Chores done I sat at my kitchen table, laptop open. I had a fleeting vision of Daffy at her kitchen table. Sitting opposite in a booster seat all his own was Little Man. Both were eating a Thanksgiving dinner in costume.

I certainly wished that wasn't what the future held in store for me.

A final check of my email showed no more questions from clients. However, something unusual was mixed in with the spam. Dr. Ethan Holtzer, Carl Wolf's former veterinarian, had sent me a note, with an attachment.

Dear Kate,

Enclosed is a picture of a local Schutzhund event held twenty-four years ago. Carl Wolf and Brownie are on my left. I'd forgotten I even had this until my wife reminded me. I'd been asked to present the awards that year and Wolf won first prize.

Note the tooled custom leather leash and collar on Brownie. He never spared any expense as far as that dog was concerned. Please tell your writer friend to feel free to use this if he likes.

Regards,
Ethan Holtzer, DVM

PS: The results of the meet were challenged because Brownie had chipped a tooth. A big fight among the participants ensued. I never sent that trophy out to be engraved with Wolf's name, which I'm glad about now. He doesn't deserve to win any kind of prize.

When I opened the attachment, the picture came up fairly small. After a little magical manipulation, I printed it out full size.

My first impression was how happy and handsome Wolf appeared in the photo, very unlike the scowling picture on the FBI wanted poster. His hair shone thick and wavy, especially on top. I'd mistakenly thought he shaved his head because his hair had begun thinning, the FBI picture having perpetuated that misconception. The date at the bottom of the photo was June sixth, three years before the murders.

Next, my attention shifted to the dog, Brownie. A beautiful specimen of German shepherd, obviously bred abroad without the sloped rear end so common in American show dogs. The image captured Werner Von Braun, attentively focused on his master. Carl Wolf looked straight into the camera, right hand on the silver trophy being presented by Dr. Holtzer. The leather leash was in his gloved left hand. That detail reminded me of a western pleasure horse-riding friend of mine who always made sure to have a single leather glove on her left hand, the hand that held the reins.

I was about to put the photo down when I noticed something interesting. Wolf wore a half-fingered glove, like race car-driver gloves. Probably for more control, I thought, since leather on leather might slip.

The picture appeared as innocent as could be, a triumphant moment captured forever. I'd stared at so many photographs of this murderer that his eyes appeared familiar, more so in this new picture than any other. I recognized that expression.

Tucker told me the first suspicious event in Wolf's life was the disappearance of his college girlfriend. Was evil hidden deep in this man's heart, even on that bright summer day? Or did it grow slowly, like a wormy apple, destroying what it fed on from the inside out?

Chapter Eighteen

Driving into town, alone in the truck, I felt sorry for myself. Perhaps it had something to do with my empty weekend, one of many lately. Everyone I knew had fun plans of one sort or another. What was I doing? Dutifully going to watch Phil the cockatoo do his bird thing.

Preoccupied, I missed the turn into the community center and had to double-back before pulling into its packed front parking lot. No snow was in the weather forecast for today, only cold and more cold.

The Oak Falls Community Center was one of the more modern buildings in town. Cindy explained that the center originally started out in the town library, then because of its popularity, moved to a building of its own. When I ventured through the door I had no problem finding Phil. All I needed to do was follow the loud singing voice that sounded remarkably like Elvis. Yes, Phil did some pretty mean imitations. After checking in with an employee, I entered the large recreation hall just as my feathered friend finished with a "Thank you. Thank you verah much."

Enthusiastic clapping filled the air. A beaming Veronica stood in front of the large seated group with a dancing Phil on her arm. Loving the attention, the cockatoo preened and bobbed his head up and down, his sulfur crest of feathers in full display, a definite hit.

I slipped along the wall to the back of the room as Phil went through more imitations of famous people. Each one got a laugh. I waved at Veronica, who smiled and nodded my way. She wrapped up the performance by doing avian addition and subtraction with her bird using some props and numbered balls.

After a spirited question-and-answer session from the audience, the community center director thanked Veronica and asked for another round of applause. Phil and Veronica moved to a small alcove, offering to take free pictures with anyone interested in posing with the talented cockatoo. Immediately, half the attendants lined up.

I was surprised at the number of families present. Young children dashed around seniors with walkers. Most of the elderly appeared active, while some clearly needed guidance. Since Veronica looked like she'd be busy for a while, I asked one of the greeters if they had a community center brochure I could look at. Pleased at my interest, she gave me an overview of the multi-use building. Partnered by Kingston Hospital, not only was there an adult daycare, but also a children's daycare. Some of the seniors volunteered to read to toddlers or comfort crying babies. Music and art therapy included all ages, and they held monthly educational events such as the one Phil participated in. The five-year program had been underwritten by a federal grant designed to evaluate how interaction between opposite age groups might benefit both.

Now I understood why Veronica had been so enthusiastic about bringing Phil to her work.

The line to take pictures with the cockatoo stretched halfway across the hall, so with time on my hands I decided to explore the adjacent rooms. For a while I wandered around, checking out a patio with a pretty gazebo used in the summer. After passing an open coffee station, I entered a large, airy space that I realized must be the crafts room. A floor-to-ceiling cupboard held art books as well as well-marked containers of charcoal, watercolors, colored pencils, and markers. Different types of paper were displayed in see-through bins, as well as all sorts of craft supplies. Regular sized tables were on one side, while stacked on the other side against the wall were tiny chairs and low tables. Obviously, it was used as a multi-generational space. I noticed a long divided cubby at my eye level, with sketchbooks and coloring books, the names of each owner labeled in big letters with a black Sharpie.

Two women sat at one of the large tables, the younger of the two busy texting on her phone. There was something familiar about them. As I watched, the older woman got up and grasped a three-pronged cane leaning up against her chair for support. Then she went over to the cubby and removed a coloring book and small packet of colored pencils.

When she turned back, her prominent profile did the trick. This was the women who'd spoken at Gloria's funeral, who said she would miss her friend.

Embarrassed to be staring, I ambled over to the wooden cupboard and selected a book on still-life painting. Although drawing fruit wasn't my thing, it gave me an opening.

"Excuse me." The younger woman looked up from her screen while the older woman kept on coloring. "Didn't we meet at Gloria LaGuardia's funeral?"

Suspicion vanished as the woman recognized me. "Yes, I'm sorry, but I don't think we were introduced."

I shifted the book and extended my hand. "I arrived a little late. I'm Kate Turner."

"Sylvia Longmire, and this is my mother, Emily."

When the older woman heard her name, she briefly looked up, smiled at me, then returned to her coloring book.

"I'm here to support my friend Veronica and her bird Phil. They were great, weren't they?"

"Fantastic," replied Sylvia. "I had no idea birds were that smart. Did you enjoy the show, Mother?"

"Loved it," she replied. "Although I think the counting was a trick of some sort."

This lady was no dummy. As far as I knew, Phil couldn't count, but he did remember which number went with which color ball.

"The center seems to offer a number of programs for town residents," I observed. The two of them looked right at home.

"Mother is usually here three or four days during the week. I drop her off on my way to work, then pick her up on my way back. She tells me she enjoys it." Her daughter, who resembled her, gave her mom a squeeze.

"I do enjoy it," her mom echoed. "Much better than sitting at home in front of the television."

"Sometimes I'll swing by and we'll have lunch together. They have daily activities and day trips, also. So far it's been a wonderful program for both of us."

While I listened to them I paged through the art book in front of me. Then I remembered something the older woman, Emily, had said. "How often did Gloria come here, a few days a week too?"

Emily looked up from her coloring. "She was here every day. Her niece worried about her being alone. If you ask me," she interjected, "Irene worried a little too much. Gloria could be a little forgetful about certain things, but I don't think she was totally gaga."

Her daughter laughed. "Gaga, I guess, is a new medical term."

"I'd love to see some of her drawings. Did she leave a sketchbook here?" I could have kicked myself for not looking earlier.

"Oh, her son came and took all her things," Sylvia said. "The day after she died."

That confused me. "You must mean Irene's son. About seventeen or eighteen, I think, his leg in a cast."

Now it was her turn to be confused. "He was no teenager. I remember I came over at lunchtime looking for mom, and a gentleman was going through the cubby. I asked if I could help and he told me he was picking up some of his mother's things that the family wanted. When I asked him who his mother was, he said Gloria LaGuardia."

"Gloria?"

"Yes." Sylvia frowned at me, as though I were obtuse.

"Then what happened?"

"Then he asked if this was the only place they kept their artwork. I explained that since the building was multiuse, each adult day guest was assigned a cubby. Open, of course. The staff encouraged their day guests to leave supplies they brought from home in their cubbies, and also to store their coloring books or whatever they were working on in them."

This sounded very odd. As far as I knew, Gloria only had a daughter, and her two remaining grandsons didn't make the funeral.

"I must be a little mixed up," I tried to be as casual as possible. "Do you remember what he looked like?"

Sylvia blushed a bit. "Well, he was extremely charming and well-mannered, dark beard and mustache with a fantastic smile. Very white teeth."

"Did he have a crew cut?"

She frowned for a moment. "Oh, that's why I don't remember. He was wearing a hat, one of those knit ones, like you wear when you go skiing."

"And his eyes?"

Again she hesitated. "I don't know. He wore those aviator glasses, the mirrored kind."

"Alright." So this mystery man hid behind sunglasses and a hat. It made me wonder how real were the mustache and bright white teeth.

"Believe me, not recognizing people can be embarrassing." Sylvia glanced at her phone. "Let's go, Mom. We have to stop off at the grocery store on the way home."

Her mother reached for the cane again. Once standing, she slid the coloring book back into her full cubby. The colored pencils went into a communal art supply bin.

"You didn't happen to catch his name, did you?" I asked as I walked them out. Veronica waved to me, almost finished with her pictures.

"No." She adjusted her mom's coat. "But I'd remember him if I saw him again."

After some quick good-byes, they started walking toward the front door.

I'd have to check with Irene and find out if one of Gloria's grandsons did pop up. But, unless I was completely off-base, I was pretty sure Sylvia wouldn't recognize that mystery man again if she saw him.

Big Bad Wolves usually disguised themselves in sheep's clothing.

Back home I wanted to kick myself. Irene never mentioned that she took Gloria to the community center each day. She probably thought nothing of it. Instead, it might have been the clue to her aunt's murder. There was no telling what Gloria had drawn in her sketchbook the last weeks of her life. If she'd really seen Carl Wolf that Halloween night, she might have drawn him in her sketchbook as he looks today.

The Big Bad Wolf must have figured it out. If Tucker were here, he would have no doubt Carl Wolf was the mystery "son" who took off with Gloria's artwork. But with no proof and no description of him, other than white teeth and sunglasses, this was another dead end.

Before I got all worked up I needed to contact Irene and clarify whether someone in her family picked up Gloria's artwork. Perhaps Sylvia misunderstood the man she spoke with. He might be one of the grandsons from out of state. That would put to rest the Carl Wolf theory once again.

So why was it exciting to think Carl Wolf was prowling around? Was it the thrill of the chase, helping to capture one of the bad guys, or all of the above? As tempted as I felt to call

Gramps and share this news, there was no sense in getting him worried until I had something concrete to tell him.

The remaining hours of the weekend plodded by as I performed the mundane chores of day-to-day living—going to the supermarket, folding the laundry, taking out the recyclables, and restocking the fridge and pantry.

By Monday morning I still hadn't decided how to approach Irene. Gloria's niece, I think, found my interest in her aunt's murder a little creepy. I needed to make some kind of decision. After another sip of coffee I came up with a plan.

I knew Irene's email address but decided to call her instead. After five rings her answering machine picked up. I explained I'd been with a friend at the Thanksgiving party at the community center and Emily's daughter mentioned someone had picked up her aunt's artwork. Then I finished by asking if she knew about the sketch artist exhibit in New York City, and left my cell phone number.

Satisfied I shouldn't allow myself to jump to conclusions without the facts, I finished my coffee, opened the apartment door, and walked into the animal hospital and another week of work.

• • ● ● •

The beautiful German shepherd in front of me was obviously in discomfort. Limping on three feet, he tried to walk, even though he couldn't place his left rear foot on the ground. Every few steps he turned to gnaw on his pad. The woman who brought him in was practically hysterical.

"My boyfriend's going to kill me," she said dramatically, flipping her pale blond hair away from her lovely face. "He's crazy about this dog."

"What happened?" I asked as I waited for Mari.

She stared down at the dog as if expecting it to answer me. "We were taking a walk and he slipped his leash. I thought he was gone. You have no idea how panicked I was."

So far I also had no idea what happened to the dog.

"Anyway, I kept screaming his name and thank goodness I saw him run up the driveway. But halfway up he slowed down, then started to limp. I'm afraid to touch his leg because he's a trained guard dog and my boyfriend is out of town."

When she paused for a breath, I asked if the dog had ever been aggressive with her.

"Viggie?" She patted the big dog's shoulder. His pink tongue lolled out as his beautifully tapered head moved toward her hand. "No, but my boyfriend keeps telling me if I have any trouble while he's away all I have to do is say his attack commands, and pow…the dog will lunge."

A gentle knock at the door caught the dog's attention first before Mari poked her head in and said, "Oh, my gosh, he's gorgeous." The black and tan shepherd meanwhile turned and tried to gnaw at his paw.

"Elizabeth was explaining that Viggie is a trained guard dog, so we need to remember that when handling him."

Mari nodded, making no overt moves and offering an out-stretched palm for the dog to sniff.

Now, there are trained dogs and just plain aggressive dogs. We needed to know what we were dealing with since I had to examine him closely to evaluate his limping.

"Was Viggie professionally trained to voice and hand commands?" I asked.

"That's right. I only know two, but I'll write them down for you in case you need them. So why is he limping?" Although obviously fond of the dog, she seemed a bit flustered. I wondered why.

"Mari, can you slip a muzzle on him for me?" There was no point in not taking precautions with this potentially dangerous dog. I'd known many veterinarians who bore war wounds from not slipping a muzzle on.

However, this dog was an angel when my assistant secured the smooth leather muzzle over his long nose. Because of the shape and length of their heads you always wanted to make sure the muzzle fit securely but comfortably. Like most animal hospitals we stocked a wide variety of sizes and types of muzzles, including leather and nylon fabric brands.

On physical exam Viggie appeared to be an exceptionally healthy, well-muscled dog. But as soon as I began to palpate his left rear leg, we began getting growls. Each time I touched it, he jerked away. The pain appeared to be concentrated in his foot, not the rest of the leg.

"He might have something wedged in his pad, or an injury to his toes," I explained to the client. "I'm going to have to admit him to the hospital for a few hours, take an X-ray, and give him a brief-acting tranquilizer or anesthesia so I can take a good look at that pad."

Elizabeth appeared horrified again. She tugged at the collar of her camel-colored suede and sheepskin vest. "He's supposed to be in a show in a week. Will he still be able to do that?"

My first impression was that Viggie's issue was in his footpad, not his joints, but until that could be confirmed by an X-ray, I wasn't able to give Elizabeth the assurance she wanted. "The sooner we can diagnose and treat him, the quicker he'll recover."

She nodded in agreement, perfect lips forming a perfect pout. "Okay, but my boyfriend is going to kill me if that dog can't compete."

I asked Mari to bring our patient to the treatment room and told her I'd join them in a minute. Then I turned my attention back to Elizabeth.

"Our receptionist will have you fill out the paperwork and give you the estimate. Can you make sure we have a good number to contact you today? Once Viggie is under anesthesia, I might need to speak to you, depending on what we find."

"You're not going to shave his leg or anything, are you? He'd kill me if you did that." Again her slender fingers tugged at her vest.

What was going on here? I hoped saying her boyfriend would kill her over and over was just a figure of speech. "I don't believe shaving him is necessary," I reassured her.

"Thank you so much." She squeezed my shoulder. "Oh, let me write out those commands for you." She picked up a small pad and pencil lying on the table next to the chair. We always had some books and toys for children to play with during their pet's trip to the vet.

Unless these words were oddly complicated, I was pretty sure I could remember them long enough to type them into her dog's medical record. When I suggested that, the answer surprised me.

"I have to write them out phonetically," she explained, "because his Schutzhund commands are all in German. Isn't that weird?"

After steering Elizabeth toward the reception area, my imagination began racing. A boyfriend she's afraid of? Schutzhund and German commands. Could I have found Carl Wolf? However, once in the treatment room, my assistant brought me right back down to Earth.

"Most of the owners of Schutzhund trained dogs use German commands," Mari explained. "I certainly do. First, they are short words and easily understood. Second, you can't inadvertently say them, like you would if they were in English. These commands are specifically for training and performing tasks. You wouldn't want to say 'Attack' by mistake."

I could see her point.

We gave Viggie a short-acting anesthesia and discovered several small sharp stones wedged in the crevices of his pads. An X-ray of the foot confirmed no hairline fractures to the toes, and a normal lower right leg. The mild swelling from the gravel embedded in the sensitive tissue would be gone in a few days. I suspected their driveway might be the source of the problem.

As soon as the diagnosis was confirmed, I called and gave the shepherd's co-owner the good news. A thankful Elizabeth made arrangements to pick him up before closing. We emphasized that

Viggie must be walked only on leash and not on the driveway. Most likely running with his full weight landing on the loose gravel caused the unusual accident.

While he was still under, I examined him head to tail and found no abnormalities. He quickly recovered from the tranquilization and when awake posed beautifully on all four paws. Still and all I was happy Elizabeth had given us his basic commands, and most importantly, Viggie's emergency halt word. *Verboten.*

Forbidden.

Elizabeth arrived to pick up Viggie just before we closed. Cindy and I had been going over some paperwork at the reception desk when she rushed in, apologizing profusely, and explained that her own doctor's appointment had run late. I texted my assistant to let her know the big shepherd was being released. When the dog appeared with Mari holding the leash, he was not limping and happy as a clam, and Elizabeth was overjoyed.

"I dreaded telling my boyfriend, Jasper, that his dog was injured," she confessed. "But now it looks like I don't have to."

"Do you have his leash with you?" Mari asked. We'd been using our all-purpose blue hospital leash looped through his fancy personalized leather collar.

For a second she appeared flustered, then dug around inside her Gucci carryall. "Here it is." While Mari swapped the leashes out, Cindy went over the bill. In this case the charges were less than my estimate. I hadn't been sure what I'd find when I first examined his leg, so I'd included some worst-case scenario tests and X-rays.

To my surprise our client pulled out a white bank envelope and proceeded to pay the bill in cash. Elizabeth must have noticed the surprise on our faces. Nowadays most clients used debit or credit cards. We hadn't seen that much cash in our receipts in some time.

"You ladies might think this is silly," she told us as she counted out loud, "but I'm not going to tell my boyfriend about this visit. If I use my credit card, he might find out. He's snooped before, the little stinker."

Her statement made me wonder how old Jasper was. Elizabeth looked to be in her early thirties. What age qualified you to be described as a "little stinker"?

Oblivious to how odd her confession appeared she took her receipt and release orders, gave us all a big smile and wished everyone a happy holiday.

"How do you like Oak Falls?" I asked her.

"Well, we come up most weekends," she explained. "My boyfriend likes it more than me. I miss my girlfriends and the shopping in the city. But it is relaxing, except for the creep who sometimes looks through our windows and takes things from the yard when we aren't home."

"What?" Mari said. "Did you report it to the police?"

"Sure, but that's mostly stopped since we got Viggie a year ago. Jasper said I needed protection if I ever came up here alone." She flipped her hair. "As if."

I'd been told some of the local teenagers targeted vacation homes in the area, although most of the pranks they pulled were minor.

"Oops, I almost forgot," Elizabeth added. "Jasper and I towed two members of your staff out of a snowdrift a few days ago."

"You're the blond lady in the Mercedes?" Mari acted as astonished as I felt.

"Yep, that was me waving at you." To prove her claim she demonstrated with a little wave. "I made him stop and help. He just wanted to zip right by you, but I said no."

Interesting. I'd only caught a quick glimpse of her in the truck's rearview mirror, but now I recognized her. It also put a face on her "little stinker" boyfriend, Jasper Rudin. Fifties, and sunglasses were about all I remembered from that day, that and a condescending attitude.

"Well, I'm glad you made him stop and help. You two were lifesavers."

"I guess now we're even." She smiled a brilliant smile, waved at all of us again, and opened the door. "I don't keep score, but Jasper does."

Mari followed close by, chatting away about our accident and how the truck was barely damaged. Viggie, I noticed, had beautiful leash manners, didn't pull, and patiently waited to climb up the portable doggie ramp into the SUV parked outside.

Cindy and I watched Mari stick her head inside the vehicle and check to make sure the shepherd was secured, before stepping away and waving a final good-bye.

Mirrored sunglasses, muffler around his face—it all came back to me. He sounded a lot like Sylvia's description of the mystery man from the community center. I felt guilty even contemplating that our Good Samaritan might be Carl Wolf on the lam.

"Hey, did you see that Porsche Cayenne, guys?" Mari excitedly said after she shut and locked the hospital door. "Her birthday present from the boyfriend. So they have the Mercedes and the Porsche. Boy, wouldn't I love to have one of those babies."

Not being a big car or truck person, I wasn't particularly impressed. However, I figured if the word "Porsche" or "Mercedes" was attached to the description, it was expensive.

"Think she's in this relationship for the money?" Mari asked us.

Cindy quickly responded, "She wouldn't be the first woman to admit money makes a man more attractive."

Then they both looked at me.

Jeremy, they both knew, had a pile of family money and a trust fund set up by his grandfather. Did it make a difference about the way I felt toward him?

With their eyes still on me, I felt forced to defend myself. "All I know is the longer I live, the less I feel I can judge anyone. Let's leave it at that."

"Well said," Cindy commented.

"Hey, I'd go for it," Mari said with a big grin.

Meanwhile, Cindy checked her watch and began putting on her coat. Because we hadn't finished everything on her list, I was surprised she was leaving early.

"Are we done?" I looked down at her printed notes.

"Sorry, but I feel very uncomfortable leaving a large amount of cash in the hospital. I want to get to the bank before it closes and deposit this."

Mari watched our receptionist close out her computer station and pick up her purse. "You know you can always use the after-hours envelope."

"For cash? Sorry, but you never know who opens those up," Cindy fished out her keys on her way out the door. "See you tomorrow."

"See you." We both watched her jump into her truck and quickly exit the parking lot, driving much faster than usual.

Mari began to clean up the treatment area, so with Cindy's to-do list in hand, I walked to my office.

● ● ● ● ●

"Want a hot chocolate?"

The interruption was perfect timing. I'd been on the phone for the last thirty minutes finishing my callbacks when Mari suggested her chocolate break. One of our clients had gifted us an expensive Italian cocoa, and I knew she'd been dying to try it.

"Be there in a sec." After a last check of my email I'd be finished for the night.

Rapidly deleting all kinds of spam offers, I paused at an email from Gramps. Tucker had been moved to a rehab facility. Things had gone downhill after he arrived. He was having some unexpected weakness again in his right arm and hand along with lingering memory issues from the concussion. Worse, he'd been taking out his anger and frustration on the staff. The rehab doctors planned to reevaluate his progress and treatment plan in a week.

That didn't sound promising.

Was anyone else looking out for Tucker's welfare except Gramps and me? How could you live twenty-eight years on this Earth and be so alone, relying on the kindness of strangers? Living a solitary workaholic life came at a costly personal price.

That solitary workaholic label also applied to me.

I think I astonished Mari when my thank-you for a cup of cocoa included an impulsive hug.

As soon as I locked up the hospital and went back to my apartment, I called Jeremy. That workaholic thing bothered me and I needed to hear his voice. We'd been trying to get together, but I had to admit I'd been more rigid with my schedule. With the weather so unpredictable, I was thinking of asking Cindy to close next Saturday. That would give me enough time to drive to the University of Pennsylvania or at least meet Jeremy halfway, maybe book a cozy B & B for a quiet getaway, the kind you see in magazines. Perhaps an historic inn with a fireplace and a king-sized bed. A smile lingered on my face especially when I heard him pick up the phone.

"Hi, beautiful," he said. "I was just thinking about you."

"Me, too. Does a rendezvous at a romantic B & B sound good? I'm going to have Cindy clear my weekend so I can spend it with you."

The several seconds of silence didn't bode well. "Sorry, honey, but I've got a family thing to go to. My aunt is turning the big five zero."

It was the first I'd heard of a party. "Want some company?"

Again I listened to an odd silence before he answered. "It's a three-day thing in Seattle. We're having the birthday party, then a bunch of us are hiking in Snoqualmie Falls. I didn't ask you because I knew you wouldn't be able to take the time off with your schedule."

Now it was my turn to be silent.

"Hey, I'm sure I mentioned it the other night."

I was sure he hadn't.

He scrambled to patch things up. "The week after next we're definitely on, even if I have to climb Mount Everest to get to you. I've got Friday through Monday off, so you name the place and I'll be there." Jeremy's charm oozed out through the receiver. "Come on, honey. You're not mad, are you?"

Sad. Disappointed. Those were my adjectives, but mad…no, I wasn't mad and told him so.

Putting that unpleasantness behind us, we talked for another half hour, laughing at silly things and sharing what our days had been like. Jeremy told me how psyched he'd become about compiling new research data based on DNA patterns, while I brought him up-to-date on office gossip and some of my clients. I deliberately didn't mention Carl Wolf, Gloria, Tucker, or anything having to do with solving a murder.

Elizabeth wasn't the only one who kept secrets from her boyfriend.

After the call ended, my thoughts drifted back to Mari's question. Was Elizabeth in a relationship with a wealthy man at least twenty years her senior for the money? And closer to home, might Jeremy's financial position be influencing my feelings for him?

Who knew the mysteries of the human heart? Not me.

I remember arrogantly thinking I knew the answers to everything when I was in my teens, and now…now I realize I hadn't even understood the questions.

Faced with another night by myself I did what any other frustrated woman would do. I decided to find some dessert. Preferably with chocolate in it.

It had been a while since I'd eaten at the Oak Falls Diner. Luke Gianetti's family owned and ran the very popular eatery, known for their homemade desserts and tasty daily specials. Truth is, I'd avoided going there, so I didn't have to interact with Luke's many cousins who worked there. There had been a time when his family thought we were an "item" or destined to become one. But given I'd maxed out my prodigious love of Chinese food, I looked forward to eating something different.

Tonight I easily found a space in the parking lot. Eight o'clock was a little late for dinner in Oak Falls, and too early for the late-night crowd. The server who guided me to the last booth at the far end that looked out at the parking lot was new, or at least someone I didn't know. Glad not to be recognized, I shucked off my coat before settling in with my back to the door and the rest of the diners. I ordered a cup of Earl Grey Tea and picked up the specials menu. Before looking at the dinners, I checked out the pies. Tonight's specials were chocolate pecan or apple-cranberry, a particularly difficult choice. I decided to order both, one slice for here and the other for tomorrow's lunch. Satisfied with my plan, I sipped some tea and turned the menu over.

"Kate?"

I didn't have to turn around to recognize Luke's voice. Before I could respond, he slid into the seat opposite me.

"Hi." After a quick look up, I deliberately went back to the menu.

"I recognized your back, and that coat," Luke said, making himself comfortable. He slipped off his own coat and shoved it in the corner of the booth by the window, along with his hat and gloves. Then with a raised hand he pantomimed a cup of coffee to one of the servers.

The next thing I knew, his cousin Rosie stood by our table, a carafe in her hand.

"Want some more hot water, Kate?" she asked while pouring Luke's java. Rosie didn't bother asking her cousin if he wanted cream or sugar. Everyone in the place knew he took his coffee black.

I checked the small ceramic teapot next to me, warmed my fingers on the curved surface and nodded. "More hot water would be great."

"Ready to order?" Her auburn curls bounced as her head turned from me to Luke and back again.

"I'll have the chicken piccata special with spinach, one slice of chocolate pecan pie for here, and a slice of cranberry-apple to go." Even on a slow night like this, the diner had been known to run out of pie so I made sure to slip my dessert order in immediately.

"You got it." Rosie turned to Luke. "What's up, Cuz?"

"Same old, you know. How's Mama G feeling? Someone said her knee was bothering her."

Mama G was Luke's grandmother, and the original pie-maker. Getting up in years now she still ran a tight ship at the diner, making sure no one cut corners with the food and baked goods. Her deeply wrinkled face, habitual black dress, and Italian-accented English did little to disguise an iron will and a fierce love for her family.

"Is she in the back?" Luke asked.

"Nope. Leo took her home a couple of hours ago, but only after she approved the chicken piccata. By the time Mama G left, the new cook was tearing his hair out, if he had any left to pull." She zipped over to the wait station and returned with some hot water for me.

"You know, make it two of the chicken piccata. I'm curious what Mama G added."

"I can tell you the lemon sauce is to die for." Rosie rested her hand on Luke's shoulder. "Mama G added what she always does, a scoop of love and a pinch of hot pepper flakes."

Of course her chicken was delicious, the balance between lemon and capers and olive oil just right.

"My compliments to your grandmother." With a flourish I took a piece of crusty bread and used it to soak up the last of the sauce. The contrast between the crunchy bread and silken sauce tasted scrumptious.

Luke finished his own dinner in the same manner, agreeing with a *mmm* sound.

Rosie must have been watching because as soon as we finished she whisked our plates away, promising to return with the slices of pie.

"Did you order dessert?"

Luke grinned at me, his eyes crinkling at the corners. That always happened when he smiled.

"I didn't have to order. Rosie knows I'm a sucker for pecan pie with my coffee."

Yep, we both had a pecan pie monkey on our backs. The dark chocolate added to the recipe made a luscious bonus.

Wait," I said, "isn't it a little late for coffee? Maybe you should order a decaf." My watch said it was nine-fifteen.

"Still got some studying to do. I'll probably be up until midnight tonight." With that he rubbed his temples with his fingers.

I sympathized. "I remember those days." During my years in veterinary school I pulled many an all-nighter before exams but never felt completely ready.

Once the pie arrived I dug in. Rosie handed me the to-go order in a small brown paper bag which I immediately stashed next to my purse. Bliss ensued by chewing the flaky crust and savoring the crunchy salty pecans embedded in sweet gooey chocolate filling.

A movement outside the window distracted me. I noticed an uneven layer of gravel left in the parking lot by the snowplow. Although there were plenty of spots, the last row by the dumpster was full of cars, probably where the employees had to park.

That got me thinking about Rosie and Luke. "Did all your cousins work here at the diner?"

What followed was a little diner history lesson, courtesy of Luke. "Everyone was expected to work here, even if only on spring break. It didn't matter if you wanted to be a lawyer, or accountant, or whatever, your parents made you help out. Take the pies, for example. We always make cranberry-apple around this time. Then, the week before Thanksgiving, they pull out all the pumpkin pies—pumpkin spice, pumpkin crème, pumpkin crumble…whatever combination you can think of, our bakers probably have done it." His voice sounded nostalgic. "That was one of my first jobs," he explained, "opening these giant cans of pumpkin and scooping the stuff into huge bowls." He told me if your name was Gianetti, the staff expected you to work harder than anyone else.

Continuing his story he leaned toward me, fork embedded in a bite of chocolate pecan filling. "To tell you the truth. I can't stand the smell of pumpkin now. At Thanksgiving I have to pretend I like the stuff."

"I've got to confess." I lowered my voice, afraid somehow Mama G would find out. "I'm not a big pumpkin fan either."

Our two heads came perilously close to touching. He smelled like nutmeg and cinnamon, and his eyes were as warm a brown as the pecans in the pie. I felt my face start to flush pink.

Luke picked up his napkin and wiped his palms. "Speaking of Thanksgiving, what are you doing? You're welcome to join us if you'd like."

My eyes reverted to the parking lot before I spoke. "I planned on joining Gramps."

"Is Jeremy going with you?" Suddenly he also feigned interest in the view of the parking lot.

"You know, I honestly don't know. We haven't talked about it."

Since Thanksgiving was only two weeks away, it seemed a little odd, in retrospect, that I didn't know my boyfriend's plans. I'm sure Luke thought the same but was too much of a gentleman to mention it.

While we waited for the checks, I made us both even more uncomfortable by blurting out what Daffy had told me, that the burglary suspect the police identified as a person of interest in Gloria's murder had been released from custody.

"I suppose you also talked to Cindy." Our receptionist had the inside track on all local law enforcement matters, since her brother-in-law, Bobby, served as the Oak Falls Chief of Police.

Of course I had to admit we'd spoken, but she'd been uncharacteristically tight-lipped about the whole thing.

"It's public record now," Luke confirmed. "The chief almost canned the guys involved in that arrest. A super sloppy job on their part, only you didn't hear that from me."

With Luke on a leave of absence and Garcia out on paternity leave, I figured the place had become a bit discombobulated.

"The morale at the station is so bad that the chief is coming back for a few days to clean up the mess. Then he's gone until New Year's or his wife is going to take matters into her own hands."

That was no idle threat. Everyone knew Chief Garcia was afraid of his wife, who, according to everyone who knew her, had a bulldog tenacity. After suffering from postpartum depression with the last pregnancy, according to Cindy, she had made her husband promise to help out with this unexpected but definitely final addition to their family.

With no other controversial subjects to mull over, the two of us settled into a comfortable silence. Rosie seemed to be taking forever with our bill, a remarkable contrast to her very speedy food service. Then Luke asked the bombshell question, "Anything new with Tucker and the whole Carl Wolf thing?"

Decision time.

Did I keep all I'd learned to myself, or involve Luke? As a police officer, even on leave, he was obligated to share anything of interest with his fellow officers. My instincts said yes and no. Luke had been a part of every other murder I'd stuck my nose into, but this one was different. With the FBI, and who knows what other agency involved, I didn't feel comfortable sharing conjecture and unproved suspicions that might get him in trouble.

Decision made.

"Tucker isn't doing so well." At least I could update him on the writer's medical condition. "Gramps visits him almost every day at the rehab place. So far he has no memory of the details of the assault, and the docs say he'll need physical and mental health therapy to counteract the effects of the head injuries."

"Poor kid." Luke's concern sounded sincere. "Recovering from traumatic brain injury is no picnic. I wish him well."

Rosie swung by, our bills in her hand. After a few joking words for Luke, she took off in the direction of the kitchen.

We parted ways in the parking lot. Holding on to the grab handle, I swung into the truck and placed my purse and pie on the floor. After starting the engine, I began to question the wisdom of not telling Luke about the odd stranger who took Gloria's artwork. Although Irene hadn't returned my call yet, I had a bad feeling that the guy was no family member.

Not to mention that a man in a baseball cap might have followed both Tucker and me.

Was a killer watching us, or was the stranger an FBI agent, keeping track of our whereabouts? Or both?

Chapter Nineteen

After another week of bad weather, sick patients, and another lame excuse cancellation on the part of Jeremy, I looked forward to my last appointment late Friday afternoon.

"Your favorite couple is here for their recheck," Mari warned me.

I blanked until my assistant pantomimed taking a picture with her phone. With a groan I said, "You go in first."

We interrupted them mid-argument. Again.

"I don't care what you say…I still don't like them." An angry Lydia stood face-to-face with her husband, ignoring the dog on the floor lying next to her foot. She didn't even realize we were in the room until Amos gave her a high sign.

"Shush, honey…"

"Don't you shush me," she continued. "When they first come around and all, we tried to help them fit in here. You took Jasper hunting and introduced him to everyone. But he sorta…"

"Kept to himself, like he was too good for us."

Lydia enthusiastically nodded her head. "And his girlfriend, forget it, she don't know her way around a kitchen, that's for sure."

Amos looked down at the ground. "She's afraid of him, at least that's what you think, right baby?"

Mari and I exchanged glances.

Taking her husband's cue, Lydia launched into a somewhat

incoherent rant about hearing her neighbors yelling at each other when the wind was blowing right. Or when she was snooping, I figured.

"Getting a permit to built that fancy garage practically on our property line. That Jasper Rudin is a two-faced..." Lydia paused, starting to run out of steam. "After all we did for them and you helping with the dog and the..."

Amos interrupted again. "I think everyone gets the idea. No need to pound it into the ground."

But that name rang a big bell. Jasper Rudin was Viggie the German shepherd's owner. The girlfriend who couldn't cook—it must be my client Elizabeth that Lydia was yelling about—the client who said her boyfriend would kill her if anything happened to his dog.

Mari indicated she'd gladly sneak out of the exam room, but my curiosity kicked in. Elizabeth and Jasper, sophisticated and rich weekenders, must be this warring couple's neighbors. How did that happen?

Although she probably could have gone a few more rounds, Lydia suddenly seemed to realize where she was, although she exhibited no embarrassment at trashing her neighbors to strangers. Amos, on the other hand, again stared sheepishly at the ground. Sam the Labrador, nudged her hand in a show of sympathy.

With the burn marks from the tick removal healing nicely, their recheck was shorter than Lydia's tirade. As I left I heard Mari ask Amos about his bull's-eye rash.

I made my exit before he could pull down his pants again.

• • ● • •

Later, in the treatment room, I questioned Mari about what had gotten Lydia so mad.

Busy wiping the stainless-steel table with disinfectant, she explained. "A lot of the locals are angry with the city people who come up here."

"Why is that?" I wondered. "They certainly boost the economy." Mr. Katt strolled by, then paused briefly to weave himself in and out of my legs.

"It boils down to money," Mari explained. "Land taxes and operating expenses eat up a lot of cash, and if farmers have a bad year they are forced to sell off some of their acreage. Who do you think buys it?"

"Got it. The people from the city."

She nodded and reached down to pet our hospital cat. "That's what's got Lydia so pissed. I think the land Jasper Rudin built on originally belonged to Lydia's people. Don't forget, some of these farms have been owned by the same families for hundreds of years."

As I helped clean the countertops, I wondered how mad or vindictive Lydia could be if pushed. Maybe Elizabeth's story of someone lurking outside her house wasn't so farfetched after all.

Ever since I'd asked Mari about Schutzhund, she had bugged me to go with her to a local training club. Under the pretext of seeing our patient, Viggie, she dragged me to an auditorium in New Paltz on Sunday, during a late afternoon snowstorm. We parked at the north entrance parking lot and entered the huge building.

Despite the weather, many enthusiastic dog-lovers filled the bleachers. Two lively couples wearing Team Schutzhund shirts strolled by us holding thermoses filled with who-knew-what. I recognized Elizabeth sitting in the front row, ready to cheer for her fiancé Jasper and his dog Viggie.

"Where do you want to sit?" I asked Mari, who had brought her portable cooler.

Instead of answering, her head turned to the right, then left, as she checked out the seating area with the efficiency of a lighthouse. "Come on," she whispered and took off in the direction of the second row, where two people were packing up their things. She sprinted past a few stragglers to file her claim, urging me onward with copious arm movements. Not as fast as my technician at the sport of capturing good seats, I waited for an elderly woman loaded down with popcorn and a large drink to pass. The path clear, I dodged another kid before catching up.

As I maneuvered past the people already sitting in our row, Elizabeth turned her perfectly coiffed head and noticed us.

"Dr. Kate," she yelled. "Did you come to see Viggie?"

I nodded and cupped my hands to my lips, for a megaphone effect. "We'll be rooting for him."

Mari stood up and flipped her an enthusiastic thumbs-up/ whistle combination. "Viggie rules," she shouted.

To my surprise I noticed two other clients sitting on the south side of the staging area. In the first row were Amos and his wife, Lydia, with their loveable Labrador, Sam, and what looked like a Doberman, enjoying the show. Cindy had assured me that Amos had indeed gone to the doctor and received antibiotics for his Lyme disease exposure.

At least some good came out of burning the ticks off his dog like a fool, and suffering through that embarrassing photo.

My eye had been drawn to them, but another figure almost directly above them loitering in the stands quickly held my attention. Alone on the very top row sat a man in a dark ski jacket, his head covered by an incongruous black watch cap, pulled low over his eyebrows.

Because we were so far away and the top rows were shadowed, I couldn't see his features clearly.

Then I got an idea. I dug around in my backpack for my cell phone, intent on taking a picture of the suspicious stranger, or at least zooming in on his face. By the time I readied the phone to take the photo, he'd left, the exit door slowly closing behind him.

Another missed opportunity.

"Hey," Mari nudged me. "You've got to see this."

Reluctantly, I pulled my focus back to the arena. "So what am I looking at?" I'd read up briefly about the sport but Mari was the expert here.

"First we'll see the tracking phase, then obedience, and finally protection," she whispered in my ear since several dogs on leashes now stood at the ready. The audience quieted down. An indoor/outdoor-like surface carpeted the arena where the dogs worked. Portable fences divided the huge space into specific areas, probably corresponding with the different skills to be demonstrated.

Mari pulled out a bag of chips and tried to silently chew them. "Elizabeth told me Viggie already earned his BH."

"That's the behavior degree, right?"

"Yes, it stands for Begleithund in German. It's the companion dog test." She stopped to munch a few, hand covering her mouth. "Both my Rottie babies have their BH degrees."

"Impressive." I knew there were four parts to the BH degree. Its purpose was to make sure each dog applicant was temperamentally suited and had sufficient obedience training to compete at the official Schutzhund trials.

The Hudson River Schutzhund Club encouraged friends and family of the participants to come and sit in the audience during training. The idea was that the dogs would get used to noise and movement in the stands, allowing them to develop focus for the real trials. Many of the club's members never competed professionally, but simply enjoyed working with their dogs.

Sure enough, I noticed many different breeds in the group. When a gunshot noise sounded with no warning, I flinched, but the dogs didn't.

"All part of the training," Mari reminded me.

One Rottweiler to our left demonstrated the protection part of the training by viciously attacking a big protective sleeve on the arm of a person, known as the decoy, pretending to attack the dog's handler. Did any dogs ever miss that padding and sink their teeth into the decoy's arm?

Mari distracted me by pulling at my sleeve. "Viggie is taking a break," she said. "Maybe we should wave to them?"

As Jasper Rudin walked toward us, I took a good look at his facial features. Thick brown hair, with cheeks, chin, and most of his mouth hidden behind a lightly trimmed beard and mustache. He had a nose whose perfect tip was more likely due to a surgeon's skill and not Mother Nature. A handsome man in his early fifties, he radiated confidence to the point of arrogance.

Sure enough, his younger girlfriend, Elizabeth, turned and pointed to us. We both waved. He briefly acknowledged us, then turned back to rummage through his pockets.

"Looks like someone took a bite out of that boot," I commented to Mari. One of his expensive work boots had a wedge-shaped divot missing just above the heel, only noticeable when the light struck it just right.

"My guys used to chew on my shoes like that, until they were almost a year old." She smiled fondly at the memory of puppyhood and ruined footwear.

After Jasper planted an air kiss on Elizabeth, the two, clad in designer sportswear, crossed the arena and said hello to Amos and Lydia. The contrast between the sophisticated pair standing next to the locals said volumes. Jasper, in Ralph Lauren country attire, stood next to Amos, whose grungy red plaid shirt barely contained a beer belly hanging over his belt. Elizabeth, with her perfectly streaked blond hair and carrying a large Coach handbag, contrasted with the oddly masculine Lydia in khaki and salt-stained combat boots.

"I guess they kissed and made up," I commented, watching Amos pet Viggie.

Mari, always a fountain of local info, said, "Well, they are next-door neighbors."

"I still find that hard to believe." I pictured Jasper Rudin and Elizabeth in some huge expensive home. Amos and Lydia, on the other hand, I saw in less-attractive circumstances, unless they were secretly eccentric millionaires.

"No, that happens all the time up here. This house Rudin built is gorgeous. Must be at least four thousand square feet or more. I went by it the other day by accident, trying to detour around an accident."

"I'll take your word for it. What about Amos and Lydia's place?"

"Oh, that's the same as it's always been, a dump. Well, I shouldn't say that." Mari decided to qualify her statement. "Her family's lived in that farmhouse for over three hundred years—and it looks it. There's an original stone part, from way back, built by the wealthy ancestors who received some kind of land grant from the British. But every time the family expanded, someone either put up another building or added on to the main house. Nobody took any time to match things up."

That sort of explained it. I wondered if the rich couple with a place in New York City and a weekend retreat here in the Hudson Valley ever resented having to look out their windows at their less-than-attractive neighbors. Or vice-versa.

Again Mari provided the answer. "We got a hint the other day of a dispute simmering away. That whole garage thing. There's a pretty wide track of forest separating the two farms and all the trees are on Rudin's side. If they'd been on Amos and Lydia's property, they'd have been cut down for firewood a long time ago."

I found it interesting that so many people moving from the city became interested in preserving the Hudson Valley, while many residents who'd lived here all their lives no longer cared about the beauty they took for granted each day.

"Anyhow, all I remember is it has to do with a building permit."

"How do you know so much about them?"

"Known them my whole life. Her family is full of crazy people. Lydia's grandfather was one of those men you didn't want to cross. If you accidently went on his property, he wouldn't warn you, he'd just shoot you."

So many pockets of anger here, I thought. You never knew what went on in some of these isolated homes with the curtains drawn that you drove by every day.

"Look at that Doberman go." Mari pointed to the middle of the arena, where several obstacles and hurdles had been set up. An extremely fit and agile Dobie with a barbell in his mouth was running up and over a six-foot slanted wall. He made it look easy.

"Must be those greyhound genes," my companion said.

I didn't comment. A professor in veterinary school advised us to never get involved in a debate on what breeds were used in 1890 by Karl Dobermann to create his namesake dog. Several studies of genetic diversity going on now might clarify the situation, but regardless, the Dobie was an elegant animal. Most veterinarians know that although Dobermans appear ferocious, these dogs would rather sit on your foot or in your lap than attack you.

"Seen enough?" Mari asked, checking her watch. I knew a bunch of her friends planned to catch a movie at the multiplex tonight, so we hustled toward the exit. On the way out we ran into Amos and Lydia and their two dogs.

The Labrador immediately wagged his tail at me and slobbered a bit. The Doberman, on the other hand, only looked up at Amos.

"Long time, no see," cackled Lydia.

"We're following you," I joked. Sam pushed his nose into my hand, while the Dobie sat like a gentleman.

Mari laughed and bent down to pet them both.

"That's a nice-looking dog," I told them, pointing to the Dobie. "Are you interested in Schutzhund training for your guys?"

Amos laughed. "Her Lab is too dumb for Schutzhund."

"Amos," his wife said, and slugged him with her baseball cap. "Don't say that in front of Sammy, even if it's true."

Sam didn't take offense, just slobbered and wagged his tail.

"We're here because our neighbors invited us." Lydia sounded less than thrilled.

"Be nice," Amos pleaded.

I took another look at the Doberman, sitting quietly, aware of everything. Sleek coat, intelligent face, this dog was a handsome specimen of the breed. I noted docked ears, something we vets no longer advised owners to do.

"Where did you get...what's the Dobie's name?"

"Hans," Lydia said. "That was his name when we rescued him, so we kept it."

Amos stroked the dog's head. "Can you imagine? Someone brought a purebred dog like this to the shelter and put it up for adoption? They'd already started Schutzhund training with him, we were told. But it's too much work to continue, right honey?"

"Way too much," his wife agreed. "Our Hans seems to remember most of it. We make sure to do his obedience commands every day or we try to. He's a very good boy and he gets along great with Sam, which is the most important thing."

Mari scratched the Labrador on his head. "They're both beautiful dogs."

"Yeah. One for me and one for him." Lydia pointed to her husband. "Good thing because Sammy seems to be holding a grudge. Ever since Amos burned those ticks off, he won't go near him."

Sure enough, the Labrador stayed close to Lydia. I noticed he'd pressed his head to her leg.

We all began to walk toward the exit, the couple arguing between themselves about why Sam wouldn't take a treat from Amos anymore. Of course he denied it and told her he'd prove it to her when they got home. Luckily, we soon went our separate ways, north entrance for us and south entrance for them. We continued to hear them spar back and forth until we hit the parking lot.

"I think those two like to fight." Mari said.

"Yes, a little of them goes a long way," I replied.

I started up the truck and eased into traffic and onto the NY State Thruway, back to the animal hospital, where Mari had left her vehicle. Baring any unforeseen problem, we'd be back in forty minutes.

Once on the highway I admitted that the Schutzhund training session had been interesting. "I bet a lot of time and dedication goes into it."

"And money," Mari added. "Which is why I'm not out there with my two sweetie pies."

My assistant loved her two Rottweilers, Lucy and Desi, to pieces. A very powerful breed. If I were a decoy facing those two I would want that padded arm sleeve to be extra thick.

Someone in a green truck blew past us. "That's certainly something to consider," I replied. "Between all the show fees, the time, and training, I bet expenses add up to over a thousand dollars."

"That's most likely why Amos bailed, because Lydia hates to spend money," she noted. "He sure is in the doghouse. Want to bet that Labrador retriever forgives him way faster than Lydia does?"

"No contest."

"So those two are counting pennies while Elizabeth and Jasper, their rich neighbors, are feasting on steaks and champagne. I need to win the lottery," Mari added.

"Me too," I laughed.

She cleared her throat. "You already have won the lottery. What do you call Jeremy?"

After Mari took off to meet her friends, I sat down in the office to think about what she said. Did I hear resentment in her voice? I hoped not. Mari had become a close friend as well as a coworker. Why did money complicate everything?

To take my mind off of it, I queried the rules of Schutzhund training and showing. Dr. Holtzer had told me that Carl Wolf was getting ready to compete on the professional level, and had been training his German-bred dog, Werner Van Braun, or Brownie, for quite some time. Would the Big Bad Wolf be tempted to repeat history? Had word of Tucker's exposé reached his ears? Maybe he'd already trained a dog, intending to show it.

But, maybe wary of the FBI and publicity, he'd surrendered Hans to a shelter to get rid of the evidence.

Although I hated to do it, I made a local call. Lydia answered.

"Hi. It's Dr. Kate calling from Oak Falls Animal Hospital."

"Didn't we just see you a few minutes ago?" Her raspy voice set at an uncomfortable decibel blasted out of the phone.

I held the receiver a little ways away from my ear. "Yes. You know, I was curious about Hans. Most dogs that do Schutzhund have to be identifiable."

"What?"

I heard Amos call, "Who's on the phone, honey?" in the background.

"Does Hans have a tattoo or a chip?"

"Does he eat chips?"

Lydia obviously was a bit hard of hearing. Amos yelling in the background didn't help things. "When he rolls on his back, is there a tattoo on the inside of his thigh?"

A familiar cackling sound on the line became a snicker.

"How'd you know that? You can't read it, though, 'cause someone messed it up good."

Why didn't that information surprise me?

After I thanked Lydia and gladly hung up the phone, I made a mental note to check into Hans and his background. Our shelters usually required some kind of history, but if Wolf surrendered the dog, it was sure to be nothing but lies.

I thought back to his original crime, the murder of his family. Before he fled the scene, he'd also gotten rid of his dog, releasing it in his neighborhood.

Did he repeat the pattern? Because that would mean the Wolf had fled the coop.

Over the next week I found myself looking over my shoulder constantly, searching for someone suspicious. Nothing. I'd deliberately ventured into the crowded Kingston Mall one night, but no one noticed me, not even the kids who bumped my arm while illegally and brazenly skateboarding past surprised shoppers.

Right on their heels the mall police on Segways rolled past in medium hot pursuit.

Unobtrusively, I moved from trash can to trash can and noticed that most were filled with half-eaten slices of pizza crust, greasy fast food bags, or empty soda cups. Many items that should have been separated out and recycled, hadn't been. The trash cans closest to the exit doors were already overflowing. It didn't take a genius to figure out how easy dumping stolen goods could be. I assumed the exit trash cans and dumpsters in the back attracted dumpster divers. The side entrances were least used. Did the killer expect someone to find Gloria's discarded jewelry and try to hock some of the items, or was that detail left to chance?

I had no idea.

Maybe Wolf hung out for a while and waited for a likely loser to start picking through the trash or watched from the comfort of his car. I doubted if we'd ever know. The police appeared to have adjusted their theory to fit the circumstances. Whoever took Gloria's jewelry realized they couldn't get rid of it easily, so they ditched it.

End of story.

But, my trip to the mall wasn't unfruitful. I purchased two pairs of warm socks, a ski sweater on deep discount, and a small camera drone for my Gramps. Mari asked me what my grandfather would do with a drone in Brooklyn. Who knew, but nothing would surprise me. Maybe make a movie starring a bunch of seniors? Take awesome photos from the Empire State Building? If it gave him some fun, it was worth it.

Surveillance on a suspicious property or person didn't cross my mind.

Not.

The next day, when Jasper Rudin came in for Viggie's rabies booster shot, I got a taste of what Elizabeth lived with each day.

As soon as I joined Mari in the exam room, I noticed the difference in Viggie. When the German shepherd had come in with Elizabeth, he'd explored everything and everyone, completely at ease, even with his sore foot. Today he stood at attention, staring up at his master. Jasper Rudin had impressive control over his dog. Normally I'd compliment the owner, but today I wasn't so sure.

I wondered if Rudin liked to control everything and everyone in his world.

"So, what brings you here today?" I started off, casually.

He glared at me. "A rabies shot. Didn't your staff write that down?" He shot a look at Mari, as if she and Cindy were incompetent.

I took the loaded syringe out of my pocket and held it in front of him. "Here's the rabies booster. I like to make sure there aren't any other health issues before I vaccinate. I'm sure you understand, Mr. Rudin." Behind me I feel the anger radiating off Mari.

Like most bullies he backed down.

"Viggie is fine, in perfect health. No need to jack up your bill."

"Actually, since you helped us out that day we were stuck in the snow, this one is on the house." I deliberately forced a wide smile his way. Was he trying to provoke me? If so, that wasn't going to happen. I knew he'd stopped to help because Elizabeth made him. He, however, proceeded to take credit.

With the compliment and freebie vaccination, his attitude visibly changed. A charming smile suddenly came out, directed to Mari and me. "Always happy to help out a neighbor."

Ready to say so long to his man, I asked my assistant, "Could you help hold Viggie?"

"I'll hold him," Rudin insisted. "He's attack-trained, you know. There's only one word that will stop him. A buddy of mine suggested this German word that worked for his dog. Nobody but Elizabeth and I know it."

Yeah, right, I thought. *Verboten.* Except, I wasn't about to get Elizabeth in trouble by letting him know she shared it with us.

After he left, Mari let her feelings be known. "Jerk."

Silently, I agreed. How long, I wondered, had he lived here in Oak Falls? Or had he appeared in his Mercedes, money in hand, no questions asked.

My Thanksgiving plans with Gramps were waylaid by a pesky thing called a flu virus. Each year the CDC and flu vaccine manufacturers try to guess which strains are going to make us sick the following year. Sometimes they're right on target and sometimes not so much. This was one of those not-so-much years. Early statistics pointed to about a twenty-four percent success rate. That left the other seventy-six percent of us coughing and feeling like crud.

How unfair was it to get sick on your days off? My plan had been to drive down to Brooklyn early Thanksgiving morning to beat the traffic, but on Wednesday night the chills and fever and coughing began. By morning I felt and looked like a bowl of Daffy's dried up corn mush. My head pounded and stomach rolled. Gramps sympathized, since several of his friends were also laid low. I told him to stay put because he really couldn't risk coming down with bronchitis or pneumonia with his bad lungs. Between coughs I wished him happy turkey day and slunk into bed. Used tissues piled up like snowdrifts on the bed. My head hurt so bad I wanted to rip it off.

By Friday my symptoms leveled off a bit. I still felt terrible but no worse. After endless cups of tea and cans of chicken soup, my throat felt a bit better and with ibuprofen most of the muscle aches and pains subsided. I knew I was on the road to recovery when I flipped on the television and turned on HGTV. Half asleep I'd drift in and out of programs. One moment I'd be watching a Victorian remodel in Boston then wake up to someone picking out fixtures for a mid-century modern in Palm Springs. My congested cough syrup brain barely processed any of it. Wrapped up in a blanket, I felt confident that all the home improvement projects, despite their various ups and downs, would turn out just fine on the magical mystery tour of home improvement land.

The ringing of my phone woke me up. Who was calling me on Saturday morning? Anyone who knew I was sick texted me, aware I was on and off napping most of the time. I dug my cell out from under the debris around me.

"Hello." After two days of disuse and coughing, my voice sounded horrible, even to me. My caller confirmed it.

"You sound horrible," Luke said.

"Thanks. I'm only pretending to be this bad." My sarcastic comment came punctuated by a deep raspy cough. Some symptoms had relapsed overnight. The ache in my muscles now matched the pain in my throat and head. All I wanted was to go back to sleep.

He waited until I stopped coughing and started breathing. "I'm dropping a Thanksgiving dinner off at your door. If you can't eat it, pop it right into the freezer," Luke said. "Everything is labeled. When you feel better you can feast on leftovers. Mama G also insisted on sending you a frozen pie with instructions on baking it in your oven when you're ready."

Right now the thought of food was nauseating but I knew sometime in the distant future I'd be hungry again. "Aren't you coming in?" I asked in a plaintive voice.

He laughed and said, "I love you dearly, but not enough to get the flu."

Was I hallucinating? Did Luke just say "I love you dearly" to me?

My foggy synapses and stuffed up nose really couldn't hold that thought. Sure enough, about ten minutes later Buddy woofed at the door. After a brief knock a car door closed, and I heard a vehicle leave. I slowly got up, rescued the two packages of holiday food then whipped them right into my empty freezer before lying back down in bed.

As the snow stacked up outside, his words floated around inside my head. *I love you dearly, but. I love you dearly, but...*until my exhausted body gave up and plummeted into a dreamless sleep.

The next day, sanity prevailed. An antihistamine cleared my nose and head and my flaming throat was reduced to a few dying embers. In retrospect Luke's thoughtful endearment sounded reminiscent of something you said to a child who wants to share her grubby binky with you. Thanks, but no thanks.

I spent the day hibernating, drinking fluids, taking medications, and generally feeling sorry for myself. When Mari texted me to tell me she was sick, too, I sympathized, realizing that riding around in the truck together was like bathing in a shared pool of germs.

After napping for a few more hours, I woke up feeling better and a little bit hungry. Once my taste buds savored the heated up stuffing, gravy, and turkey, I turned ravenous. Half the portion disappeared in record time.

However, I didn't risk my first few hours of recovery by baking and eating an entire pie.

The next time I woke up it was two in the morning, my mind finally sharp and clear and ready for work. My brain didn't care that it was the middle of the night. I'd passed from too little sleep into the too-much-sleep realm. But at two a.m. my options were limited.

Even Buddy refused to get out of bed to play.

Besides reading there was only one other thing to do this late at night—surf the Internet and play Spider Solitaire. I started to wonder what the FBI website had to say about Carl Wolf, so I queried the Ten Most Wanted List.

Directly under his last known picture, Wolf rated only a brief overview of the murders of his wife and children. An icon encouraged the curious to download the full FBI poster, which contained several sketches showing Wolf with different hairstyles, light stubble beards, and a small mustache. Oddly enough, I thought, they didn't really age him with much weight gain, or jowls or the common facial wrinkles associated with aging. I suspected the artist in Gloria would have been disappointed.

So why wasn't the Big Bad Wolf living it up in Costa Rico, or Belize or Mexico? With a new identity and passport you could hide anywhere today, especially if you had computer skills and the foresight to stash money away in an untraceable account. A different persona allowed you to form new relationships, slip smoothly into other cultures and create a whole new life.

I closed my eyes and tried to think like a fugitive.

If I were Carl Wolf, twenty-one years down the road after killing the people closest to me, why would I risk everything to come back to the United States?

Then I realized, killer or not, Wolf might be very much like some of my friends who are uncomfortable in strange places and unfamiliar situations. Not adventurous. Not eager to learn a new language or eat ethnic food.

With his white supremacist leanings, maybe Wolf preferred staying in the USA. To risk living here with the FBI actively searching for him, he must have physically changed enough to feel pretty confident no one would recognize him. It must have been a shock to come face-to-face with a pair of elderly eyes from the past, a well-trained, observant pair of old eyes not fooled by superficial changes, eyes that barreled on through to the nitty-gritty.

Someone evil is here. Oh, Gloria, if only you were able to tell us what you saw.

I stayed up far too late thinking of crazy reasons why an FBI fugitive might stay in the States. Perhaps he won the lottery? Right. What if he came into estate money or property some-how linked to his new identity? Or maybe he wanted to enjoy the things he used to enjoy. You couldn't go elk hunting in the Caribbean, snowshoe across the sand, or savor a Philly cheese steak sandwich or New York hot dog in the Amazon.

Then I realized I was only focusing on the man. Wolf would have had time to father an entirely new family by now. Maybe the wife wanted to relocate so their kids might graduate from an American high school, then go on to a stateside college.

Or not.

By the time the sun began to rise I had long since peaked and fallen asleep, head aching with possibilities—possibilities all predicated on the assumption that Carl Wolf would want to live in the good old USA.

Things came to an abrupt head the following morning when I received an urgent call from Gramps.

"This is a big mess."

No hello or small talk. Something was definitely up.

"I'm calling you from rehab. Tucker has been on the phone with the FBI for the past twenty minutes. He's told them every-thing, all about Gloria and Halloween night and ended up accus-ing them of not investigating the Wolf case properly." Barely stopping for breath, he continued. "Now he's threatening to go to the *New York Times* and the *NY Post* with the story."

I sat up on the sofa. What was going on?

Through the receiver I could vaguely hear a voice that sounded like Tucker screaming in the background. After a few random noises, silence ensued and Gramps got back on the line.

"Alright. He's hung up the phone and the staff is calming him down. We're not sure what set him off, but he's definitely got his memory back. All he's talking about is Wolf and the book."

"Do you think…?"

"Oops. There he goes again. I'll call you later."

That upset me. What the heck had I been thinking to drag my grandfather into all this? After Tucker's phone call from rehab to the FBI, our amateur investigation would be out in the open. Maybe they'll take into consideration the person who called suffered from a recent head injury. All I knew was that threatening the FBI was never a good idea.

Without my normal schedule I barely knew what day it was. After losing a few days to the flu, it was a struggle getting back up to speed. I started by calling Cindy to go over Monday's appointments. Our cheery receptionist reminded me that it would be business as usual, regardless of the weather. She felt confident we could work around sick staffers for now, as long as I was feeling better.

I assured her I'd be ready to rock 'n' roll by tomorrow morning.

After I got off the phone I looked around at the results of three days sick in bed with no one to help. Almost every surface had some item draped on it. Wastebaskets overflowed with used tissues. My sweats could probably stand up and walk around without me.

With some Aretha Franklin playing to get me moving and grooving, I scurried around and straightened up the place. The washing machine soon hummed with a load full of yukky stuff, and I'd even put clean scrubs out to wear in the morning, like I did with my school clothes in middle school. After a quick inventory of the pantry and fridge, I felt confident to brave the world outside.

Unfortunately, as soon as I took a deep breath of cold air, I started to cough. To remedy that, I wrapped my muffler tightly around the lower part of my face and jumped into the truck. Enough was enough. I was tired of being sick.

Getting out and moving around was the best decision I'd made all day. With each completed task, I became more and more invigorated. Delighted to be vertical I enjoyed prowling the grocery aisles and stocking my pantry against future storms. Several times clients stopped me to say hello, many happy to share their tales of being sick with the flu. There was nothing more satisfying than commiserating with another victim of this nasty virus going around.

Loaded down with grocery bags, I made several trips back and forth to the apartment, careful not to slip on the watery mush that was slowly turning back into ice. I'd noticed the temperature dropping so I was more than content to wind up my first day out with a quart of ice cream in front of the television. Buddy happily munched on a new chew bone with a tummy full of doggie treats I'd picked up on sale.

Spoon fully loaded with ice cream, squeeze bottle of fudge sauce at my side, I knew all was right with the world.

When the phone rang a few minutes later, I assumed Gramps was calling me back. Instead, everything that had been right flipped to wrong.

"Hello, Dr. Turner?"

"Yes, who is this?"

"Special agent Steve Frendell. FBI."

You know how being near a police car on the road makes you feel vaguely guilty you've done something wrong even when you haven't? Well, multiply that times a thousand if you find yourself talking to the FBI. Even though I knew why they were calling me, I still felt uneasy.

Which is probably why I went on the defensive immediately. I'd seen too many made-for-television movies to stay passive.

"Agent Frendell, is this conversation being recorded?" I said this in my best pseudo-legal voice.

"No, it isn't."

"Am I being investigated for any crime?"

"No."

"Well, good." That out of the way I couldn't think of anything else to say except to throw myself on the mercy of the court.

"Can I help you?"

"We certainly hope so. I understand you are acquainted with Tucker Weinstein?"

"Yes." So, this call had been prompted by Tucker's conversation with the FBI that Gramps told me about.

He cleared his throat. "Would you be able to meet me tomorrow to discuss some allegations Mr. Weinstein made?"

"Certainly. I'm at work tomorrow until five."

"Then I'll meet you at your office around five-thirty?"

"Five-thirty it is."

As soon as I hung up I realized my mistake. I should have suggested another meeting place. Cindy, the gossip queen of Oak Falls, would be sitting at the front desk tomorrow at five-thirty.

Chapter Twenty

I didn't want everyone in Oak Falls to know the FBI came to call on me, so I resolved to try and keep this meeting with Agent Steve Frendell a secret. That lasted about thirty seconds.

The mistake began by mentioning an after-hours appointment to Cindy.

That morning, while sipping my first cup of coffee, I casually told her I had an appointment of a personal nature at five-thirty and implied she could leave at five tonight.

"Viggie's owner is coming in at four-forty-five to pick up that Schutzhund health form. If it's Elizabeth, she usually runs late."

"Right. Thanks for reminding me."

"No problem."

By trying to be casual, I ended up waving a red flag in front of my receptionist. "Then just let me know when my…ah…appointment gets here, please."

"Should I prepare a medical record for him?" she began ever so casually, "or is it her?"

"Him, and it's not necessary." The more I said, the more likely I'd be to put my foot in it.

"Do you know the pet's name and info so I can load it into the computer?"

This was starting to be a little tricky. "Ah, don't worry about that. It's an informal consultation." Satisfied I'd skirted the issue, I took another sip of coffee and tried to walk away.

"What's his name?"

That made me stop. "Why do you need to know?"

"Well, how will I know if he's your appointment or some random stranger?" Cindy arched her brows as though I had made a terrible faux pas.

What she said sounded reasonable, but why did I feel I'd been outmaneuvered by a pro?

"Okay. His name is Steve, Steve Frendell. Just text me when he gets here, please."

Once again she halted my escape.

"What does he look like, you know, so I can recognize him when he walks in?"

I'd walked into a trap. I had no idea what Frendell looked like. I tried to punt. "Steve's pretty ordinary. He looks like a guy."

Determined now to flee before she wrangled anything else out of me, I tried to escape into my office, walking away at a fairly swift pace.

I heard footsteps close behind, keeping up with me on the tile floor. Rats.

"Should I put him in an exam room, or let him wait in reception?" Another deceptively simple question loaded with innuendo. My instinct told me to get him away from Cindy as quickly as possible. That meant an exam room. However, it also involved a punt to Mari, who would definitely run with it to the goal post.

I would have been better off not saying anything. Then I realized all Agent Frendell needed to do was hand someone his card and it was all over. Not to mention Cindy's brother-in-law, the Chief of Police for the town of Oak Falls, most likely knew if an FBI agent arrived in Oak Falls to interview one of the town's residents. For all I knew, they'd called him first.

With too much on the table, I gave up. "He can wait in reception with you."

Those words opened the way for Cindy to ask whatever she

wanted in the short time Agent Frendell was in her clutches. I'd be curious to learn how much he'd be willing to tell her.

Around five-thirty I had my answer when Cindy's text popped up:

Agent Frendell is here.

No need to hide anything anymore, which actually felt like a relief. If Carl Wolf had taken up residence in the Hudson Valley, we'd need all the help we could get—including guidance from the FBI.

When I walked into the reception area and saw Steve Frendell for the first time, my guard went up. This guy looked like he meant business. In his fifties, he had close-cut military-styled gray hair, a black suit with a dark blue tie, long winter coat, and a face set in a permanent frown. His stern expression, I'm sure, dampened my staff's initial enthusiasm at meeting a real life FBI agent. Did they expect a black SUV packed with agents in the parking lot, ready to stream out on the least provocation?

Frendell also could have passed as a grumpy IRS agent.

I noticed Cindy and Mari both found reasons to stand in the reception area while waiting for me to arrive, expressions suitable for attending my funeral.

He stood and acknowledged me as I approached. "Dr. Turner?"

"Agent Frendell?" We shook hands. I'm five-ten and judged him to be about six-one. Although older, he appeared lean and still muscular, with a physique like a runner. He also didn't appear to be in the mood for idle conversation.

"Is there somewhere more private where we can talk?"

A slight gesture of his head away from our audience prompted me to escort him to my office. He shut the door behind him, and gave the room a quick once-over before taking the chair opposite mine.

Now, my only experience with the FBI was taken directly from massive amounts of television. Unsure how this interview would go, I'd decided to let him do most of the talking. Of course, I'd still answer all his questions truthfully, but succinctly, and I vowed to try not to embellish. Just the facts, like the fictional Sergeant Joe Friday used to say in the classic 1950s television series *Dragnet*. I'd seen every one of those old Jack Webb black-and-white episodes a million times with Gramps.

Frendell put his leather briefcase down on the floor, and slipped off his coat.

"What can I do for you today?" I asked. In the harsh overhead light, I noticed something about his face, an asymmetry that signaled plastic surgery or a healed facial injury.

"Your friend, Tucker Weinstein, made a phone call yesterday to our main office in New York City, which has prompted my visit."

"I see." So far, so good. "This must be about Carl Wolf. Is it safe to assume there are other FBI agents here in Oak Falls?"

He sort of did and did not answer my question.

"We at the Bureau are well aware of Carl Wolf. The untimely death of Gloria LaGuardia raised some flags in our Albany office, especially with Weinstein's implication in a news interview that her death might be tied to Wolf somehow." He looked up at me, gauging my reaction. I tried to keep a poker face. Gramps would have been proud.

"As we've investigated this report of a possible sighting, your name came up several times."

"I see." My fingers fiddled with a few stray papers on the desk.

When I glanced up at him, he tilted his head, as if he heard something. Did he think my staff might be listening at the door? After a moment his steely attention turned back to me.

Neither one of us said anything. It felt like we were sizing each other up in a poker game, but a poker game in which chips represented pieces of information. All I really wanted to do was blurt out everything I knew, but caution kept me, well, cautious.

"Let's start from the beginning, shall we? Do you mind if I

record our conversation?" He removed a small electronic device from his jacket pocket.

Recording again? The inevitability of telling my story once more and having it on tape again crashed down on me. I took a deep breath and agreed.

For the next half hour I told him everything I remembered, starting from Halloween night with Gloria to visiting Tucker at the hospital. With a few prompts he steered me toward the adult daycare center, and my curious conversation with Sylvia about the man who came and removed the contents of Gloria's cubby.

"You've had a very adventurous time here in Oak Falls, Dr. Turner," he commented while turning the recording device off.

"Meaning?" My head started to throb from having to concentrate on telling all the facts he wanted in a logical and clear manner. Plus, I hadn't had any dinner or much lunch.

With the first hint of being human, he gave me a semi-smile, "You're not a stranger to murder investigations."

"Just bad luck, I suppose." All in all, the interview had been straightforward, and I must admit I felt better now that I knew the FBI was on board. However, it was time to get him on the road so I could go home and crash. Escorting Frendell through the now-empty hospital we unconsciously fell into step. I didn't realize it until I heard only our in-tandem heels clicking on the tile.

"You seem to know quite a bit about Carl Wolf," I tentatively commented before we entered the reception area.

His body seemed to tense for a moment. I had the impression he consciously willed himself to relax, and after a beat he replied.

"I think there's only one person on Earth who knows more about him than I do."

"Who is that?" A feeling of dread came over me since I suspected I knew his answer.

"Why, Carl Wolf himself." The look in his eyes when he spoke chilled me. Did Agent Frendell have a personal vendetta against Wolf, or was there something much more sinister to his story?

After he left I bolted all the doors and checked the window locks. The hospital screamed out its silence. Cindy and Mari were long gone. I paced back and forth and looked out into the empty parking lot. Why did this FBI interview make me so upset?

The facial scarring, the right age, another man who fit the Carl Wolf profile. Was I imagining things? This needs to stop, I thought. Was my well-developed sixth sense trying to tell me something? If so, I hadn't deciphered the message.

My body felt as though ants were crawling up and down my back. Only one solution I could think of. Pie.

The parking lot at the Oak Falls Diner was more crowded than usual this time. I squeezed the truck into a narrow spot one row from the edge of the highway and quickly walked to the entrance. Rosie, Luke's cousin, saw me and with a free hand signaled me toward the last seat at the counter. The temperature inside was a stunningly hot contrast to the freezing outdoors. As I walked I began sliding my coat off. Unfortunately, my move ended up knocking a man on the head. He dropped his glass of soda on the floor.

The commotion made everyone in the room look over at me.

By the time I'd apologized and maneuvered past another guy whose long legs stuck out in the narrow aisle, the seat at the counter had been taken. Resigned to takeout, I heard someone call my name.

Agent Frendell sat at a small table for two. "You can have this extra seat if you like." He stood up and helped me with my coat.

"Thanks," I told him. "Be careful. My coat attacked someone."

"I saw."

Unburdened, I gratefully slid into the chair, suddenly aware of how hungry I was.

"The special is chicken piccata. That's what I ordered."

Rosie stopped at our table on her way to the kitchen and I quickly ordered the same thing.

We made idle chatter for a while. Frendell turned on the

charm and told me snippets of his personal life. Divorced, two kids, wife had remarried and moved out of state. His life revolved around work.

I didn't bother to share. I had a feeling he knew everything about me.

We didn't talk about Carl Wolf, either.

When our food came I tried to be ladylike but didn't make it. Instead, I sliced off a slab of chicken, bathed it in lemon sauce, and stuffed it in my mouth. Heaven once again.

"A woman with a healthy appetite. That's refreshing."

A compliment? I chose to call it that. His remark slowed me down, but only temporarily. I raided the bread basket, and began buttering a piece of Mama G's handmade French baguette. Sitting opposite me in the diner, Steve Frendell didn't appear as intimidating. I turned the tables and asked him a question. "What do you think your department will do with the information I gave you?"

He debated for a moment before answering. "Everything will be turned over to the case agent and all our offices updated. You know, this kind of call from your friend Tucker isn't anything new. We receive reports about sightings of Carl Wolf and many other fugitives at least once or twice a month."

"After all this time?" My astonishment was real. I had no idea.

"The FBI Internet site is viewed by millions and millions of people worldwide. There's always someone who starts thinking that the ex-boyfriend or old coworker looks like Wolf or some wanted guy they saw on a true crime program. Most often the person calling in just wants to stir up trouble for someone they're mad at."

"What a waste of time and resources that could be put to better use." I'd learned the hard way that the vindictiveness of some people had no bounds.

"True. However, in your case, there are enough odd markers to draw our attention. The problem with Wolf is he's very smart, and very computer savvy. He's been successful at avoiding capture for a long time. With all this publicity, I doubt he's still hanging around here."

Another reason occurred to me. "Maybe he hasn't been caught because he's dead."

Frendell's frown deepened. "We have reason to believe he is still alive. Average life expectancy in America for a man his age is eighty-three or four. Wolf is only fifty-one and had no known health issues when he disappeared."

I bet those statistics masked something unsaid. "Has he contacted the FBI?"

"I'm not at liberty to comment on that."

Rosie came by and freshened up our drinks. Seeing we weren't quite finished she said she'd check back. The diner, meanwhile, was packed. With the noise level approaching extra loud, I didn't worry about anyone overhearing us. Out of habit I took a quick look around the place, concentrating on the counter clients. There were no single guys in baseball hats or any other hat to be found. I realized that was the one detail I had left out, my feeling of being followed in the Kingston Mall. It hadn't come up and I wasn't about to appear to be a hysterical female.

When I turned back, Frendell was staring at me.

Rosie swooped in, removed our entrée plates, and came back with dessert and coffee.

Despite our casual surroundings I didn't have any illusions that this seemingly friendly FBI agent was probably evaluating me to decide if I was a truthful witness or a nut job.

"So, what do I do next?" I'd finished my piece of cranberry-walnut pie, and looked around for Rosie, who seemed to have disappeared.

Agent Frendell also appeared to be closing up shop. "You do nothing. If something comes up that concerns you, call me." He slid a card out of his business card holder, then turned it over and wrote down a different number. "This is my personal cell. Don't put yourself or anyone else in jeopardy. Our profilers describe Wolf as a narcissist and a sociopath, with a genius IQ. Protecting himself and his identity will be paramount to him. In a confrontation, you won't win."

I opened my purse and put his card in my wallet. Rosie appeared out of nowhere and dropped off our separate checks.

Frendell picked up his check and turned downright chatty. "The agent in charge is issuing a press release, warning Hudson Valley residents of a possible Carl Wolf sighting in this area. It reveals that the Bureau is on hand and actively investigating."

"Won't that make him run?"

"That's the plan. We'll be watching for anyone remotely fitting his description making sudden travel plans in the next few days. Don't forget, we've had several supposed sightings of Wolf before and none of them have added up to anything. I admit, this one is very promising, but we might still be barking up the wrong tree."

It sounded straightforward and logical. But what if our logic didn't match up with the killer's logic?

I had one more question. "Do you mind if I ask why you joined the FBI?"

Frendell stared out the window. "Someone very close to me was murdered."

He quite obviously didn't want to go into it any further. From his prickly demeanor I gathered this was a very personal matter, one he preferred to keep to himself. To breach the silence between us I decided to voice a thought that had only now occurred to me.

"You know," I mused as we waited, "let's say it is Wolf. I keep wondering what prompted him to be here? Why did he kill Gloria? If he thought she recognized him, he could easily avoid her, he didn't have to kill her. Or would her presence upset some plan he has going?"

His pupils widened briefly before he deliberately looked down at the bill. My Gramps called that a "tell."

"You might be overthinking this," he responded. "Most criminals on the run want to get as far away from the scene as possible.

Remember, Wolf has vanished before. The FBI searched for months and months, in and around New Jersey, and never found a trace of him. No full set of fingerprints and no DNA are on file for him, which is quite a feat."

I nodded as though I agreed with him. Oddly, he sounded as though he admired Wolf for not getting caught.

"However," he paused for effect, "those are the kinds of scenarios the agent in charge will be exploring."

I suspected the FBI knew a lot more than they were letting on. It wouldn't be the first time. With my bill in hand, I stood up. So did he.

"May I ask you one more thing?" This time I looked straight into his eyes.

"Of course."

"If Wolf is around, what's the possibility he's the guy who assaulted my friend, Tucker? Don't forget, Tucker gave a very extensive and somewhat exaggerated interview about his book to the local paper and television station. It's also blasted all over the Internet. He implied Wolf was behind Gloria's murder."

Frendell didn't flinch. "Anything's possible. But Kate, you're seeing Wolf's hand in everything." That hinted that I, too, had become paranoid, like good old Tucker.

We each paid our separate bills, put on our coats, and made our way toward the exit. When I paused to zip up my ski jacket he waited at the exit door for me.

I held out my hand. "Well, thank you for being so professional. I'm sure the Carl Wolf case is in good hands.

There was an awkward moment between us, with my hand sticking out toward him, before he reached out and shook mine.

That's when it happened.

Sometimes when I examine a new animal patient, I get a funny feeling—a feeling of danger. The first time it happened to me, a Great Dane, weighing about one hundred and fifty pounds, lunged at me for no reason and pinned me to a wall.

The second time, a mixed breed dog on a leash unexpectedly jumped up from behind and bit me on the arm.

The touch of his flesh on mine set off a danger signal.

"Let me walk you to your truck," he said, his eyes averted. With more force than necessary, he took hold of my arm. "I don't want you going out there alone."

Just then two chatty couples came through the diner entrance door. I recognized one of them.

"Dr. Kate, so nice to see you. Peaches is doing so much better on that new medication."

Frendell still held my arm.

"That's wonderful." I turned to Frendell with a big smile plastered on my face. "You know, I think I'm going to go back inside and order some takeout for my dinner tomorrow. Thanks for sharing your table. Have a great night."

My client overheard and said, "Please join us while you wait. If you don't mind, I have a few questions about my other cat."

I turned away from Frendell and started to move along with her group, listening politely to a recap of how many hairballs her kitties vomited each month. While the five of us waited at the reception desk for a table, I glanced behind me. In the dim parking lot Frendell's strangely familiar back stalked away.

How old was Frendell? My guess was that he was in his late forties, or early fifties? Wolf's mother-in-law mentioned Carl originally wanted to join the FBI.

What if he did?

I hung around until my takeout order was ready, then made sure to exit with a big noisy group. Lady Luck stayed with me because they too had parked in the last row, near the road. A quick glance inside my truck confirmed no monsters lurking inside.

Better to be paranoid than paranoid and dead.

When I turned into the animal hospital parking lot, I noticed how isolated the entrance to my apartment was, set all the way in the back of the building in the renovated garage. The front entrance of the hospital, on the other hand, was well lit and visible from the road. We had an excellent new alarm system for both buildings that automatically alerted both the police and fire departments, but that wouldn't protect me in the time it took to walk from my truck to the back door.

Gramps made me promise to carry pepper spray with me at all times and tonight was no exception. With nerves on edge after dinner with Agent Frendell, I decided to go in through the front entrance. Slowly I inched the truck smack up against the concrete parking space marker.

The motion-activated lights immediately bathed the entire front of the building and parking lot in a bright clear light.

I removed my keys and the pepper spray from my pocket before I opened the driver's side door. After a deep breath I exited and semi ran to the front door. It only took a few seconds for me to unlock the deadbolt and turn the main lock. Before I knew it I was inside. With practiced skill I threw all the locks and put my code into the alarm panel, arming it again

On silent kitty feet, Mr. Katt ambled up to greet me. That was when I truly felt safe. Mr. Katt dislikes strangers, sometimes dive-bombing them from the tops of cages in the treatment room, nor was he particularly fond of other animals, including Buddy. If this kitty calmly walked our halls, I could be certain that no one else was in the place—personally guaranteed by our 24/7 feline security guard.

To show my appreciation, I opened a can of stinky tuna, his favorite, and fluffed it up in his dish, just the way he likes it. He rewarded me with a deep purr before turning his back and concentrating on the food.

More tired than I'd realized, I turned off the lights and went into my apartment. Buddy greeted me with yips and kisses, happy and relaxed. He would be barking and growling if anyone was hiding in my apartment or outside in the parking lot.

All the alarms were set and functioning—my high tech electronic alarm system, the cat motion detection system, and my default canine bark alert.

Armed with my cell phone, pepper spray in my pocket, and a knife from the kitchen, I predicted an unsettling night.

Safe in the apartment I went back over my conversation with Agent Frendell. I wasn't sure what to make of him. Was I seeing Wolf's hand in everything, like he suggested? Maybe I felt danger emanating from him because he was capable of violence—something to be expected of an FBI agent.

I wasn't sure. In fact, I wasn't sure of anything anymore.

Tucker's anxiety and paranoia seemed to be contagious.

To take my mind off the Big Bad Wolf, I opened my email. Then I realized Irene had never called me back about Gloria's drawings.

I looked at my watch. Ten o'clock, a little late to be calling about her aunt's sketchbooks. Tomorrow would have to do.

Alone again with only my dog for company, I realized this long-distance relationship with Jeremy wasn't working for me. I needed him here tonight. Perhaps I was feeling a little sorry for myself again. During our last conversation, Jeremy had let slip that one of his colleagues at the New Mexico dig was the Italian who'd taught him how to cook—and this colleague's name wasn't Marcello, like I'd been led to believe. No, her name was Marcella. The two of them had been friends for some time. Unfortunately, this scenario sounded horribly familiar, a story direct from the relationship advice column of a women's magazine. Even though Jeremy still talked a good game, I didn't see him hurrying back to be with me.

One of us needed to compromise.

Would it be Jeremy or would it be me?

I'd just gotten comfortable in bed when my cell rang.

"Hi, there," Jeremy said. "Finally back in my apartment. It's been a crazy day."

I almost countered by saying I doubt your day has been more crazy than mine, but instead I asked him to tell me all about it.

"Ken and I got into a huge argument about creating a database to compare cave drawings found in Europe, Asia, Australia, and North America for similarities."

"No kidding," I said as I walked over to the kitchen, opened the refrigerator and poured out a big glass of wine.

As he continued his lengthy story, I lay down on the sofa and finished my drink, thankful for the distraction. I'm sorry to admit that my focus drifted away. The next thing I knew, Jeremy was saying my name.

"What?" I sat up, confused.

"Did you fall asleep while I was talking?" His voice sounded hurt and accusatory.

While I scrambled for an answer, he continued, "That was a snore I heard, wasn't it?"

Shoot. No defense. "Perhaps," I admitted, "I'm a lot more tired than I thought."

"Or maybe I'm not as interesting as I used to be." The hurt voice morphed into an angry one.

"I'm sorry, honey. I've been having some weird dreams and between not getting enough sleep and the FBI interview today, I…"

"The FBI interviewed you? What about?"

Before I could answer he said in an accusatory tone, "You promised you wouldn't get involved in that woman's murder, Kate. What the heck is going on down there? Didn't you learn anything from the last time you did that?"

If I wasn't sure he was mad before, his words removed all doubt from my mind.

"Honey, calm down." I tried to appease him. "They showed up because of that writer, Tucker Weinstein's interview. Remember? Tucker said I was an expert in the human/animal bond and I was helping him with his book. I sent you a copy of it."

That appeased him a little. "So, they interviewed you because of that article."

"Exactly. An agent came to the office, asked me a few questions and left." Except it wasn't—and he didn't—but I knew I had to stop before another argument erupted.

"Well." He cleared his throat, obviously back-pedaling. "I guess I didn't have to go on and on about all the petroglyphs and pictographs and artwork we need to organize and catalogue."

"It's fascinating, honey," I told him honestly, "and probably ten times more fascinating delivered in person."

"Ahhh, so that's how it is. I'm boring over the phone."

We both laughed and proceeded to have a peaceful conversation about nothing at all.

After we said goodnight I found myself wide awake. There were two important men in my life, Gramps and Jeremy, and both expressed concern about me, for good reason. For some reason I deliberately kept both of them in the dark. Why didn't I confess my growing paranoia?

Maybe I didn't tell them because I knew it sounded crazy.

I was beginning to understand how Tucker felt, as each little suspicion appeared and piled up, one on top of the next, until it became a huge jagged tower looming in front of you. Who would I suspect of being Carl Wolf next?

Using the same lopsided logic I decided to make it three guys in a row. Now it was Luke's turn to tell me to keep my nose out of it.

To my surprise, he didn't.

Chapter Twenty-one

"What's it like to talk to the FBI? I can't even imagine."

It was the following morning and Cindy had been pestering me with questions about Agent Frendell since she spotted me pouring my first coffee.

"I don't think I should talk about it." I'd been trying to go over the day's appointment schedule with her but she kept changing the subject.

"Oh, please. Like there's such a thing as a secret anymore."

"There is if someone's life is at stake." When she looked up in astonishment at me I realized that came out way more dramatic than I intended. The truth wasn't dramatic at all. Besides, the FBI was in contact with the local police and Cindy's brother-in-law happened to be Oak Falls Chief of Police. She'd find out everything sooner or later from her sister. She always did.

My receptionist turned her monitor toward me so I could see the appointment list. With uncharacteristically clipped diction she unemotionally went over my callback list, pending lab tests to address and gave me a giant list of tasks to do that she usually allocated to various staff members. Like ordering more toilet paper for the client bathroom.

I knew defeat when I smelled it.

Time to tell all.

Fifteen minutes later Cindy raised an eyebrow and said, "That's the craziest story I've ever heard. You think some serial killer is hiding out here in Oak Falls? Don't you think we'd notice a crazy stranger lurking around the village? Maybe this is wishful thinking on your part. You know I consider you a friend and a wonderful person and veterinarian…"

That pause set the stage for the rest of the sentence.

"Of course you've been sick with the flu, with nothing else to do, but you really need to stop poking around Gloria's murder and begin concentrating on your own life. Especially your personal life."

I'm not sure when this started to happen, but all my friends and some acquaintances had no qualms about giving me suggestions on how to live my life. I think they considered me some clueless blonde in a lifeboat adrift in the Dating Sea. Everyone meant well but drifting sometimes took you to unexpected places. At least that's what I hoped.

"Did you tell Jeremy about being interviewed by the FBI?"

Her eyes bore into me. "Sort of."

"Hummmph."

Cindy didn't need words to convey her opinion. She kept going. "What did you think of that FBI guy?"

"Agent Frendell?" If Cindy was going to continue to interrogate me she was going to have to work for it. "What did *you* think of him?" I countered.

"He was a bit scary."

"Oh," I agreed, "you have no idea."

Finally finished with the schedule and being grilled on both sides over Cindy's fire I made a beeline for the storage room. With a perverse pleasure I hauled bags of cat litter out to the truck, happy to concentrate on the physically challenging task. There's no room for idle thoughts when you have to be careful not to tear those bags and free the messy litter to dribble out. Scooping thirty bags of litter, each weighing twenty pounds, from the Ford's floor carpet would be a daunting task.

To avoid dealing with any dust or smell, I wrapped the whole wall of litter I'd created in plastic, then covered it with a canvas painting tarp.

An additional three hundred pounds behind the driver's seat could almost guarantee we wouldn't get stuck on the ice anytime soon.

The added weight slowed the truck down a bit, but it felt nice and solid over the packed-snow driveway of Sun Meadow Farm, our last house call of the day. One of the snow-burdened trees that lined our way had bent ominously across the road. Its branches scratched across the roof of the truck. In my imagination I could almost hear that loud crack before it snapped. Sunset was approaching fast. Since we'd last been there the twins had plunked some reflectors down into the snow alongside the driveway to keep vehicles from straying off the road into the ditches on either side.

I was glad this was a quick pregnancy check.

"They said they'd put up a big sign for us in the barn," Mari explained, "in case they aren't back in time."

"Okay. Let's make this quick."

Their main barn was as nice a barn as I'd seen, with the sheep in one big pen and the goats in another. A smaller pen, obviously new, with shiny metal bars, contained only their ornery goat, Billy. Technology had invaded animal husbandry too. Every animal sported an electronic tag around its neck programmed to open the doors to the outdoor fields. Outside, the women had added additional metal fencing, wisely not trusting the picturesque stacked stone walls to keep jumping goats from escaping. Exceptional owners, the twins spared no expense for the safety and well-being of their animals.

The warm farm smell of hay and animals always made me nostalgic for my student days. I'd spent many a morning in the cow barns, milking and mucking out to earn a little extra money in school.

"I see her." Mari pointed over to the shearing station, where a brown speckled goat stood chewing away at a pile of hay. Her downward hanging ears identified her as a Nubian, like Billy, a premier breed of dairy goat that produced very rich milk and plenty of it.

We set up our portable ultrasound machine and went to work. The twins said this female was bloated, her abdomen much larger than the other pregnant does. As new goat owners, they worried she had a tumor, because she wasn't that fond of old Billy either, not letting him get too close in the outside mating pen. They were positive he hadn't been able to romance this doe.

The plump young goat placidly chewed away, her horizontal pupils staring at me. It only took a few passes of the ultrasound probe for me to confirm it—old Billy must have done something right, because this little lady was pregnant with triplets.

"That's why she's so big," I told Mari as we were packing up. "Billy is batting one hundred percent. Why don't you text them the good news?"

Thanks to modern technology our clients could be quickly updated about their animal's health.

"Shoot," Mari said. She squinted at her phone. "I've got one bar that keeps popping up then disappearing."

"Don't worry about it. We'll do it later." With the portable ultrasound machine safely packed up, we headed out of the barn, passing by a small storage shed, the door slightly ajar. A big shiny lock hung open only on one side of the metal hasp. I peeked in to make sure no animals were inside before closing the door. If a sheep or goat got loose, they'd gorge themselves on all the grain and supplements stored on the shelves and that could prove disastrous.

"This needs to be closed," I told Mari.

"Last time we were here the lock was on but not completely shut. I wondered if they did it on purpose."

"Glad you noticed." I secured the door, latching it properly but not locking it, before continuing out the barn entrance. Mari held the ultrasound case while I lifted and slid the big wood plank they used to secure the double doors into the metal stays. Definitely goat-proofed.

Our day had dragged on later than we'd thought. Sure enough, by the time we inched down the driveway the nearby trees were silhouetted in the pinkish rays of the fading sunset.

Next to me in the passenger seat Mari was still fussing about her phone. In the dim light I followed my fresh tire tracks, carefully using the reflectors that marked the way. Once again the low-hanging branches sounded like fingernails scratching the roof. It wasn't until we were on the main road and stopped at a red light that we finally got cellular service.

With my bright lights bathing both sides of the road, I slowly drove back to the office, wary of deer, elk, raccoon, or whatever else felt like running across the road. It was all I could do to concentrate, since my thoughts kept circling back to Agent Frendell, the FBI, and how the local police were dealing with the Feds showing up.

Cindy could be counted on to know the latest news, but she may have already left the office.

"Alright, so I've texted the twins about the pregnancy, and shutting their storage closet. Anything else to add?"

"Don't think so. If they have any questions, tell them to email me tonight. Make sure they understand that this doe might have some problems. She's young and this is her first pregnancy. Carrying triplets takes a lot out of the mother, so I suggest we recheck her if they notice anything unusual."

Before Mari could finish texting my message, her phone rang.

"Oh, hi. Sorry we weren't able to call sooner but we couldn't get a cell phone signal in the barn or on the driveway." Mari mouthed the words *Jane and Lorraine* and pointed to the phone.

Being able to call out was essential for us on farm house calls. Often the owners were away and simply left us instructions on where the animal patient was. A quick glance to my right showed Mari with her phone to her ear. She made another hand signal indicating one of the twins was chatting away.

I concentrated on the road. We were only ten or fifteen minutes away from the office and the end of a series of long days. Come to think of it, they all seemed long now.

"Is that the only way we can call out?" I heard my assistant say. "Okay, well next time we'll try that. Yes." Another pause. "You have a good night too. Bye now."

Snowflakes started to drift past my windshield, but I didn't care because I could see our Oak Falls Animal Hospital sign shining in the distance.

"So, you're never going to believe this one," Mari said, stowing her phone in her purse.

"Okay, clue me in. Do we have to climb up on the roof to get a signal?"

"Better than that. The best place to make a call in the barn is the bathroom. She said hold your phone to the window over the toilet." Mari started giggling.

"I'll have to remember that for next time," I commented. "Very convenient, I suppose. You can take care of two things at the same time."

• ● ● ● •

With Cindy and Mari gone, I relaxed, amazed I'd been able to hide something from them both. In response to my impromptu text the other night, Luke had suggested we meet over Chinese food at my place.

I'd barely had time to shower and get the goat smell off before Luke arrived at my door, takeout bags in hand.

"I give up," he said as soon as he lined up the takeout containers on the kitchen table, although he smiled when he said it. Those killer crinkles around his eyes were smiling too.

He'd caught me off guard. "What do you mean?" I asked, my

chopstick poised in mid-air. We were doing what we did best together, eating Chinese food. I'd baked the frozen pie from the diner that he'd brought me at Thanksgiving, and left it cooling next to the stove.

"I mean just that. It's useless to tell you not to snoop around this Carl Wolf thing. Instead of telling you not to do it and then you ignoring me, I'm going to go with the flow." To punctuate his statement he picked up his mug and drank the rest of his jasmine tea in one gulp.

"Go with the flow? What are you? Lost in the sixties?" I joked, not sure how to respond to him.

He held up his hand, formed his two fingers into a "V" and said, "Like my Great Aunt Mirabelle used to say, 'Peace'."

We laughed and for the first time in several days I stopped worrying and obsessing over the FBI, Carl Wolf, reporters, and all the other trappings of Gloria's murder. The only thing on my mind was claiming the last shrimp left in the shrimp in black bean sauce.

Buddy, of course, sat directly under Luke, happily waiting for his forbidden under-the-table treats.

Our conversation drifted here and there, touching on the weather, studying for exams, and his family's various do-it-yourself projects that he'd been roped into. We deliberately steered clear of any law-enforcement talk until halfway through the meal.

Luke's "go with the flow" statement made me decide on full disclosure, so between bites I updated him on everything: baseball cap dude in the mall, the mysterious guy at the Schutzhund trials, Jasper Rudin with the German shepherd, my growing paranoia, and reluctantly, FBI Agent Steve Frendell.

He shook his head. "That's a lot of anxiety for you, Kate. What did Gramps say when you told him all this?" A slight frown settled on his forehead.

"I didn't tell him," I answered. "He'd just worry too much."

"Well, what was Jeremy's reaction?"

This time I looked down into my soup while I confessed. "Ah, I didn't tell him either."

"The worry thing again, I suppose?"

"Right," I told the wonton floating in the bowl in front of me.

His voice became a tad playful. "I guess I should take it as a compliment that you don't mind worrying me?"

I looked up, straight into those dark eyes that held a hint of mirth, a bucket-load of pride, and something else. "Yes. It's definitely a compliment."

To cover the awkwardness that sprang up between us after my candid admission, I excused myself to put on more water for tea. Luke busied himself by scooping out the remainder of the fried rice onto his plate, then spearing a piece of chicken and sneaking it under the table to Buddy.

"Hey," I said, "I saw that."

Although he did his best not to show it, Luke had a very pleased look on his face.

I didn't think it was because he fed the dog.

● ● ● ● ●

One hour later that pleased look had vanished, replaced by a different upset face.

"Can you explain why you still want to be involved in this investigation when the FBI is on the scene?"

What happened to the "I give up" speech, and "go with the flow"? We were back to arguing, exactly as if that conversation never happened.

Still in the kitchen an hour later, we sat at the table, the leftovers put away. Remains of fortune cookies and a half-eaten chocolate-pecan pie littered the table. We now both were drinking coffee. Maybe all the caffeine put us on edge.

"Loose ends, Luke. I can't stand loose ends. I need to put my suspicions to rest, regardless of what anyone else is doing."

He cut himself a sliver of pie and ate a forkful. Then with resignation, he said, "Now, Kate, that I can understand."

Revved up on chocolate and caffeine after Luke left, I tied up loose ends from work. Sure enough, a long email from the twins sat waiting in my inbox. Before I answered them I decided to bone up on any new advances in goat husbandry. During vet school I'd spent a summer working with sheep, goats, llamas, and pot-bellied pigs as well as cows and horses when I interned with a large animal vet. I also experienced all kinds of different critters up close and personal through a close college friend who lived near Ithaca, where I went to veterinary school. She and her farmer boyfriend had gone off the grid and raised just about any animal you could think of. They'd also dedicated a portion of their enormous acreage as a rescue center, and I spent many a weekend doing everything from feeding and cleaning to helping one of the local vets do an emergency caesarian on a guinea pig.

However, doing a C-section on a goat with triplets was a whole other ballgame, best left to the twins' large animal veterinarian. I tried not to encourage my small animal clients, who also owned other species of animals, to use me as their large animal vet. Often, I got waylaid by an owner trying to bundle their veterinary services to save money, figuring I was already there, so what the heck? I was always upfront if I felt they needed to consult someone else, or needed a specialist, such as a veterinary ophthalmologist, orthopedic surgeon, or dermatologist. Not everyone realized veterinary medicine had board-certified practitioners, and just like in human medicine, they were uniquely qualified to see complicated cases.

I realized the twins felt a little anxious, since this would be their first year of breeding goats, but luckily, most goat births are very efficient and on time. They already knew quite a bit from years of raising sheep, so I was confident they would be able to handle this multiple birth with a little coaching. If not, they had an excellent support team at their fingertips.

Oddly, after such a long day, with more coffee and chocolate than usual, and a dinner with Luke, I had no problem falling asleep. A strange dream kept interrupting my slumber, startling me awake time after time. In the dream I stood on a huge toilet seat aimlessly waving a toy cell phone with one hand, while balancing a gigantic pie with the other. Below me frolicked three baby goats. Each goat wore a black jacket with the letters FBI flashing red then green, in perfect rhythm to a loud selection of Christmas songs.

Chapter Twenty-two

It wasn't until my lunch break the next day that I realized I still hadn't heard from Irene about the mysterious stranger at her Aunt Gloria's adult daycare. Since I didn't start my afternoon appointments for another twenty minutes, I took a moment to call her again, this time on her cell phone. She answered immediately.

Halfway through my explanation, she stopped me.

"What are you talking about?" Irene asked in a somewhat puzzled way. "What message?"

Now I had an inkling why she didn't return my call.

"I left a message for you several days ago."

A noise of disapproval was followed by a caution to never trust a teenager to listen to your messages.

"So, what were you saying?" Irene sounded distracted, which I was beginning to suspect was normal for her.

I explained everything again, first telling her about the court quick sketch exhibit in the city, then asked, "Did you send someone from your family to pick up Gloria's things from her cubby?"

"Hmmm. You know, I completely forgot about that cubby. Maybe one of her friends took it?" Her answer sounded unconcerned, already moving on.

"Did Gloria have any sons, or grandsons, or nephews that came into town for the funeral?" Although I doubted it, I had to ask.

"No, only the local family and friends were at the memorial service. She didn't have a son, only one daughter, and her two grandsons couldn't attend on such short notice. They're going to try and visit this coming summer. It's been a while since I've seen them…probably five or six years, I suppose."

Trying to loop this conversation back to Gloria's cubby, I hesitated. Irene sounded ready to end our conversation.

"Well, thanks Irene." Then something else occurred to me. "Did you know that Tucker Weinstein is in the hospital?"

"No. Did he have an accident?"

"Not an accident, he got beaten up outside a bar in Brooklyn."

"It's New York City. I'm not surprised."

Irene, like many people in the country, seemed to dismiss violence as part of city life. Then she continued.

"He's a nosy little guy. Maybe he rubbed someone the wrong way with" she searched for the politically correct adjective, "his lifestyle choices." A voice yelled in the background. "Alright, got to go. Thanks for the call."

Before I could respond, she hung up the phone.

Now I knew two new things about Irene, and Gloria wouldn't have been happy with either one of them.

With my appointments wrapped up early I dutifully texted Agent Frendell of this new wrinkle in the Gloria LaGuardia story. Almost immediately my phone rang.

Instead of texting me back, the FBI had decided to call.

"Hello?"

"Are you sure about this?" Steve asked.

"Positive. Also, Gloria's grandsons were in different states when this impersonation took place. Do you need anything more from me?"

"Don't think so. I'll speak to her directly. Is your hospital alarm system on?"

Odd. That question came out of the blue. "Of course it is." For some reason I wasn't surprised he knew where I was. "I also sleep with pepper spray and a vicious dog," I joked.

"Good idea."

He wasn't joking.

"No need to worry." This time his voice sounded calm and relaxed. "That stranger probably was a reporter, or some crime fan collecting memorabilia. We see that quite often."

"Sure." Was he trying to make me feel better by dismissing my fears? My self-preservation instincts kicked into overdrive. The Big Bad Wolf had at least five murders attributed to him and one attempted murder of poor Tucker. At this point I wanted him gone.

"Still, it doesn't hurt to be prudent and careful," he added casually.

Prudent and careful somehow didn't sound like me. I get itchy if I'm not doing something.

"I'm not known for my prudent behavior," I reminded him.

"I'm very aware of that," he answered without a hint of sarcasm.

"By the way, is there another number at the FBI I can call, in case I can't get hold of you?" Or want to talk to someone else, I didn't say.

The audible silence on the other end of the line disturbed me. "This number is the best one," he said. "If I'm unavailable, your message will roll into our communal mailbox."

That relieved me somewhat until he added, "If it concerns Carl Wolf, I'm always available."

I paced around my apartment with so many conflicting thoughts bouncing around my head that I had to get out of the house.

Since it was only four o'clock I wandered into town with the vague idea of going to Judy's Café, but when I passed by the community center I made a hasty detour. Something had been bothering me about Gloria's cubby, but I wasn't exactly sure what. Maybe if I took another look around the place it would shake loose.

When I entered the crafts room, after saying hello to the staff member on duty, I saw Emily Longmire sitting at the long table in front of the cubbies bent over a coloring book.

She looked up and smiled. "You were here the other day. Ahh…"

"I'm Kate, Emily. How are you today?" The picture she was working on featured an intricate floral design, the kind you'd find in a tapestry.

"I'm trying to decide what color to make the main flower." With a slow gesture she pushed the coloring book toward me. Sure enough most of the borders were finished, but the large iris in the center remained white.

"Aren't irises usually lavender, or purple?" I asked.

"They have all kinds of hybrids now," she explained, "but purple has always been my favorite. Thanks for helping me make a decision."

Her fingers separated out several different purples and lavenders from the pencil box before she started coloring again.

The white iris began to take on lovely lavender tones.

"Do you mind if I take a look in your cubby?" I asked her. "I'm still searching for pictures Gloria might have left behind."

"Go right ahead, dear. I think there are some teaching drawings toward the back of one of them."

Emily's cubby held a few sketchbooks, some notecards, and an apple along with various markers and an old glass doorknob. Although I was dying to find out what a doorknob was doing in there I decided to concentrate on my task.

With her drawing books and paperwork piled in front of me, I began searching everything, one page at a time. Meanwhile, Emily continued coloring, humming happily to herself.

The first twenty pages or so of a sketchbook with a bright red cover were filled with drawings of lopsided apples, odd flowers, and some other unidentifiable objects. All were in pencil, with multiple erasure marks, some going right through the paper.

However, then I came across a series of sketches in a style I instantly recognized, with notes printed at the bottom. A lovely still life, depicting apples in a blue china bowl, illuminated one page. Printed at the bottom were pointers on how to shade a round object. Next I discovered illustrations of various flowers, leaves, and seedpods drawn in a confident manner, along with additional drawing tips, again written at the bottom of the page. Gloria must have been giving Emily a short course on how to draw. A little further on, I saw studies of hands, some roughly drawn but others achingly expressive.

When I turned the page, I hit the jackpot.

Gloria had drawn scenes from Halloween night. I recognized the couple in rabbit costumes, the man with his bunny nose leaning against a brick wall having a cigarette. There followed a quick sketch of a baseball player with a question mark under it. Several crowd scenes captured robots, vampires, and one of the town police officers followed by a surprise—a quick sketch of me.

Turning to the next page revealed Irene and her kids, a tiny Cinderella waving a wand and a menacing-looking devil with dark glittering eyes all captured in pen and ink. Gloria's artistic memory for faces and events had remained intact. But did these drawings mean anything?

"Can I borrow this sketchbook?" I asked Emily, still busy with her bearded iris.

It took her a few seconds to focus back to me. "Of course. I'm not drawing that much now that Gloria isn't here. The coloring books are my favorite things to do now." As if to demonstrate she turned to the front of the book and showed off her carefully completed pages.

"They're lovely." By choosing the colors, concentrating on the design and working within the lines, Emily not only enjoyed herself but was having a good cognitive workout.

Seeing I was getting ready to leave, Emily asked, "What time is it, dear?"

I checked my watch. "Almost five o'clock."

"Then I'd better hurry," she told me. "Sylvia will be here soon and I'd like to have this finished by then."

"Say hello to your daughter for me. I'll return these to you as soon as possible," I promised her.

"Take your time, dear. You might learn something from them."

I certainly hoped so. Carefully securing my newfound clues in my backpack, I fired up the truck and drove back home.

• ● ● ● •

I cleared off the coffee table and arranged the sketchbooks in some kind of order, pages marked with Post-it notes. Small details became sharper the longer I stared at them. I was studying the Halloween drawings when Gramps called.

After a quick hello I told him about the cubby and Gloria's artwork.

"That's good thinking, Katie," he said, his voice sounding particularly strong over the phone. "You're giving the FBI a run for their money."

"There's nothing so far but I've got high hopes. Gloria drew a pretty good portrait of me, by the way, only wish she'd signed it." I paged to my picture. The artist had captured something familiar in my face, an expression I recognized from looking in the mirror.

"Take a photo of it and send it to me." Gramps loved getting texts and pictures, now that he'd mastered his phone. "Things are going well on this end too."

"How so?"

"That little guy Tucker is as tough as a nail. You wouldn't think it to look at him. They're predicting he'll be out of rehab in a few weeks if he behaves himself." An element of pride came through in his voice.

"Wonderful. I'll text him congratulations tonight." Lately, I'd been getting all my Tucker news from Gramps, who still saw him every day. With the cover design of his book completed, his publisher was contemplating pushing up the release date. Thanks to several news stories, and multiple Internet postings of sightings of Wolf, they wanted to take advantage of the public interest and any free publicity.

Gramps continued with more surprising news. "I'm going to look for typos in the ARC for him. We're breaking out of rehab tonight and I'm taking him to get some real food."

"What's an ARC?"

"The advanced reader copy. Those are the copies they send to reviewers. Tucker says they're the last opportunity to make changes to the finished book."

"Have fun," I told him, once again aware that my grandfather had a more active and interesting social life than I did.

My eyes slipped to half-closed by nine o'clock, as sleep snuck in. I turned off the television and paged once again through the open sketchbook. One section demonstrated how to sketch eyes. Through sleepy lids I scanned them again. A pair at the bottom of the page struck a distant chord. Why did they feel familiar?

When I glanced at the baseball figure drawing, however, I noticed something I'd missed before. His boots. Instead of sneakers he wore boots. There was something familiar about those too, but what was it?

Have you ever tried to recall something that's right at the edge of your consciousness? The harder you try the further it slips away. After trying to remember for ten minutes straight, I gave up, walked the dog, and went to sleep.

The memory was waiting for me the next morning. At the Shutzhund show I remember Jasper coming over to his wife sitting in the stands. He faced away from Mari and me, but I'd noticed the back of his boot had a wedge-shaped gouge in the rubberized heel. It was barely noticeable, but was it a coincidence that the baseball player Gloria drew in Emily's sketchbook had the same mark on his boots? Between that and their similar body type, I could swear this sketch was of our Good Samaritan Jasper Rudin, Viggie's owner.

I concentrated on what I knew of him. His girlfriend found him controlling. She told us he would "kill her" if anything happened to the dog.

Strike One.

His dog was a purebred German shepherd, Schutzhund-trained and attack-trained, just like Carl Wolf's dog. Even the hand-tooled collar and leash were similar in design.

Strike Two.

The last time I'd seen him at the office his manner had been stiff, impersonal, as if putting on an act for me. Wasn't that what Agent Frendell had said about psychopaths? They pretended to show emotions, but really had no empathy for their fellow humans.

Strike Three.

Could Rudin be Carl Wolf? Did Gloria's drawing unmask a killer?

Who did I trust with this information? For a brief moment I thought of talking it out with Luke, even though he now had no official capacity with the Oak Falls Police Department. Then I thought of calling Chief Bobby Garcia. Drat. As a new father, the chief was unavailable because of paternity leave.

Although my first loyalty was to our local police, I knew I needed to contact the FBI with this new information—contact the same agent I once thought might be the Big Bad Wolf himself.

"Explain it again," Agent Frendell said. We'd been on the phone for fifteen minutes already, as I went over my discovery step by step with him.

"Jasper Rudin fits a lot of Wolf's profile," I explained. "I'm not saying he is Wolf, I'm only suggesting he could be. Remember, Gloria penned a question mark under his picture."

"I understand," he repeated for the fourth or fifth time.

"You might ask him some questions. Maybe get his finger-prints on a glass or recover some DNA from a used tissue."

"Kate. You've been watching too much television." His joke came unexpectedly. "Besides, we only have some partial prints on Wolf and no DNA. He was never in the military, never was arrested or detained on any charges."

That surprised me but I continued with my suspicions. "He and his girlfriend seem to have plenty of money, from the cars they both drive. Wolf worked online, investing in the stock market. Maybe he made a killing, no pun intended."

"If the agent in charge thinks all of this is worth a follow-up, believe me, the Bureau will investigate him."

Charged up by now, I repeated my warning. "I'm not saying he is Carl Wolf."

"I understand."

That second time he'd been impatient. Forget Jasper Rudin. They probably were starting a file on me right this moment in some FBI office. But with my conscience now clear, I backed off. "Okay. You've got the pictures I sent you?" I'd texted photos of the pictures in the sketchbook to his phone.

"Right."

"Any questions?"

"No."

"Well…then, good luck." Was it dumb to wish the FBI good luck?

"Good night, Kate. Remarkable work, by the way. I'm quite impressed once again."

"Thanks."

I didn't think he'd be quite so impressed if he knew I still had a tiny suspicion that he was Carl Wolf. And if that was the case, I'd just played right into his dirty hands.

Chapter Twenty-three

If I expected something momentous to happen overnight in the Carl Wolf investigation because of my conversation with Agent Frendell, I was wrong. Since Cindy had a direct line to the police department via her brother-in-law, I pumped her for information first thing the next day.

"Nothing yet," she informed me. "Oh, that new client with the six puppies canceled and rescheduled for later in the week, so you have two hours until your next appointment. Why don't you get out of here? Get your mind off things." Her meaning was icy clear.

Of course I immediately wanted to run down to the police station, but sanity prevailed and instead I decided to return Emily's sketchbook. I'd already stored pictures of every page in my phone and sent copies to the FBI.

The drive into town was short and peaceful, little traffic and a piece of blue sky played peek-a-boo above.

This time I parked in the back parking lot and walked through the side entrance, hoping to be in and out quickly. In a hurry I turned a corner and stopped short. I was in a medium-sized room with multiple computer stations, not the crafts room. Veronica had mentioned they taught computer skills to seniors and in conjunction with the library offered Internet services to residents who couldn't afford service at home. Somehow, I must have gotten turned around.

There was only one person in the room, but he didn't look like he needed help with his computer skills. Agile fingers flew across the keyboard, but stopped as soon as he saw me standing in the doorway. After a suspicious look my way, he closed out the window he'd been working on, closed the window of the computer next to him and started to leave.

"Excuse me," I said. "Do you work here? I'm looking for the crafts room."

His face folded into what I assumed was his smiley face. It was hard to tell with the carefully trimmed reddish-brown beard and mustache covering his upper lip. Did every man in the Hudson Valley wear a beard?

"That's the next room on the right."

Something about this situation felt odd. Had I caught him on some naughty website? Why work on two computers at the same time? And he hadn't answered my question. About six feet tall, well-built and muscular, with dark eyes, he didn't strike me as a stereotypically pale, socially awkward geek.

"Are you tech support for the community center computers?" I persisted.

"Yes." Obviously he was dying to get away from me, and my questions.

"Do you have a business card? I've got a friend who needs help with her laptop," I lied. "It's so hard to find anyone local to do that kind of work." With an effort I smiled at him, trying to put him more at ease, or less on guard. There was something about this guy—an edge—that bothered me. Above the Van Dyke beard his dark hair was streaked with gray. Was he older than I originally thought? Fine lines around his eyes put him maybe in his late thirties or early forties.

Carl Wolf's profile popped into my mind. Just as quickly, I dismissed it. I had started to think every big guy over forty might be the Big Bad Wolf. Still, his suspicious behavior made me curious.

He looked quickly around the room, as though making sure all the screens were showing the community center screensaver before he answered. "Sorry, I'm pretty booked up right now. My customers are exclusively local business and Internet subscribers."

Halfway out the door, I again asked for a business card.

"Out of them."

Before I knew it he'd gone around the corner. Odd guy. I made a note to ask someone at the center for a little more information about him.

With Emily's sketchbook back in place in her cubby I headed for the parking lot when I remembered that IT guy working the computer room. One of the student volunteers walked past me so I stopped and asked her.

"We have a service, I know, that comes and takes care of our systems," she answered vaguely. "My supervisor has their number. Are you looking for computer support for yourself?"

"Yes." Another lie.

"Well, let me find out. She's around here somewhere. Oh, there she is." With a quick gesture she signaled to a very tall women with streaky white and gray hair, who quickly changed direction and began walking toward us. Dressed in a long skirt and a hand-knit sweater, she resembled an old hippie.

"Helga, do you have the name of our computer guys? This lady is interested."

When Helga turned to answer me any resemblance to a laid-back hippie evaporated. She radiated efficiency.

"Dr. Turner, nice to see you."

I racked my brain but knew I hadn't met her before. "This center is very impressive," I began. "You provide some great resources here."

"Yes," she glanced around with pride. "For a small town we do very well, I believe. Welcome to Oak Falls, by the way." Her laser focus came right back to me. "Now, what's this about computers?"

"Oh, I just met one of your computer technicians and I…"

"Excuse me," she interrupted. "What did you say?"

A bewildered look had replaced the confident stare.

"Your technician…" This time I didn't even get the rest of the sentence out.

"What technician? We have no one working on the computers today. You must have met one of our resident users." Confidence once again reigned supreme.

Arguing with her would be useless, I guessed. "Perhaps so. But if you don't mind, can I have the name of your computer services company?"

"Of course," she answered. "It's very easy. Catskill Computer Support. Just Google their website." Helga held out her hand and we shook in a business-like manner, now that everything was right with her world.

"Helga," I tried again. "You might mention this to your tech support, just to be safe. The impression he gave me was that he worked here. Reddish beard. Nice looking, dark hair streaked with gray, in his forties, I would estimate."

This time something clicked. "He said he worked here?"

"Yes, he did."

"Sage advice. Better to be safe than you-know-what."

The volunteer standing next to us giggled. "Tall dark and handsome. Maybe I should go and look for him."

"He's much too old for you," snapped Helga, appearing slightly annoyed at the suggestion. After the reprimand to the student, she focused her attention back to me. "Please, Dr. Kate, come back any time."

With a nod to both of us she strode off, secure that I had made a mistake.

But there was no mistake.

A man had been inputting something into one of their computers. Was it an innocent Internet search or something not so innocent?

I hoped they hadn't been hacked.

• • ● • •

When I arrived back at the office I asked Cindy about freelance computer people working in the valley.

"Can't really think of anyone offhand," she said. "There used to be four or five retired IBM employees who did local advertisements, but I haven't seen their ads recently. I know some of them moved down to Florida.

Looking out at the snow piled up on the edges of our parking lot I understood why.

"How familiar with the community center are you?" I asked her.

"Not very," she admitted, "but my friend Delia works there part-time. Why?"

"Just curious."

There was a nasty sound from her. "You're never just curious. What's up?"

It was hard to fool Cindy or get much past her. "There was a man on the computers at the center who didn't look like he belonged there." I wasn't exactly sure how to describe it. "When I asked him some questions he took off."

"Did you tell Helga the Hun?"

"Yes."

"Well," she suggested, "maybe you scared him off. You can be a bit intimidating when you want to be."

"Intimidating?" I suppose my barrage of questions might have been off-putting.

"Some of our local guys spend too much time in the woods," she joked. "Those are the ones who live with their mothers until they're in their late forties or fifties. Never date or marry. Then once mommy dies they begin to hoard stuff and it's downhill from there."

"Got it."

We discussed my schedule and I gave her a message for one of my clients. On the way to the treatment area I went over my encounter with the unknown computer dude. He didn't look like a lost mommy's boy.

He looked like he knew exactly what he was doing.

But he looked way too young to be Carl Wolf. At least I hoped so.

I'd hate to think I met the Big Bad Wolf and didn't recognize him.

With another plea to Cindy to keep me posted if anything happened regarding the Wolf investigation, I checked in with my first appointment. Just after lunch Mari took me aside and told me the FBI had brought all the members of the New Paltz Schutzhund club down to the police station for interviews. Cindy had hinted to her that the man they were most interested in was one of our clients.

I acted surprised. "Who is it?"

"Viggie's owner. Jasper Rudin. I can't believe it."

"Just because they're interviewing someone doesn't mean he's going to be arrested or anything." For some reason, I felt it was important for me to make a disclaimer. I had started to feel guilty bringing our Good Samaritan to Agent Frendell's attention.

"Why don't you ask that FBI guy what's going on?" Mari said, her head in the fridge.

"I've got work to do," I reminded her.

"Right," she said, pulling out some vaccines and placing them in our portable cooler. "Before I leave I'll restock the truck for you."

"Thanks. Have fun at the doctor's office." Even though she worked at an animal hospital, Mari loathed going to the doctor. She had forced herself to make an appointment for this afternoon because this particular physical was about a year and a half overdue.

"One of my Facebook friends said I should meditate in the waiting room."

"You posted your OB-GYN appointment on Facebook?" I said with astonishment.

"Sure."

Cindy and Mari were frequently on all the social media sites, but I'd never really got in the habit. The big reason, I think, was a desperate attempt to keep my personal life from melting into my professional one. I felt an intense need to protect my privacy, what little I had left.

Ready to leave I walked into the reception area only to see a familiar back leaning over the counter.

"Hi, Amos," I said while quickly walking to the other side of the reception desk. "What brings you here?"

The printer started up at that moment and Cindy slid her desk chair toward it. "Just in the nick of time. Can you sign these rabies and health certificates for me?" She picked the copies out of the printer and placed them on the desk.

"Sure. Are these for your Labrador?"

"That's right." Amos leaned over and asked us both, "Anything else we need to travel with the dogs?"

Cindy explained. "Amos and Lydia are spending the rest of the winter in Florida. How long do you two lucky folks plan to stay this time?"

"That's up to the little lady. She tells me where and when— and I follow along." He took the pages Cindy handed him and stared for a moment, unsure of what to do.

"Let me get you an envelope for those." Our stationary had the office name and address, and made everything much more professional. "Wait, I'll put one of our cards inside, too. Do you have paperwork for your Doberman?" I didn't recall ever examining the dog or giving it any vaccines.

"Yep," he assured us, his eyes wide behind the bifocals. "Lydia's got all that stuff they gave us at the shelter. She usually handles all this, but she had a quick errand to run." He looked out into the parking lot searching for their vehicle.

"Perfect. Well, have a good trip."

"Thanks Doc, Cindy. Don't you gals work too hard now."

Amos moved over to one of our white plastic chairs where he'd created a colorful pile from his coat, gloves, and hat.

"That reminds me." I turned back to Cindy. "How many house calls do I have this afternoon?"

"Only two. Should be short day for you, although Jane and Lorraine asked if you might stop by their place for a sec on the way back. The goat expecting triplets has them worried. They said it's in their email and you'd know what they mean."

"Actually, I do. Did Mari leave yet?"

"You just missed her," Cindy told me.

Staccato honks from the parking lot interrupted our conversation. Amos jumped up like someone had lit a fire under the seat.

"Shoot, that's Lydia. I better get hopping." He put his winter gear on as fast as he could, but dropped first one, then the other, glove on the floor before scurrying out the door.

"Old Lydia is a rip. How she found someone to marry her, I'll never know," Cindy said as she sent an electronic copy of the health certificates to Sam the Labrador's file. "No one believed it when she got hitched last year. Amos is way too nice for her."

I checked my pocket for my stethoscope. "I've given up trying to figure out why some couples get together. The two of them seem pretty devoted, though, in an argumentative sort of way."

My receptionist agreed. "Guess so. Sometimes love is blind, and deaf and, well you know."

"Boy, do I ever," was my final comment on the subject.

While tucking my pants inside my boots before getting in the truck, I decided to call Jeremy. To my surprise he answered on the second ring.

"Hi, honey. You must be a mind reader," he said.

"Why do you say that?" My finger stuck inside the back left boot as I tried to talk with the phone jammed between my shoulder and my cheek.

"Well, I've got a few days free and thought I'd come and visit you. Maybe do some skiing or snowboarding?"

Now that Jeremy had acclimated back to winter conditions from the African heat, he'd begun to embrace the cold weather sports we used to do all the time.

"That might be fun. Honestly, I can't remember the last time I went skiing." Did I even have any of my ski clothes left in my closet?

"How did that whole Carl Wolf thing turn out?" After our last conversation he'd made a point of steering clear of the subject. Since his question came out of the blue I wondered if he'd seen all the chatter of sightings of the killer on the Internet. Jeremy seemed to run hot and cold about my involvement in the Gloria/Tucker/Wolf story. Sometimes he pumped me for details and at other times, all I heard was criticism.

"The police and FBI have a person of interest, but that's all I know." No way did I want to admit I guided Agent Frendell to the suspect. Better to lay low right now. Once Wolf was caught and identified, the media focus would be off the charts and I hoped I wasn't swept up in it.

"You're keeping out of it, right?" His voice took on a concerned tone.

"Of course," I lied, wondering what sort of couple we'd become.

It felt odd driving to house calls without Mari chattering away in the truck, but at least this was a relatively short day.

Back in the truck after finishing my two brief house calls I kept thinking about my encounter with the computer dude at the community center. Should I call someone or leave it up to the supervisor to investigate further? No crime had been committed so why call the police or the FBI? I'd been bothering Gramps about every little thing to the point where I was embarrassed to mention yet another "premonition." Tucker didn't need any more stress and Jeremy assumed I'd let go of my odd amateur sleuthing hobby. That left Luke.

We'd argued the last time we met, so what did I have to lose? What was the worst thing that might happen? More arguing?

I texted him to call me and turned the truck toward home. It felt strange to be finished so early, but I wasn't going to complain about it. A few minutes later, while stopped at the gas station I heard my text chime sound.

Can u come 2 my place?

His place?

The whole time I've known Luke, I'd never been to his home, in fact, I had no idea where he lived or who lived with him. Come to think of it, there were plenty of things I didn't know about my elusive friend. Curious, I told him no problem, and asked for his address. After all, he'd been to my place a million times. Tonight I got to experience his messy old apartment.

Not wanting to drive back home and then get in the truck again, I decided to go in my scrubs, as is. With the directions securely entered into my GPS, I followed along, his place situated in a more remote area than I'd expected. Most of the travel took place on the main road, before veering onto side streets, past the homes of many of my house call clients. In the daylight and with clear roads, it didn't take more than twenty minutes for me to spot the turn-off to a long driveway, thanks to my bossy GPS voice. Not quite sure where the heck I was, I pulled up to a modern A-frame home tucked into the woods, invisible from the road. White bark glistened in the fading light as I noted a stunning grove of white birch that circled the house, standing tall in the clearing. The metal roof was free of any snow, and was a surprising clear blue color—like the sky on a sunny day.

The sound of my tires alerted him. He opened the front door and walked out onto the huge front deck. Dressed in worn jeans and a green flannel shirt, Luke and the house looked like they belonged together.

"Mind the steps," he said. "I sanded and salted but there can be some slippery spots."

The curved wooden stairs made a graceful pathway to the wide deck and front door. Pale gray planks blended with the woods directly behind us. I bent down to touch it.

"These are resin planks, aren't they?" I asked.

He nodded, seemingly pleased that I noticed. "Very little maintenance and made from recycled materials. Glad I made that decision when I built the place."

His words made me spin around. "You built this house? By yourself?"

"With a little help from my friends."

He told me the story during our walk inside. "My grandfather deeded land parcels to all the kids and grandkids before he died. If you were old enough, you could pick out where you wanted to build, so I chose Silver Hollow Drive. I loved the birch trees and looking out at the mountain."

Presence of mind made me stop before I blurted out *what mountain?* The road had curved and dipped into such a heavily forested area I'd lost track of exactly where I was. Sure enough, when I looked through the towering wall of glass in his living room, I saw a craggy mountain, outlined in red and gold by the fading sunset. No other homes were in sight.

"Have a seat." He gestured to one of the two tobacco-colored leather sofas arranged in an L shape in front of the fieldstone fireplace.

Now I was embarrassed. All this time he'd been coming over to my place, with the old saggy sofa, messy kitchen, and Formica kitchen table he'd gone home to this?

Girlfriend Dina must have helped decorate, I realized, my heart sinking for some reason I preferred not to think about.

"Want something to drink?" Luke didn't seem to notice my stunned state.

"Sure. Water or juice or something." My vague answer reflected my astonishment. His home looked like something out of a magazine.

Finally, he noticed my confusion. "How do you like the place?"

A mischievous smile seemed to anticipate my response. "Luke," I searched for an appropriate answer then blurted out, "It's spectacular. Gorgeous. I didn't realize you were," again I struggled for the words, "such a decorator."

"Me? I didn't do this," he laughed.

"Well, Dina…"

"She hated this place. Too isolated for her. When we were together, we lived in her apartment in Kingston near the hospital. All modern stuff."

"Then who…?"

"My cousin, Bella."

Another cousin? Luke had cousins coming out of the woodwork.

He continued his explanation. "Right after I built it I moved in with Dina at her apartment so I never did anything but camp out here sometimes, especially when we fought. Bella came up one weekend with her husband from the city and asked if she could stay with me, instead of at her sister's place, which is full of kids and dogs and cats. I said sure, but when she walked in the door and saw my stuff, she almost had a heart attack."

By now I'd settled on the sofa and Luke had started a fire for us. "Why's that?"

"She's an interior decorator in the city, does magazine work and set design. Her husband was a stockbroker. Very well off, no kids, the sophisticated members of the Gianetti family."

"Why didn't they just buy their own house?" My ginger ale didn't taste as satisfying as a glass of wine, but I needed to keep a clear head.

"They were trying to decide between a country place here in Oak Falls, or go for the Hamptons and the beach. Bella decided to do a trial run, so to speak. And when Bella decides to do something, it's best to jump out of her way. Bossy women run in our family."

Luke took a sip of coffee from his mug. Books, a pile of notes and a second coffee cup were stacked across his dining room table. I'd most likely interrupted his studying.

"So your cousin decorated the house?"

"Yep. I gave her a key, told them they could come up anytime they wanted. Bella would text me the night before and I'd make sure it was ready for them. I'd put a few bottles of white wine in the fridge, lay fresh bread and her favorite cheeses on the counter, make sure the driveway was clear and the lights turned on. She repaid me by furnishing the whole place."

I wished someone would do that for me. "Well, she did a fabulous job."

"Actually it worked out great for her, too." He got up and poked the fire. Sparks showered up then floated down like tiny red stars. "A photographer friend used the place for a photo shoot. Then it wound up being featured in one of those home magazines, and several people called her with job offers."

"So did they buy another home here?"

He sat back down on the soft rich leather. Bronze nail heads reflected the light of the fire. "Nope. They got divorced. Bella met a Hollywood actor on some location shoot, got remarried, and they moved out to California."

That beat anything I'd imagined.

"So the furnishings are…"

"…all mine." His arms made an expansive gesture. "And I've got a standing invite to visit her in sunny Los Angeles anytime I want."

I shook my head in astonishment. "How many cousins do you have, Luke?"

He thought for a moment. "About thirty or so first cousins, I think. I'm a little foggy on the rest."

A huge Italian family—a real family that kept in touch with each other, helped each other. Something I'd never experience.

"So, what did you want to talk to me about?"

The tables had flipped. He sat comfortably on his expensive

sofa and I was the visitor. The only thing missing was Chinese food. With the fire burning, sitting together in this remarkable, comfortable living room, the still woods outside, Carl Wolf seemed a million miles away.

Luke crossed his leg, work boot resting on his opposite knee, an expectant look on his face.

My turn to spoil the party once again.

He listened without interrupting, although my account of the last few days and the parade of Carl Wolf look-alikes came out a bit disjointed.

"I agree with you about the computer guy," he began. "But Helga will look into that, I'm sure. Maybe I'll give her a call and tell her to keep me in the loop, unofficially of course."

I'd ceased being surprised that everyone seemed to know each other in Oak Falls.

"What I don't like," he continued, his relaxed pose gone, "is your feeling of being followed. Believe me, I don't argue with female intuition. I've been surrounded by it all my life."

Luke wasn't kidding. For several years he'd been the only boy in the family. His girl cousins and sisters treated him like their own personal Ken doll.

"Would the FBI have any reason to follow me?"

"Not that I can think off. But I doubt we'd get a straight answer from them if we asked. From what I hear, they're investigating someone right now."

Jasper Rudin. For a panicked moment I worried they might include me in their investigations for some unknown reason and told Luke. After he finished laughing he gave his take on that.

"If the Bureau was following you, I would think it's because you intersected with an existing investigation. Unless you're hiding a wicked past from me."

The playful manner of his voice reassured me. "No secret life here," I confessed.

"Not true," he countered. "You are Kate Turner, veterinarian by day and secret sleuth by night."

That struck me as funny. "You have a point, but I'm missing the magic outfit." I jumped up and twirled around like the famous woman superhero.

Luke laughed, flipped on his phone and took a picture of me twirling around.

"I know. My stethoscope could shoot laser beams." Although a little dizzy I was starting to get into this. "What do you think I would turn into?"

"Some kind of animal, I suppose," he answered. "But all the good ones are taken."

My head spinning I crash-landed on the sofa next to him. "True. Maybe I'd end up being Badger Woman, you know, always digging up the dirt."

He reached over and took my hand. "You're much too pretty for that."

This compliment felt different. A warm feeling radiated between us. His shoulders started to lean perilously close when my phone rang.

"Hello."

The moment broken, he stood up and brought our empty glasses into the kitchen.

"Hi, honey, bad time?" Jeremy sounded happy. I figured Luke could hear him even across the room.

"Ah," I stared at Luke's back. "Hi, Jeremy. No, it's fine. What's up?"

"Well, you sound enthusiastic," he said with a touch of petulance in his voice. "I wanted to solidify those plans with you. Maybe rent a ski chalet for a few nights, not that I don't like your place. I'd prefer to have you all to myself for a change."

The petulance had turned into seduction, a little too fast for my liking. "That's wonderful. Listen, can you text me the dates? I want to clear my schedule a little and I don't have anything to write with."

"Sure."

"I'll call you later. I'm about to get back in the truck and head home."

"No problem, sweetie. Drive safe. Talk to you later."

"Later."

Although he made kissy noises at me I didn't make them back. After I hung up, I went to get my coat.

"Party over?" Luke had rinsed off the glasses and dishes from the dining room table and was loading them in the dishwasher.

"Party over."

I joined him, once again impressed. Bella had gone to town in the kitchen, with high-end stainless steel appliances, custom tile work—everything needed for that designer cabin look so popular in glossy magazines. Somehow, she'd suggested a warmth and coziness. Maybe next time we could have Chinese at his place.

Then my real life and Jeremy snapped firmly back into focus. To put us on a different track I asked Luke, "What should I do if I think I'm being followed again?"

He promptly answered. "Let me go over some strategies with you, although you probably know most of them. Try and take a picture of him. That way the FBI can run the photo through their systems and pull out details in the photo we can't even imagine."

"Good point."

"Get a small mirror, compact size, and carry it in a pocket, or someplace you can get to it easily. That way you can check behind you in an unobtrusive way."

This sounded like cloak-and-dagger stuff, but I gave him my full attention.

Luke then shared with me the short version of what to do in surveillance and counter-surveillance that he'd been taught. Some of the self-defense techniques I knew, but it served as a refresher course.

"If we're dealing with Wolf, his pattern is very specific. He'll wait until you're alone to move. This guy doesn't bump into you on the street and stab you, or drive by and shoot you. In a way he's sneaky, so be careful. Isolation is not your friend."

That last sentence triggered my sarcastic response. "I live by myself, you know."

"I'm very aware of that, Kate." We were standing by the front door by then. "Keep your pepper spray handy at all times, and if Buddy starts barking for no reason call 911 and then text me. Remember, you've got a very sophisticated alarm system now. No one can just clip a wire and disable that alarm."

"Thanks to you." Luke had insisted on upgrading our hospital system after my last run-in with a cold case murder.

"You're very welcome."

"But I'm not going to stop working, or living my life." For some reason I'd started to get irritated, thinking of how much of my time I'd invested in the study of Carl Wolf.

"Not asking you to." He helped me on with my coat. "Just promise me you'll be careful."

"I promise."

"Meanwhile I'll try to track down the computer guy, or at least give the chief a heads-up. I wonder if they have a surveillance camera in their parking lot?"

"No idea."

We walked together across the expansive deck, mostly free of snow. The moon and stars shone above the silhouetted mountain, the vast forest rising across the road. Behind us white tree trunks glowed silvery in the moonlight. The tangy scent of pine mixed with the fragrant wood smoke rising from his chimney.

"What a beautiful setting," I said to him. "You are so fortunate to live here." My hand rested on the deck railing. "I can hear my heart beating in this stillness."

It happened so quickly I didn't realize for a moment that I was in his arms.

Luke's kiss felt soft and gentle on my lips, gone so quickly I thought I'd imagined it. But the look in his eyes was no dream.

"I...I have to go," I said, thrown off balance, wanting to stay but needing to leave. My car keys jingled in my pocket when I pulled them out and clicked the opener.

Inside the familiar confines of the truck, I glanced in the truck's rearview mirror, my foot gently resting on the gas pedal. Luke stood motionless on the deck, backlit by the cabin's light, as still as the unforgiving mountain ahead of me.

I can't say that I remember driving down his driveway that night. My brain had shut down, emotions taking over. Confused and surprised, I hadn't been ready for a kiss I'd thought might never happen. Jeremy was my focus, supposed to be my soulmate. I'd known him for years. He was funny, dedicated to his work and, let's face it, if we married, rich enough to ensure a type of life I'd never dreamed about. On paper, the perfect catch.

Luke, on the other hand, had been on and off with his girl-friend Dina since the day we'd met. A brief kiss didn't change that. With Dina moving back to town, who knew what would happen between them?

I didn't want my heart to be broken again.

It must have been five minutes later, as I slowly navigated the curves in the pitch blackness, that I noticed headlights behind me. Usually people were courteous on these roads at night, backing off a bit not to blind you with their high beams.

Not this driver.

There were no turn-offs on this unlit country road to get out of his way. Snow remained piled up on either side of the road, obliterating any shoulder. The only signs of civilization were the mailboxes at the end of the driveways as I slowly drove past.

A side gust of wind shook the truck.

Well, they'd just have to wait if they were in a hurry, I decided.

My mind drifted back to my personal dilemma until the truck behind me flashed his lights. Where could I go? If he wanted to pass, he'd have to go around, because I certainly wasn't pulling over to the shoulder. There was no shoulder on this road.

Suddenly acutely aware of the darkness all around my imagination kicked in. Was the Big Bad Wolf making his move?

With both hands firmly on the steering wheel, I sped up,

thankful for the new winter tires and heavy double grill welded to the front and back of the hospital truck.

The headlights behind me dropped back. It looked like he was slowing down, about to make a turn. Maybe this was a local, impatient to get home with his takeout pizza while it was still hot.

Sure enough, he'd put his turn signal on leaving me alone once again on the rural road.

As the mailboxes slid past, my high beams illuminated a familiar shape. Day-glow yellow paint outlined a sun, the trademark of my twin clients at Sun Meadow Farm.

Hadn't Cindy asked me to stop in on them? On an impulse I made a quick turn into their driveway, barely slowing down, the truck fishtailing past a dead tree leaning precariously close, bent down by the weight of the snow. My back tires slid out but the front dug into the gravel under the surface and held. The same dead branch as before scratched the truck's roof. Pointed in the right direction I slowed down and drove toward the house. No lights were visible on the road behind me. The twins had once boasted to me that they both owned shotguns and had no problem using them.

Unwelcome visitors to Sun Meadow Farm were greeted with a nasty double surprise.

With a roar the old Ford crested the hill and broke through the forest into the double pastures and clearing in front of the house and barn. Their home stood still and dark with only the light over the front door shining. Six o'clock and no one home yet?

I'd forgotten Cindy mentioned the twins were at the Hudson Valley Arts and Crafts Fair, where they displayed their woolens and yarns. It was running all this week. They made loads of their contacts from people stopping at their booth.

Without the owners or my assistant to help, I would have put this house call off until tomorrow. But in the back of my mind I knew they were worried about this young doe and her triplets, so I decided to make sure she wasn't in distress. The twins would probably be back here by the time I finished.

To make it easy on myself, I pulled right in front of the barn. Above, dark clouds rolled by, blocking the moon, which I hoped didn't portend more bad weather. Mari had loaded all our equipment into the truck before she left. Hoisting up the ultrasound machine and carrying case loaded with gel, different sized probes, and all the rest of the stuff needed, I carted everything inside. The smell of hay and animals hung in the warm inside air like a funky musk.

Florabelle was right where she'd been before, in the smaller holding pen, happily munching away. Her belly was now enormous. We were getting close to her estimated due date. I set up the ultrasound machine and plugged it in to warm it up, then did a quick external exam on the expectant mom. She did have a slight discharge, just as the twins had described, but nothing that particularly alarmed me. I took a quick sample to be sure there were no nasty bacteria involved. Finished, I placed the culturette into the lab sample bag, and sealed it, then placed it in the case.

I felt her ligaments for any softening, checked her udder and carefully looked at the set of her tail, shape of her abdomen, and her general demeanor. Florabelle couldn't have cared less, although she did ask for a friendly head scratch. There were no outward signs the triplets would be born any time soon.

After loading her belly up with gel I got a good look at the three little babies she was carrying. I noticed they all were approximately the same size, which decreased the likelihood of one being a smaller, weaker kid. Although a petite goat, she had strong wide hips and a calm personality—all positive traits. When I got back I'd get measurements and forward the ultrasound to Jane and Lorraine's large animal vet.

I made a note to discuss installing a camera with video and sound in the kidding stall, which might be helpful and come in handy for all kinds of future husbandry issues. I'd also suggest they speak to some of their other farming friends to compare available systems on the market.

Since I was finished I let Florabelle out into the larger pen to mingle with her flock mates. Ten of the goats had kidded, four or five more were pregnant and expected to give birth next week, with our expectant mother of triplets due in about one more month. I checked everyone's food and water and bedding just because and then lugged the ultrasound and stuff back into the now chilly truck.

Since I wasn't in a rush I braced myself against the cold, started the truck running and ran into the bathroom, not to use it but to make a phone call back to the office. Sure enough, I didn't get four bars until I was practically standing on the toilet.

"Hey, Cindy. Everything is fine with Florabelle. I'll type up my notes and email the twins when I get back to the office."

Rustling and then a loud bang came over the receiver. "Oops. I dropped the phone. Sorry."

More extraneous noise on the line. As soon as it stopped, I finished my update. "That's it for me. See you in a few."

"No, you won't. I'm taking advantage of everyone being gone and going to the grocery store. You don't mind, do you?"

"Of course not. No sense in waiting just for me." The thought of the warm truck outside made me happy. When I opened the cab door the hot air would envelope me like a Florida tropical breeze.

The chime of Cindy logging out of the main reception computer pinged in the background. "Tell you what," she said. "I'll walk Buddy so you don't have to rush home. Oh, wait a second. I heard Irene recognized a piece of jewelry Elizabeth had on. It belonged to Gloria, and Elizabeth's boyfriend, Jasper, is the person who gave the piece to her."

"Oh, my gosh."

"It looks like they found Carl Wolf, but don't tell anyone I told you. I bet we have more reporters calling us tomorrow."

She sounded excited at the prospect of talking to the media. Maybe Cindy craved her fifteen minutes of fame. "Okay. That's good news."

I climbed off the toilet seat and hung up. Sure enough, my phone now registered no bars at all. Happy the nightmare was over, I gathered up the rest of my stuff, shoved the phone into my jacket pocket, and checked the pen gate to make sure it had latched shut.

The only goat I didn't see was handsome Billy the Goat. There were a few outdoor pens still being used by the sheep and goats, but eventually everyone came into the barn through the automated doors at night. I assumed the large male was somewhere close by, plotting cantankerous things. Now that all the female goats were taken care of by the big guy, his stud lease was up. In a surprise move, the twins had purchased him, Billy's endlessly curious personality winning them over, not to mention his baby daddy success rate. There had been talk of loaning him out to stud to some of their friends with dairy goats, which would partially pay his purchase price. I'd have to ask the twins more about that.

Securing the barn door with the large wood crosspiece, I turned toward the truck, which was merrily spewing out exhaust in the driveway.

With my work behind me I started down the driveway thinking about that kiss on the deck. The whole night and his house had been a huge surprise. Would Luke acknowledge what happened tonight the next time we saw each other? And should I or would I tell Jeremy?

Preoccupied, I didn't see the obstacle in the road until the last moment.

Blocking the driveway in front of me was a long shadow. That tree I'd noticed when I'd driven in had finally succumbed to gravity. Thankfully, not while I was driving under it.

Leaving the truck running, I tried to move it, but it didn't budge. The darn thing probably weighed several hundred pounds and some of the broken branches had embedded themselves in the snow. Predictably my phone had no service down here, so I had two choices: driving back up to the barn or hiking down to the main road.

No brainer, it was back to the warm barn, call the twins with a heads-up, and wait for someone to come home.

The crunching of snow under tire chains made me look up. A van was coming slowly up the driveway. It stopped on the other side of the tree, about twenty feet away.

The driver, when he got out, was someone I immediately recognized.

"Boy, am I glad to see you," I called over to Amos. He stepped down from the running board, his Doberman pincher, Hans, waiting in the passenger seat. "What are you doing here?"

"Came to get some of the sisters' honey before we left. Lydia sent me. She's got to have that honey with her tea when we're down in Florida. I told her they got honey there, but she said it just ain't the same." He turned to his truck and made a hand signal. Immediately, Hans jumped down like the superb athlete he was and stood next to his master.

"Where's Sam?" I'd become fond of the happy Labrador I'd treated for match burns from when Amos tried to burn some ticks off the poor dog.

"Oh, he's Lydia's dog. Doesn't like me much anymore."

His tone was unapologetic. Like he expected the Labrador not to like him.

That's when I sensed something—call it a chill—or a sixth-sense warning. Friendly, slightly goofy Amos was standing in front of me, but he wasn't the Amos I knew. His posture, the way he held his shoulders was different. Normally a little hunched over, apologetic, tonight he stood very straight and tall, with eyes that showed no emotion at all.

His eyes. He wasn't wearing those thick bifocals that made his pupils all huge and weird. I thought I recognized those dark eyes now.

Both figures stared at me like I was a rabbit, or a fox, or another piece of prey. The man stared with a sick pleasure. The dog stared by command.

Could I have sent the FBI on a wild goose chase, focused on the wrong person?

"Just a second, Amos." I reached for my phone trying to buy some time and think this through. I glanced at the screen as though getting a text message.

What if Amos didn't find Hans at the shelter? What if Hans was his dog all along?

Amos must be the neighbor who got Jasper interested in Schutzhund.

Amos loved to hunt.

But why would Wolf subjugate himself and play the submissive husband to someone like Lydia?

Then I recalled an offhand remark of Mari's. Lydia had inherited her parents' farm, over five hundred acres. Developers were paying a fortune for these large tracks of buildable land.

My glance lifted from the cell phone screen to meet cold eyes. Money. With his money running out, it was the perfect legitimate way to make a fortune. On vacation in Florida, or the Bahamas, or somewhere Lydia would pass away, her grieving husband inheriting everything. Wolf was a careful guy. No one would suspect anything.

As I watched he morphed back into the role he'd been playing. With an affable grin, Amos slouched a bit, and scratched his short scraggly beard. He felt around in his jacket pocket and pulled out the bifocals. Now his disguise was complete.

"Dr. Kate, why don't you get in my van? I'll take you back to the animal hospital if you like, no sense waiting here."

First mistake.

"Thanks for the offer, Amos, but I'll go up and use the twins' phone. They'll be back real soon." I moved toward my driver side door. We stood directly opposite each other, separated by the dead tree across the driveway.

"Now, you know I can't let you do that." Amos whispered a command and the Doberman bared his teeth at me.

"What are you talking about?" I feigned ignorance. As the dog kept growling, I reached for the door handle.

Now he dropped all pretense and the real Big Bad Wolf came out to play.

"You know perfectly well what I'm talking about. Lydia told me about your call the other night. Once you found out Hans didn't come from a shelter you'd start suspecting something was wrong. I saw your mind working at the show the other day, the suspicious look you gave me. Maybe you guessed I burned that stupid dog Sam for the fun of it."

The Labrador's reluctance to take anything from this man made sense now. "Sam didn't obey you, right?"

From the narrowing of his eyes behind the glasses, I knew I'd guessed correctly.

"No one else suspects, so I got time. But once the FBI realizes Jasper Rudin isn't me they'll start asking questions. You and that writer fellow, Tucker Weinstein, have too many of the right answers now."

"You're the real Carl Wolf, I take it." As much hatred as I could muster was put into that sentence but it wasn't enough. It would never be enough. "Let's see, the famous Carl Wolf. You killed a sweet old lady, an innocent woman and children, beat up a young man, and got rid of a few others who didn't bend to your way. Did that include your high school sweetheart, Nancy?"

For a second I thought he registered surprise at how much I knew, but if I expected my words would get a rise out of him, I had miscalculated. "Nancy? That's a trip down memory lane. Let me tell you, the first kill is always the sweetest."

He took off the glasses. No need for a disguise now. His flat steady stare appeared completely noncommittal. Unemotional.

That lack of empathy for the human condition marked a sociopath. He must have studied the people around him so he could mimic emotions he never felt. Acting may have helped to hone those skills. Like Ted Bundy he could be a charmer when he wanted to be. But Gramps and Luke had him pegged. Wolf was a coward. The odds had to be stacked in his favor for him to make his move. This time he'd brought along his dog.

"Who was the real Amos?" I asked.

"A hunting buddy. Lived alone in the woods, bit of a hermit. I buried that Amos behind his cabin."

"And stole his identity."

"It wasn't hard. Only downside was I had to make myself look like this." Wolf gestured to the stomach always hanging over his belt. "Got him real drunk one night. After he passed out on the sofa, I helped him go to his final reward, so to speak."

"You're a real tough guy, Amos." I deliberately used his alias.

Anger flashed and he moved his hand. The dog growled again. "You need to get into the van now. Unless you want me to send Hans over to get you." A sardonic smile flickered across his face.

A plan started forming in my brain but I needed to distract him. Make him think he'd won again. Tucker had fought and I intended to do the same.

I scrunched my face up, as though giving up. "Please. Don't sic the dog on me. Can't we talk this out?"

"Alright. Climb over the tree now, but carefully. Wouldn't want you to stumble and hurt yourself." His voice sounded completely reasonable.

"I can't believe you're Carl Wolf. You certainly had me fooled." I hesitated, as though looking for a path through the branches. "How were you able to escape from the entire FBI? They had their best agents working your case."

This time I noticed a tiny relaxation in his posture. I'd admitted he'd beaten the most powerful law enforcement agency in the country. He'd won again.

Predictably, Wolf boasted, "They never had DNA on me and before I set the fire, I obliterated every fingerprint with bleach. Their official file only contained a partial they lifted from something, most likely the wrong guy." He laughed at that. "After I killed Gloria, I planted a piece of her jewelry near Jasper's car. The moron picked it up. He is such a conceited know-it-all. Thought his dog was better than mine."

"And the cat hair?"

"That's from one of Rudin's useless barn cats. Call it my artistic touch."

"You don't think...?"

"Jasper's only a diversion. I wish I could stay for the fun and games while he's humiliated in front of everyone, but Lydia and I have a plane to catch."

"The FBI is probably on to you by now." I shifted my weight, prepared to make my move.

"Doubtful. Now get in the..."

Before he finished his thought, I turned, grabbed the handle of the truck door and dove in. Slamming it in reverse, I backed up the driveway, swerving and sliding at the curve near the outdoor pens.

When I looked back at Wolf, he was calmly jogging up the driveway, Hans by his side. In his hand was a claw-tooth hammer.

I pulled the wrench out of the truck's driver's side pocket. Do it yourself was about to begin.

No way was I letting him trap me in the truck. I grabbed my backpack, threw it over my shoulders and jumped down, leaving the truck door open so he wouldn't see me run. The only place I knew with cell phone service was inside the barn so that's where I headed.

Unfortunately, so did Wolf.

The wooden beam closure was my downfall. It took me too long to lift it up and slide it off to the side. By then he'd come close enough to grab me.

His hands clutched my backpack, pulling me toward him. With a free hand I pivoted and wacked him in the left eye with the wrench.

He screamed and lunged at me, tightening his hold.

My elbow dug into his side. In a fury he tore the wrench from my hand.

I karate-chopped his wrist and the tool fell to the ground.

Undaunted, he jerked the backpack again, straps digging into my skin. Any moment I expected a blow from the hammer so I opened the front clasp and shrugged the backpack off my arms. With the pressure gone, I ran. I'd sprinted halfway across the barn when Wolf yelled out a German command.

In seconds the dog was on me. Snapping jaws latched on to the puffy fabric of my ski jacket and held on. I heard a tearing sound, felt cold air, and the sudden wetness of warm blood.

The dog's extra weight threw me off balance. I stumbled toward the feed closet, trying to shake him off. Hans let go, then attacked again, lunging at my leg. Sharp teeth grazed my leg, and sunk into my calf muscle through my jeans. Even though I was in pain I didn't blame the Doberman. He was only doing what his master told him to do. I didn't want to hurt him, but I would if I had to.

Strong jaws now pulled and ripped my boot.

Had Amos shared his German commands with Jasper Rudin? With nothing to lose I tried Viggie's stop command.

In my deepest voice I called out, "*Verboten.*"

Hans immediately let go. Trained to stand down he stood, confused, looking at me for guidance.

I leaned against the shed. If I gave Wolf a chance to override my command it would be all over. I flung open the door, grabbed the surprised dog by his leather collar, shoved him inside and slammed it shut. A quick click secured the big lock. I tossed the key behind the bales of hay, my back blocking his view.

Leg aching, I touched the back of my calf and three fingers came back slick with blood.

When I turned I saw Wolf headed toward me. Blood dripped down the side of his face, his left eye puffy and swollen.

"You bitch," he said.

"You've got that right," I said.

My goal was to reach the bathroom, but Wolf's body blocked the way. I needed to maneuver him away from his Hans, frantically barking in the storage shed. The noise from the dog started frightening the sheep and goats. They milled around their pens, restless with fear. Wolf's good eye focused on my bloody hand then took in the torn jacket and ripped boot.

"Hans got me good and broke some fingers," I lied. "You trained him well." I limped a few steps, making my leg injuries appear much worse than they were.

"Then I'll just have to finish the job."

The claw-toothed hammer came out of his coat pocket.

He started toward me, hammer raised in the air, but I bolted toward one of the pens, ducked under the rails and waded through the goats, searching for a weapon. I remembered the twins had some metal pen railing lying around, but where?

Wolf started to follow, ignoring his wounded face. The does blocking his path seemed to confuse him. When he angrily waved his arms at them, they bolted past, forcing him to get out of their way.

Wolf was a gruesome sight. Clotted blood covered one side of his face. His swollen eye now cracked open a slit and evil glittered at me.

Animals scattered as I slowly waded through them, arms at my side. The mucky ground slowed me down, which made pursuit easier for him. Dog bites now throbbing, my limping was no longer exaggerated. The wounded muscles clenched with a sharp pain that knifed close to the bone and I crashed down onto one leg. Fingers splayed out into the cold mud, breaking my fall. When I lifted my head Wolf loomed above me.

He raised the hammer and aimed at my face.

I lifted my arm to block the blow, ready to kick out with my good leg.

The blow never came.

Instead something lifted Wolf off the ground and violently

flung him sideways into the mud. The hammer slipped out of his grasp and fell a few feet away as he tried to break his fall.

Protecting his flock, Billy the Goat stood behind him, curved horns ready for another round.

I didn't wait for Fate or the goat to give me a second chance. Fighting the pain I pulled myself up, dragged myself over to the hammer, and tightened my hand on the handle. Wolf made a move to rise. Billy lowered his head.

I moved slightly to the right, Billy securely in my sights. Like a discus-thrower I put my good shoulder into it and wacked the Big Bad Wolf across the bridge of the nose with the side of the hammer.

"That's for Gloria," I said.

His crushed nose gushed blood. The claw of the tool caught the lid of the remaining good eye. A curtain of blood obscured his view. Bonus point.

"That one's for your wife and children."

Effectively almost blind, Wolf tried to lunge at me.

I used the tool to smash his kneecap like I was hammering a nail to the floor.

"Nancy sends her regards."

He screamed so loudly Hans stopped barking.

When he struggled again to stand up, I slammed the other knee. It must have hurt like crazy. His eyes rolled back and he sank slowly into the muck.

"That one's from Tucker."

I left Billy to guard the Big Bad Wolf while I limped to the toilet to call 911.

When help arrived they found me propped up in the corner of the pen, scratching Billy's long Nubian nose and feeding him some hay.

Carl Wolf lay passed out in the mud, surrounded by curious goats.

To my surprise, I saw FBI agent Steve Frendell mixed in with the police. As usual, when men showed up unexpectedly, I wasn't exactly looking my best. Streaks of mud and muck plastered my blond hair flat to the side of my head. I'd used a strip of torn ski jacket to bind the bloody leg and stop the bleeding. Wolf's claw-toothed hammer lay across my lap, ready for work as needed.

Funny thing, though, Frendell stared at me like I was Miss America. As we waited for the EMTs, several officers stopped by to congratulate me on taking Carl Wolf down. So as far as I was concerned, if this had been a beauty pageant I'd nailed the talent part of the show.

● ● ● ● ●

When I woke up after surgery I was in a hospital bed, three men in the room. Jeremy held my left hand just below the blood pressure cuff; Luke stood at the foot of the bed grasping the railing; and Frendell sat on a chair to my right, a gorgeous bouquet of flowers next to him. A nurse stood next to me checking my vitals flashing on multiple screens and checking out the guys at the same time.

Luke gave me a quick update. "I called your office to cancel your appointments and Jeremy called your grandfather. Everything's going to be okay. They found some puncture wounds and several deep gashes which had to be cleaned out under anesthesia, but nothing's broken."

"Dr. Turner. When was your last tetanus shot?" the nurse interrupted.

"Two years ago. Also I had a rabies titer done last year and I've got plenty of antibodies."

"Good. I'm going to get you a little something for the pain." She tucked the sheet under my arm and stole a sideways glance at Jeremy before smiling at me. "Press the call button if you need anything."

I swear she winked at me, but maybe it was the medication.

"I'm going to hang around and take your statement," Frendell said. "More fantastic work, by the way. Are you sure you don't want to quit veterinary medicine and join the FBI?"

Luke spoke up. "She's risked her life enough. Besides, she's a great doctor. Everyone here in Oak Falls loves her."

Frendell continued, "Sorry I spooked you by following you that day at the mall, but I thought Wolf might target you, like he did my sister."

"Your sister?" Was his hatred for his sister's killer what I'd felt when I shook his hand?

"She was his high school sweetheart. It killed my mother, not knowing what happened to her youngest, never being able to give her a proper burial."

"So your sister was…?"

"Nancy Frendell. I was in Germany with the Army when it happened. After I got back I joined the FBI."

"Never mind all that," Jeremy said, squeezing my hand. "After Kate gets better, I'm taking her as far away from here as I can get. Maybe Bali or a sunny beach in Tahiti." His confident smile enveloped me.

Someone in scrubs moved past and checked my arm. The sharp smell of alcohol was followed by a warm sensation that tingled through the IV line as the nurse injected the pain meds. The bright hospital lights started to blur around the edges while at the same time the inside of my mouth felt dry. Everything stopped aching. My body sank into a pit of warm soft wool, enveloping me from the tips of my toes to the top of my head.

As I slipped away, only one male came to mind.

Billy's goat eyes calmly gazed into mine, his curved horns protective. "Take a nap, Doc," he bleated, his breath sweet from the half-chewed bouquet of wildflowers between his teeth.

Chapter Twenty-four

All's well that ends well, Shakespeare wrote, and I second the sentiment. With Wolf safely in custody, his identification had been confirmed with fingerprints lifted from the Schutzhund trophy he'd handled so long ago. The FBI was lucky retired veterinarian Dr. Ethan Holtzer never threw anything out.

When Tucker heard about the arrest, he catapulted out of rehab and wrote a final update chapter. His publisher rushed the book into print to benefit from all the publicity being generated. With projected sales exceeding everyone's expectations, he texted me a list of book-signings scheduled across the country. It looked like Tucker's dreams of fame might come true. My red-haired friend's agent had also booked appearances on two late-night shows and had started negotiations for a movie deal.

Lydia, strangely enough, stood by her man, certain there had been some sort of government conspiracy mistake until, during a strategy session with his high-profile lawyer, Carl/Amos told her to "shut her stupid trap." The next day she filed for divorce, packed up the dogs, and moved to Florida.

Taking advantage of the situation, Jasper Rudin's real estate agent made a deal for him to buy his neighbor's property.

Always thinking, Tucker contacted Lydia with an offer to co-write her memoir, tentatively titled *The Murderer in Bed with Me*.

Wolf's lawyer immediately cut a plea deal in exchange for revealing Nancy Frendell's burial site. Since that murder took place in New Hampshire, the death penalty had been taken off the table and replaced with life imprisonment.

Agent Steve Frendell would finally be able to bring his little sister home.

The stream of psychiatrists, sociologists, anthropologists, writers, publishers, and groupies who requested time with Wolf increased every day. He relished the attention. But, like Ted Bundy before him, he gave deliberately conflicting statements, trying to manipulate each one. Lately, he'd hinted at even more bodies hidden in different states.

Only the Big Bad Wolf would ever know the truth about his crimes.

In Oak Falls things started getting back to normal. No, I did not go to Bali on vacation with Jeremy. After one day of hospitalization, I checked myself out, took my antibiotics, and threw in some ibuprofen for pain and went back to work. A few bite wounds from a dog weren't going to slow me down.

I heard through the grapevine that Helga the Hun and the community center computer had indeed been hacked. A search was on for the fellow with the Van Dyke beard, captured on video leaving the building by the parking lot security camera. All the center computers were scrubbed of data and reloaded, with each user being warned not to use public machines for sensitive materials.

Four weeks after Wolf's arrest, I was sitting on the sofa in my sweats when I received a call from the twins, Jane and Lorraine. Florabelle had given birth to her three babies, two girls and a boy, who looked just like daddy. Billy the Goat, meanwhile, had had his fifteen minutes of Internet fame as the goat instrumental in capturing serial killer Carl Wolf. The twins now featured him and his distinctive heart-shaped markings on their extremely popular Sun Meadow Farm tour. Of course, Billy had his own website.

That was good news, because I'd become quite fond of the stinky old guy. Whenever I passed by their farm, I stopped and took some time to give Billy the Goat one of the goat-approved treats I stocked in the truck. We'd become buddies, but I never turned my back on him.

As for my personal life, that was complicated. So far Luke had been very attentive, but who knew what would happen when Dina came back to town? I'd turned the temperature down to low and slow with that relationship. After a long talk with Jeremy, he confessed that he had "renewed" his flirtation with Marcella in New Mexico, the two of them living it up before she flew back to her husband in Italy.

That relationship was now on hold. Truthfully, I felt most of our problems had to do with being apart so much, but trust shouldn't come with an extraneous circumstances clause.

Gramps, as always, took the long view.

"There are plenty of fisherman in the sea of life, Katie. Your boat will collide with the right boat one of these days."

Boating and fishing metaphors aside, I felt I needed time on shore.

My year in Oak Falls would be over in five months. Did I want to stay, or were there new adventures in new places waiting for me?

The segment of HGTV's *House Hunters* I'd been watching drew to a close. Wind howled outside and the windows rattled, but nothing penetrated my warm cocoon. I had my dog, a cold glass of wine, and a velvety blanket over my feet.

No place I had to go. No one I had to see. No urgent plans or emergency agenda. Bliss.

After a long slow sip with my head resting on the pillow, I watched the young couple on the screen review the pros and cons of all three homes.

Which would they choose?
I had a sentimental favorite.
They couldn't go wrong with the house on Billy Goat Lane.

To see more Poisoned Pen Press titles:

Visit our website:
poisonedpenpress.com
Request a digital catalog:
info@poisonedpenpress.com